C000165417

UNDER THE SYCAMORE TREE

BOOK ONE IN THE FOREVER LOVE TRILOGY

JAMES KEITH

Editing Services Provided by Dark Raven Edits
www.facebook.com/darkraveneedits

Cover Created by Phycel Designs
www.phycel.com

SYNOPSIS

A story about the hunger for food, life, and opportunity.

After stealing a loaf of bread, Edward was running to escape when he slammed into Dorothy. In that moment, fate intervened, and a love began that would span the years.

Desperate to make a better life for himself and be a man worthy of Dorothy, Edward takes a job in the mines. When catastrophe strikes, he finds his world in a state of upheaval once more.

But his isn't the only future at stake. War is looming and the desire to stand for his country is staring Edward in the face. In the midst of battle, surrounded by pain and suffering, it's his love of Dorothy that keeps him fighting.

Will he find his way back to her, under their favorite sycamore tree? Or will his hunger to be a better man end in tragedy?

From author James Keith comes, Under the Sycamore Tree, a gripping tale of life, love, and hope.

CONTENTS

For my amazing and wonderful wife Claire and my beautiful daughter Leah-Jane.

YOUNG LOVE

Love can find us in unique ways, whether it be friendship at first or an untimely event. Love is the most powerful of all emotions and can be found when we least expect it.

IT WAS a warm spring day in Birmingham the year of 1937. The sun was shining and the sky was clear blue without a cloud in sight. The shops were bustling with life and people were going about their business as usual.

Among the crowd was a 13-year-old boy called Edward. While walking down the street, he stopped off at the bakery. He was so hungry and had not eaten for many days. Edward looked in the bakery window and saw all the fresh bread that had just come out of the oven. The aroma of freshly baked bread made Edward's mouth water, causing his smile to stretch from ear to ear.

Looking around, he thought, *I am so hungry, I could grab one and be gone before anyone would notice.*

Edward walked into the shop, the bell ringing loudly as he did, and grabbed a hot loaf of bread off the shelf. He ran out of the shop as fast as he could, making it down the road as the baker shouted, "Come back here you nasty little thief!" Edward continued to run, looking behind him to make sure that he wasn't being chased. As he turned to look forward, he bumped into a young teenage girl, causing them to both fall down onto the ground.

"Look where you are going, stupid boy," said the girl.

Edward stood up. "I am terribly sorry, my lady," he said to the girl.

As the girl looked at Edward, his heart began to rise. She was so beautiful with long, golden hair that went down to her hips. Her beautiful lips reminded him of a blooming pink rose while she stared at him with the most mesmerising blue eyes.

Edward began to stutter. "I... I... I... am so so sorry, my lady. My name my name is Edward," he said.

The girl looked at Edward and said, "Well I am Dorothy and you should be much more careful next time."

She then looked at the loaf of bread all squashed on the sidewalk. "Did you steal that?" she asked Edward suspiciously.

"Yes, my lady. I haven't eaten in three days," replied Edward.

Edward was hungry and desperate. But he could not go as low as lying to anyone.

Dorothy looked at Edward and smiled. "Come with me, silly boy. I'll make sure to get a good meal down you today." Edwards's heart began to flutter as he walked with Dorothy back to her house.

Dorothy opened the front door to her house and held

it for Edward to walk in. As he stepped foot in the house, he was greeted by Dorothy's mother.

"Well, young man, you know it should be you who holds the door open for a lady," said Dorothy's mother.

"Sorry, ma'am," replied Edward.

Dorothy then explained to her mother that Edward had bumped into her on her way home from school and was hungry. Dorothy's mother glared at Edward, concerned that he may be bad news.

"So, young man, where are your parents?" asked Dorothy's mother.

"I.I.I don't have any parents," stammered Edward.

"Well, where are they?" replied Dorothy's mother.

"Dead," said Edward.

The room suddenly fell silent. Tears began to roll down Edward's cheeks just as the door flew open.

In came a towering man, causing Edward to look up. He hadn't seen such a giant of a man before. Dorothy ran over to the man and gave him a huge cuddle.

"Welcome home, Father," she said.

Edward thought if that was her father, he'd best be on good behaviour.

"Who is this?" asked Dorothy's father.

"This is Edward. We bumped into each other earlier, and he is very hungry. I thought I would bring him here to have some food," replied Dorothy.

"My name is George," said Dorothy's father. "My wife is called Anna."

Edward looked at both George and Anna and said, "It's nice to meet you both."

George then sat down at the table and asked Edward if

he was going to join him so they could get to know each other. Edward sat down at the table next to George. He couldn't believe how massive the man was.

George looked at Edward and told him, "I am only going to say this once: There are very few people in the world who help strangers in need. My daughter is well brought up and very dear to me. If you upset Dorothy in any way or hurt her, I am going to bury you alive."

Edward's heart began to beat harder and faster. He started to panic. "But I.I.I.I d.d.d.d don't want to hurt anyone," said Edward.

"Well that's good to know," said George.

Anna then started to bring some trays over filled with chicken, potatoes, broccoli, carrots, and gravy.

Edward looked startled. He hadn't seen a meal like this in a long time. His mind drifted to his young mother working in the kitchen and humming a sweet poem with a fresh aroma swirling out of the kitchen.

Edward was brought back from his memories when the food was put on the table.

Edward began to eat hurriedly. He was starving. Dorothy was amazed at this skinny boy eating like he had never seen food before.

"Excuse me Edward," called Anna from across the table. "Where do you live and sleep?"

Edward stopped eating. He looked down at the table and replied,

"I don't sleep in the same place twice, ma'am. I move about. I have no home, so I go where there is shelter and food." Everyone around the table just went silent. They didn't know what to say.

Dorothy was looking upset, she went pale, her eyes blurred out. Her lips were trembling and the cup she was holding in her hands began to shake. George turned to her concerned and said:

"what is it darling?" Dorothy replied with,

"We cannot let him sleep outside, what if something happens to him, it's not safe outside".

"Dorothy come into the kitchen with me please," asked George. Edward could hear Dorothy and George talking in the kitchen he could George's overpowering voice

"he cannot stay here Dorothy". Edward could hear Dorothy pleading with George, begging him to allow Edward to stay. After a long argument, George shook his head and said:

"alright he can stay for a while, but he needs to get a job and earn his keep". Edward was amazed. He could not believe what he was hearing. The generosity of these people that he had only just met gave him a glimpse of hope. Edward thanked them all, he continued to thank them for the rest of the evening.

IT WAS GETTING LATE, George shouted out

"right everyone time for bed". With that Anna and Dorothy started to go upstairs. Edward was unsure of what was happening and began to follow Dorothy up the stairs to her bedroom.

"Excuse me, young man, where do you think you're going?" said George.

"I.I.I.I. a.a.a.m going up to bed," said Edward. George shook his head and said to Edward

"no boy, you're not sleeping upstairs with Dorothy, you young man are downstairs on the floor". Edward then realised what was going on. There was no way he could sleep in Dorothy's bed with her. Edward walked back down the stairs; he was given some blankets by Anna. Edward snuggled down onto the floor. He wrapped himself in the blankets, closed his eyes and thought this house is lovely and warm, no more sleeping in the rain and cold. Edward finally felt safe. He had a roof over his head and he was relieved. The house soon fell silent and everyone fell asleep. However, Edward was tossing and turning throughout the night, the sounds of creaking around the house caused his sleep to be unsettled. He could hear George's loud coughing from upstairs constantly. Edward felt that this was just too good to be true, he would feel paranoid and anxious but finally managed to drift off to sleep.

THE SOUND of the cockerels woke Edward the following morning. It was raining, a typical day in Birmingham. Edward then heard a huge bang from upstairs. Edward ran up the stairs to see where the sound came from only to find George standing at the top of the stairs.

"Can I help you?" said George.

"I.I.I heard a loud bang," stammered Edward.

"That was just me getting out of bed," said George.

"Now get downstairs and get yourself ready we have to

find you work today". Edward quickly hurried down the stairs and put his outfit on. George was an intimidating man to say the least. Edward knew he had to keep George and Anna pleased if he wanted to stay there.

A few moments passed and Dorothy came downstairs.

"Hello Edward, did you sleep well?" asked Dorothy.

"I.I.I s.s.lept really well," stuttered Edward. Dorothy was wearing a long red and white dress. Edward could not stop staring at her, his mind thinking how beautiful Dorothy was. Edward knew Dorothy's presence made him nervous

"Young man, don't make it so obvious," said Anna. Edward turned and said,

"excuse me ma'am". Anna just smiled at Edward and said

"don't you have somewhere to be now young man?" Edward quickly jumped up and followed George out the door, wondering what work would be coming his way today".

GEORGE AND EDWARD walked for what seemed miles. Edward struggled to keep up with George. George walked very fast and very aggressively. He was very dominating even in his mere gestures. Edward could not believe the strides George was taking and was in complete awe of this giant of a man. Eventually, they arrived at the entrance of a mine shaft. George said

"where is Harry, I got someone here who can help out in the mines". The miner on duty informed George that he would go and get Harry. Edward thought to himself, how would he work in a mine, he isn't even strong enough. Harry arrived and took one look at Edward.

"What am I supposed to do with him, he's tiny," said Harry to George.

"Well Harry you owe me a favour this boy needs work and needs turning into a man, so please will you give him a chance?" Harry shook his head "ok, come on then boy I'll take you into the mine and show you what you need to do". Edward hesitated, he did not like the fact that he was being ridiculed. He started to feel worthless and that he was going to be a failure and let everyone down. He then hesitated but eventually followed Harry into the mine.

They walked about 400 metres into the mine. As they walked through the mine Edward could smell the damp horrible smell of stale water. The darkness and the narrow tunnels would make Edward feel; claustrophobic. He was scared, he did not know what to do. He knew he had been thrown straight into the deep end. The mines were like a maze with tunnels veering off in every direction. The tiny small lights barely creating any light to see clearly. Edward was always afraid of the dark and now he was surrounded by the darkness. They then stopped at a large clearing. Harry handed Edward a pickaxe.

"Do you know how to use one of these?" said Harry.

"Ummm, no," said Edward. Harry shook his head looked at Edward and said:

"just watch me". Harry then swung the pickaxe into the wall of the mine which caused some coal to come loose.

"We want this". Harry showed Edward the coal, and

told him that was what he must do for the rest of the day. Edward thought to himself, this doesn't seem so hard. This seems easy. Edward then went to swing the pickaxe but realised he was not strong enough to get the momentum Harry got. As Edward swung the pickaxe he slipped and fell onto the floor.

"Are you going to get this, or do I need to let you go already?" said Harry.

"I can do this," replied Edward. He then used small swings to hit at the wall. Harry then left Edward alone. Edward worked all day long, he was exhausted, thirsty and hungry and wanted to go back to the house.

He couldn't get Dorothy out of his mind. As he swung the axe time after time, he would vision Dorothy in her beautiful red and white dress, her incredible smile and eyes. The emotions were overwhelming to Edward, he didn't understand them. He kept telling himself, what is going on. What am I feeling? Am I in love with Dorothy, surely not? I have only known her a day. Then there was a loud sound. It was the horn to signal the end of the day. Edward was delighted, he was burned out, he couldn't wait to get back to see Dorothy.

As Edward left the mine, George was there waiting for him.

"Well boy how did you get on today?" Edward replied,

"it was exhausting I am so tired".

"Well, you better get used to that," said George,

"you're going to be working here six days a week". Edwards heart sunk, he thought to himself, I barely got through today. How am I going to be doing this six days a week? Edward looked at George and said,

"6 days a week, yes I can do that". Edward really didn't know what he was going to do. But he couldn't look weak, he wanted to impress Dorothy.

———

As the pair arrived back at the house they were greeted by Anna and Dorothy.

"Edward, I'll go and run you a bath," said Dorothy. Anna looked up and said,

"oh please do Dorothy, Edward you are filthy do not touch anything I have been cleaning all day". Edward was covered in soil and soot from head to toe. His clothes were black, his skin was filthy. He stank of stale statement water; he knew that he was dirty but he did not like this being pointed out to him.

"Edward come upstairs, I shall run you a bath," called Dorothy. Edward went upstairs behind Dorothy, where she started to fill the wooden basin up. Edward could feel some rumbling in his tummy, a feeling like lots of butterflies floating around. Dorothy looked at Edward and told him,

"you really are a sweet boy, aren't you?" Edward became nervous and replied

"I think so my lady". Dorothy then left the room and told Edward to be quick as dinner was almost ready. Edward jumped into the bath. He was smitten. He knew then that Dorothy was going to be the girl for him.

Edward enjoyed a long nice soak in the bath. He hadn't felt this warm heat around his body for such a long time. As he lay there he thought about his parents. His mind went back to when he was 10 years old. His father worked in a smelting factory; his mother was a housewife. Edward closed his eyes and said to himself,

"I miss them so much". He thought about his mum, how she became sick. His mind went to when she was in her bed, she was struggling to breathe. He was sat with his father each holding his mother's hand. She looked at Edward and she said to him,

"follow your dreams my son, I will always be with you". She turned and looked at his father and said softly

"I love you". She then took her last breath and closed her eyes. Edward was heartbroken and cried on his mother's chest. His father stood up walked downstairs and left the house. Edward would always think of his mother's tenderly smile. How she used to brush his hair. Get him dressed looking nice for school. His love for his mother was unconditional and every time he closed his eyes, he could see her big beautiful blue eyes looking at him with all the love in the world.

Edward then remembered the following day, the day after his mother passed away, his father went into the living room and opened the gun cabinet. He looked at Edward and told him that he was sorry. He then loaded his pistol, placed it in his mouth and pulled the trigger. Edward opened his eyes and jumped up out of the bath. His breathing became erratic and he began to cry, as he tried to get out of the bath he slipped and fell. Hitting his head on the floor. Dorothy was in her room; she heard a loud bang. She ran into the bathroom to see Edward lying on the floor naked, bleeding slightly from his head. She wrapped him in a blanket and held him tight.

Edward opened his eyes, and saw Dorothy looking down at him.

"Are you ok?" asked Dorothy.

"I.I.I.I think s.s.s.so," stammered Edward.

"Thank you for helping me".

"That's ok," replied Dorothy. Dorothy was rather concerned about Edward and told him that he needed to get himself dressed and come downstairs so everyone could keep an eye on him. He looked at Dorothy shook his head and said, "yes, of course, my lady, I don't want to worry anyone. I just slipped that's all". Dorothy was not convinced that Edward had just slipped, however, she gave him the benefit of the doubt and left the room to allow Edward to get dressed.

Edward came downstairs, as he was reaching the bottom of the stairs, he could smell the amazing meal that was being prepared. He couldn't believe how lucky he was that he was being fed warm meals and given a place to stay. As he came into the living room he was greeted by George,

"are you ok boy?" Y.y.y.yes sir," stammered Edward. Edward sat down at the dinner table. Dorothy was sat opposite. As the food was served onto the table Edward could feel something rubbing up against his leg. He wondered what it was, he looked across at Dorothy who was smiling at him. Then he realised that Dorothy was rubbing her leg up against his. Does she like me? He thought to himself. Edward then decided to rub his leg back against Dorothy's and the two gazed into each other's eyes throughout the meal.

Once the meal had been eaten, Anna asked Dorothy

and Edward to clean up. They both took the pots into the kitchen and began to wash them. Edward was nervous, he could feel himself trembling. He really liked Dorothy and wanted to tell her. Little did he know that Dorothy also liked him. They stood close together at the sink. Edward reached for a dinner plate, Dorothy reached for the same plate and their hands came together.

"I.I.I'm really sorry," said Edward.

"No, it's ok," said Dorothy. Edward tried to pull his hand away, but Dorothy held onto it. Edward looked into Dorothy's eyes he could see a sparkle he knew something was there. He went to lean in for a kiss. Dorothy leaned into towards Edward then...

"Excuse me what is going on here?" George had come into the kitchen.

"You two were not about to do what I was thinking are you?"

"N.n.n.no sir," Edward was terrified. He was worried that he was going to get a beating from George. George looked at them both. He smiled and said,

"why don't you two go out and get some fresh air?" Dorothy smiled at her father.

"Come on boy, let's go to the canal we can go for a lovely walk there". With this Dorothy grabbed Edward by the arm and whisked him out the front door.

THE WALK to the canal was quiet, Edward was still thinking about how close he was to kissing Dorothy. Dorothy was smitten, she really wanted to kiss Edward but knew she couldn't kiss him on the way to the canal. She was worried that they might be seen and that her father would not be pleased. When they arrived at the canal it was, quiet, the only noise that could be heard was the sounds of the birds in the trees. The water was still and silent. Dorothy grabbed Edward's hand.

"It's ok boy, you don't need to be nervous". Edward accepted Dorothy's hand and they began to walk down the canal together hand in hand.

They walked quietly, looking around at the trees and the water. Dorothy asked Edward about his childhood and what happened to his parents. Edward told Dorothy that he really didn't want to think about this right now as he was really enjoying his walk and he didn't want to spoil it. Dorothy then asked Edward if he went to school.

"No, my lady, I haven't been to school in a very long time".

"Can you read?" she asked. "I can read some words," he replied.

"Well, I can teach you how to read if you would like," replied Dorothy.

"R.r.really?" stammered Edward. Dorothy just looked at Edward and smiled.

They continued walking past the old dockyard. The smell of the smelters made Edward think again of his father. He paused and looked at the factory. It brought back memories of when he would come and see his father at work. Where he would help his father melt down the metals.

"Boy what is wrong, come on let's keep walking," shouted Dorothy who had continued walking past the factory. Edward then turned and ran down the canal to catch up to Dorothy. They continued walking and then came to a part of the canal that had an opening into a field. In this field was a large sycamore tree. The tree was enormous, it looked somewhat magical It was the only tree around. The gnarled exposed roots were showing. Dorothy grabbed Edward's hand

"come on let's race to the tree". They both began to run towards the tree. Edward tried hard but Dorothy was too fast for him.

"I win," she said.

"What is this tree?" asked Edward.

"This tree is my safe place, I come here when I want to feel safe and gather my thoughts," replied Dorothy. Edward looked at this remarkable tree.

"It's astonishing," he said. Dorothy sat down at the base of the tree.

"Come boy, sit down with me". Edward was so nervous, he sat down next to Dorothy.

"Have you ever kissed a girl before?" she asked". Edward paused. He had never kissed a girl and was so worried that Dorothy had kissed boys before.

"It's ok boy, I have never kissed a boy before myself," she replied. She then placed her arm around him and leaned into Edward whispering

"hold me". Edward turned, he placed his arms around Dorothy's neck and closed his eyes. They both leaned into one another and swiftly placed their lips upon one another's. They both felt this magical feeling in their tummies as if this kiss was both their destiny's.

They leaned back, after what had just happened. They

had their first kiss under the sycamore tree. They opened their eyes. Dorothy giggled and smiled at Edward. Edward went bright red.

"Don't be shy boy, that was absolutely amazing," she told Edward. Edward smiled and just gazed deeply into Dorothy's eyes.

"W.w.w.what happens now?" he said.

"Now, we watch the sunset together". Dorothy then moved closer to Edward, and they cuddled into one another to watch the sun go down over the horizon. They both felt like they were in heaven. It was a magical evening for them both.

As TIME PASSED they would do everything together, as soon as Edward would finish work they would go for long walks together. Dorothy's parents knew that something was going on. One day George called for Edward.

"Hey boy, come and sit down, and we can have a chat". Edward was very nervous. His instincts were telling him that something was wrong and George was going to be very angry with him.

"I know something is going on with you and Dorothy, care to explain?" asked George.

"W.w.w.well i really like her," stuttered Edward.

"It's ok boy, you have my blessing." Edward was shocked this was not what he was expecting. He started to smile. Then in a very deep voice George told him

"you do not go into her bedroom unless Anna and I are in the house. Do you understand that?"

"Yes sir," replied Edward.

Dorothy then came into the room.

"Is everything ok father?" she said.

"Yes, my dear, everything is fine. You two have fun, but be careful," he said. Dorothy then knew that her father knew about her secret relationship with Edward. The fact that her father did not mind made Dorothy feel very relaxed.

"Come on Edward," she said.

"Let's go out to the sycamore tree". As they walked up to the tree hand in hand, they could feel each other's arms trembling. What was this feeling they both thought. Something that neither of them had felt before. The tree towered over them both. They looked up and could see all the beautiful sycamores glistening in the sunlight. This was where they loved to be together. They would both visit the tree many times a week. It was a place where they could both feel safe and be passionate with one another. They would spend the entire evening kissing and cuddling. They sat down in the usual spot under the tree. Dorothy would sit on the raised mound of grass; Edward would sit beside her. Edward was nervous, he kept thinking should I say it. Should I tell her I love her? What if she doesn't love me? Would that make me look foolish? Edward continued to go over this in his mind until his hands stopped shaking. He then knew that the time was right to declare his love to Dorothy. Edward looked at Dorothy and stared deep into her eyes. He softly said

"I love you". Dorothy fell silent. She didn't say a word. Edward felt foolish. He thought to himself maybe this was too soon. Dorothy then lunged toward Edward and kissed him deeply. She then leaned back and responded,

"I love you too". Edward's heart began to melt, he was in love. An emotion that he had never felt before.

They walked home hand in hand, past the smelting factory, past the old docks down the street. People looked at them both. Dorothy could hear the whispers,

"that's George and Anna's daughter isn't she too young to be holding another boys hand?" Dorothy didn't care. She was happy. Edward was still very smitten. He didn't even remember the walk home. He was in love, and he didn't have a care in the world about anything that was going on around him. When they got home, they were met by Anna.

"Well you two, what time do you call this?" she said.

"Sorry mother, we didn't realise the time," replied Dorothy. Anna did not like Dorothy's tone. She then raised her hand and gave Dorothy an almighty slap across the face. Dorothy grabbed her face and began to cry. She ran upstairs to her room and slammed the door. Edward stood there in shock. He couldn't believe what had just happened. He was worried about Dorothy, but he knew he couldn't go upstairs and see if she was ok. Anna looked at Edward.

"Well, if this happens again and you bring her home this late, you'll be back out on the streets". Edward dropped his head. He looked at the floor and replied,

"sorry ma'am, this will not happen again".

Edward felt truly awful that night. He blamed himself for Dorothy being slapped by her mother. If he only thought better this could have all been prevented from happening. Edward could not get Dorothy off his mind. He was worried about her, how she was feeling. He was sure at times in the night that he could hear her sobbing in her bedroom. Edward felt so uncomfortable in the house. He knew that this was his one and only chance of bettering his life and making a fresh start again. He knew that this could not happen. He cared for Dorothy and did not want to cause any friction between mother and daughter.

SEVERAL MONTHS PASSED, Dorothy and Edward were very careful about what time they came home. They did not want to keep getting in trouble. Their relationship had blossomed. They were both now 14 years old and very much in love. One Saturday Edward did not have to go to work. So, Dorothy decided to take him into the city. Edward used to sleep rough in the city so he knew his away around this very well. When they arrived, Edward started to remember all the times where he would have to steal food, search through bins for food and clothes. Dorothy could see that something was not right with Edward.

"What's wrong?" she asked. Edward turned and looked at Dorothy.

"This is where I spent 3 years of my life, starving, freezing and worrying if I will wake up the next day". Dorothy had no idea how difficult it was for Edward. She did not want to upset him. So, she grabbed his hand.

"Come on, let's go and get some sweets."

Dorothy pulled Edward all the way to the sweet shop. When they got there Edward began to panic.

"I.I.I.I.I cannot go in there," he said.

"Why can't you?" she replied.

"I stole from here once, what if the shopkeeper remembers me?" said Edward.

"Don't be silly, it's been a long time. He will not remember you, so come on let's go inside". Edward agreed and walked into the sweet shop with Dorothy. His eyes lit up when he saw all the beautiful coloured sweets in the jars. He was amazed at how many choices there were.

"Well kids what can I get you?" asked the shopkeeper.

"Liquorice?" asked Edward.

"Great choice," said the shopkeeper. Dorothy then smiled at Edward and took some money out of her purse and bought the sweets for them to share. Edward had never had anyone buy him sweets before. He felt so flattered.

"I do love you so much," he said to Dorothy. She giggled and replied

"I know you do".

They both then hopped onto a bus towards the canal. Their plan was to eat the liquorice under the sycamore tree. When they arrived at the sycamore tree they sat down together and began to feast on their sweets. They began to cuddle up together and then noticed the shadows of 3 people.

"What you doing here?" yelled the voice of another boy. Edward stood up and saw 3 teenage boys. These were all a lot bigger than him. They approached Edward and

Dorothy and snatched the bag of sweets out of Dorothy's hand. Edward was scared, he did not know what to do.

"D.d.d.d.d don't do that," he said. The boys laughed at him.

"What's wrong little boy, are you stupid?" Dorothy jumped up and said,

"leave him alone and get out of here".

One of the boys took offence to this, he did not like being shouted at by a girl. He pushed out his chest and stood tall making himself look as big as he could. He then lunged towards Dorothy and pushed her down on to the floor. She whimpered as she hit her arm hard on the ground. Edward was angry, his legs began to twitch. His heart begun to pound he lunged towards the boy, and a fight broke out. Edward jumped onto the boy knocking him onto the floor. Edward hit the boy in the face repeatedly in a fit of rage. He was screaming

"don't you ever push my girl". Edward was then grabbed by the two other boys and then pulled him to the floor, where they proceeded to hit him and kick him. Edward was screaming in pain. The boys continued to attack Edward until one of the boys said,

"let's go, before someone else comes". The boys left. Edward was lying on the floor, his face all battered and bruised. Blood pouring from his head and his nose. Dorothy crawled over to Edward.

"I am so sorry," she said.

"Let me help you". Dorothy helped Edward to his feet. She managed to walk him to the canal. He then collapsed onto the floor. Still bleeding and hurting from his injuries.

"Edward I need to get help". She ran into the smelting factory.

"Please can someone come and help me?"

Two men came out to her aid. They went with her to Edward who was lying on the floor appearing to be unconscious.

"What the bloody hell has happened here?" said one of the workers.

"We were attacked," replied Dorothy. They lifted Edward and took him to the factory. Edward woke after about an hour. Dorothy was sat with him holding his hand.

"I will be ok," he said to Dorothy.

"I have been so worried about you," she replied. She then gave him a kiss on his cheek.

"Let's go home," Edward said to Dorothy.

"I don't think you're in any fit state to walk home," said a mysterious voice. Edward thought to himself who was that. A man then came into the room.

"I carried you up here boy, now tell me where you both live and I shall take you home". Dorothy told the man where she lived and thanked him for being so helpful. The kind worker took them both home.

When they arrived home, panic arose in the house. George was angry as to who would put their hands on his daughter. He saw how beaten Edward was.

"Listen Edward," he said.

"Any man that can take a beating for my daughter to protect her is a special man in my eyes". Anna took Dorothy upstairs.

"I am so sorry mother, I didn't expect anything to happen". Anna just smiled at Dorothy, she replied,

"it's ok my baby, you are safe now and we won't let anything happen to you anymore". Dorothy was so pleased that her parents were being supportive. She gave her mother a close tight hug.

"I love you mother," she said.

Meanwhile, Edward was being looked after by George. George filled the basin with hot water, he got some cotton wool and begun to clean Edwards wounds.

"You did your best boy, you stood up for my little girl and for that I am eternally grateful," Edward then told George that he was in love with Dorothy. George smiled and told Edward that he already knew this and this was ok.

"Now boy after you've all healed up, I'm going to teach you how to defend yourself." Edward was pleased, he had never been able to defend himself let alone anyone else before in his life. Edward then knew that he had a family. A loving family that cared for him. Something that he hadn't experienced in a very long time.

2

COMING OF AGE

There is a time in all our lives where we become either a man or woman, where we make the decisions that will shape the future of our lives.

A FEW DAYS had passed since the violent assault on Edward and Dorothy. Edward had been too unwell to go to work and spent all his time in the house. He was still badly hurt, struggling to walk around the house. Dorothy would tend to his wounds every day, keeping them clean. This only brought them closer together. The house would often be quiet, Dorothy would sit with Edward cuddling into him all day long. She began to teach him how to read and write, so he was capable of so much more. As his mind became occupied with learning new things, he became interested in how the body worked. Dorothy made him her mother's chicken broth which was wholesome comfort food, he was gaining strength every day both in body and spirit.

True to his word George wanted to teach Edward how

to defend himself. He took him to the mines where there was an unofficial boxing club. It was where the miners let off steam. Edward saw this horrible dark, smelly room. It was very dusty and the lighting was very poor. Edward felt so claustrophobic as the room was so busy. People were placing bets on the fights. Edward did not feel that this was the right place for him. George leaned down to Edward

"Right boy this is where I will make you a man". Edward scowled and watched in horror as two miners were battering each other with bare fists.

"T.t.t.this is brutal," stuttered Edward.

"Of course, it is," said George.

"This is where boys are turned into men" Edward's knee's begun to tremble, he had never actually had to fight anyone properly before, he didn't know what to do.

"Remember boy, you need to keep your fists up, defend yourself and think that this man is going to try and kill you," George said to Edward. With this, he pushed Edward forward into the makeshift ring.

Edward was terrified, he looked across at this other boy who was taller and broader than Edward. Edward knew that this was not going to go well. He walked forward to his opponent. He looked him in the eye. He knew now there was no escape, and he needed to impress George. Edward raised his hands over his face and threw a punch. He completely missed his opponent, who then started to punch Edward in his ribs. Edward fell to the floor in agony. Begging for no more. George then stepped in,

"enough," he said. He lifted Edward onto his feet,

"come on boy let's get you home".

They arrived at home.

"Father what has happened?" cried Dorothy.

"Nothing, I was helping him to become tough," replied George.

"Please father, Edward is not a fighter. I don't want to see him getting hurt". She pleaded with her father not to allow Edward to fight anymore. George looked at Dorothy, he could see how much this was hurting her. He promised to not allow Edward to fight anymore. Edward then looked at Dorothy, he reached out for her hand. She took hold of his hand and told him that she loved him, and he did not need to be big and strong to impress her. She then took Edward and sat down with him. She lifted his shirt to see large bruises to his ribs.

"Oh Edward, I am so sorry that this has happened," she said.

"It's ok Dorothy," replied Edward.

"I will be ok." The two then embraced with one another. Edward promising Dorothy that he would not fight again.

THE NEXT MORNING it was time for work, Dorothy wanted to walk with Edward to the mine to keep him some company. The two walked together hand in hand to the mine. Dorothy gave Edward a kiss and told him that she would see him later in the day. Edward said his goodbye's and walked into the mine ready for another day of hard work.

There was a pungent smell in the mine that day. Edward sniffed many times, he thought he could smell a considerable amount of damp and water.

"Excuse me Harry," called Edward. Harry looked over, "what is it boy, I am busy," Harry replied.

"Well sir there is a really funny smell here today and I don't know what it is," said Edward.

"Don't you be worrying about any smells boy; you just get on and do your job," replied Harry. Edward thought to himself ok, I'll just carry on. Edward continued to mine and after a few minutes, he felt some soil drop onto his shoulder. He knew something was not right. Edward backed away from the wall of the mine. He looked up and could see that the beams supporting the mine were bending.

"Uh, Harry I think we have a problem," called Edward. With this, Harry got very angry. He stormed over toward Edward.

"What is the problem, you are really getting on my nerves today," replied Harry. Edward pointed up. Harry then looked up

"Shit!!" he called.

"Everyone out now!" He pushed Edward.

"Get out of the fucking mine you fool".

Edward turned and ran, he ran as fast as he could, there was a loud bang, the supports started to break, the roof of the mine started to collapse. Edward continued to run, looking behind him. The roof started to fall behind him. Edward ran his heart out and made it to the entrance of the mine. He stopped and paused.

"Harry," he thought. Edward turned around and

waited for Harry to come out of the mine. Some miners came out after a few seconds but there were no signs of Harry. Edward began to panic. He fell to his knees. He was unsure of what to do. He then stood up, he walked back into the entrance of the mine. He could see someone was trapped under the rubble.

Edward ran over to the miner, he then saw that it was Harry. A beam had fallen down and had crushed Harry underneath it. Edward tried to move the beam, but it was covered in soil and it was just too heavy to move. Edward then pulled away at the soil. He could see Harry's face, his eyes wide open, no movement in his eyes, his jaw. He was lifeless. Edward knew then that Harry had been killed. He closed Harry's eyelids and said

"I am so sorry, I wish I had made you come over sooner. It's all my fault". Edward then began to sob uncontrollably. Someone else he knew had died.

"Edward, I am coming," called a voice. Edward turned around. It was Dorothy, she had come to the mine to see him. She grabbed him and pulled him close.

"We need to get you out of here, it's not safe," she said. She put her arm around Edward. They walked out of the entrance to the mine together. Edward did not say a word, his eyes streaming with tears. Dorothy took Edward home where she helped him in the bath to clean him up.

"Are you hurt?" she asked. Edward just looked at Dorothy, he did not speak. He just shook his head to indicate that he was fine.

AFTER EDWARD WAS CLEANED UP, Dorothy took him out of the house. They walked together and ended up at their favourite place. The sycamore tree.

"Edward, please talk to me," she asked. Edward looked into Dorothy's eyes

"this is all my fault," he replied. Dorothy just stared into his eyes.

"This is not your fault; you did not cause the mine to collapse. You did everything you could to save Harry". She then pulled Edward in close, his head lay against her chest. He could hear her heartbeat.

"You're safe now," she said. Edward closed his eyes, the sound of Dorothy's heartbeat made him feel at rest, he felt safe and secure, and he knew that everything would be ok in the end.

They both fell asleep under the sycamore tree. Dorothy woke, it was dark. She was so worried that her mother would be very angry with them both for staying out so late.

"Edward wake up, we need to get home now," she called. Edward opened his eyes, he realised it was dark. His heart started to race. He remembered when Anna had told him that if this happened again, he would be back out on the street.

"Oh, Dorothy. Let's run". They both ran home as fast as they could. They got to the front door; the house was dark.

"Maybe they haven't noticed," said Dorothy. She then quietly opened the front door.

"What time do you call this?" They were greeted by Anna who was sat in her armchair holding a rolling pin.

"I am so sorry mother, we fell asleep".

"Don't talk back to me child," replied Anna. Edward then stepped forward

"I am so sorry ma'am this is all my fault. There was a terrible accident at the mine and some people died". Anna scowled at Edward. All of a sudden, the front door then flew open.

"Oh, thank goodness you are okay". It was George. He had heard of the tragedy at the mine. His eyes lit up when he saw Edward was ok.

"We have been searching for you, we all thought you were caught up in the accident". Edward felt relieved. George had come to his rescue. Anna then changed her tone.

"Well it's good to see that you were not hurt". Dorothy let out a huge sigh of relief. She was so terrified that her mother was going to hurt her.

THE MINE REMAINED CLOSED after the tragedy. A funeral service was held for Harry. Edward and Dorothy attended with George and Anna. George began to sob. Edward could not help but stare at George. This mountain of a man who appeared so strong was emotionally upset. Dorothy noticed this also and she turned to Edward.

"I did not know that my father and Harry got on so well". The service was beautiful and Harry was given a beautiful send off. George remained quiet throughout the day. Anna by his side holding his arm and comforting him. Both Dorothy and Edward were very intrigued to learn more about the relationship between George and Harry. But they knew now was not the time to be asking these sorts of questions.

Edward knew that he needed to find another job. He thought long and hard to himself about what he could do. He decided to head to the market and asked the traders if there were any vacancies available. He started at the blacksmith. Where he was asked if he had any experience. Edward knew this was a no go. He tried the fishmonger.

"Do you know what these fish are?" asked the fishmonger. Edward had no idea

"sorry sir, I don't know".

"Well then there is no work for you here boy," replied the fishmonger. Edward started to feel defeated. Then something popped into his head. The smelting factory. He then grinned. He knew this might work, as he would sometimes help his father there when he was younger.

EDWARD MET UP WITH DOROTHY.

"Dorothy my love, I know what I can do now," he said.

"Well, what is it, Edward?" she asked.

"The smelting factory, I know all about the metals and ore's and how to help separate them. My father showed me when I was younger". He was so excited, he grabbed her by the hand and dragged her out of the market and down the street towards the canal.

"Slow down Edward," she called.

"Sorry my love," he replied. They then began to walk

casually. He was so excited and couldn't wait to see if there was any work available.

They arrived at the factory. Edward looked at the large entrance. He walked inside and approached a worker.

"Excuse me, sir, may I speak to whoever is in charge?"

"Well that would be me," said the worker. Edward asked the worker if there was any work available and if there was anything he could do to help out. The worker stared at Edward, he appeared to recognise him.

"I know you don't I?" said the worker.

"I.I.I.I don't think so," stammered Edward. The worker then paused, he looked at Edward and then said,

"I do know you, you're Thomas' son". Edward stared in disbelief. This man knew who his father was and knew Edward.

"Well, Thomas was my friend," said the worker. Edward smiled; he knew luck was going his way this time.

The worker thought very highly of Thomas.

"Thomas was not just my friend," he told Edward.

"He was the best smelter I have had the privilege to work with". Edward was shocked. He had never heard anyone speak so highly of his father before. This made Edward feel proud. The worker continued to tell Edward that Thomas was so dedicated to his work that he would stay after and always help the cleaners and that he was so kind to anyone who needed any help. Edward was amazed. This was all new to him. He just listened as the worker continued to praise his father for all the good that he has done.

Dorothy stepped forward.

"Hello, sir I am Dorothy". The worker looked at Dorothy and said to Edward.

"How does such a beautiful girl end up with a skinny little guy like you?" Dorothy giggled and smiled. Edward frowned but then began to smile. He knew it was only a joke.

"Anyway, said the worker, seeing as you are the son of our famous Thomas, we can help you out, you can start today by sweeping all the floors". Edward could not believe his luck. He jumped up into the air raising his hands shouting yes.

"T.t.t.t.thank you so very much sir," he said. He turned to Dorothy and gave her a tight hug. He then kissed her with such force that she had to push him away.

"Calm down Edward," she said. Edward apologised. The worker then handed Edward a brush.

"It's time to get to work now boy". Edward could not stop thanking the worker. He turned to Dorothy and told her he would see her later.

EDWARD STARTED to sweep the floor, he swept away all the dust and debris that he was previously standing on. The factory was so incredibly hot. The smell of molten metals filled the air. Edward continued to sweep the floor, he moved around the factory and bumped into the worker he had spoken to before.

"How are you getting on boy?" asked the worker.

"Very well sir," replied Edward. The worker asked Edward to come with him upstairs to his office. Edward was concerned, he was worried that he hadn't done a good enough job and that perhaps he was about to be laid off. Edward walked up the stairs, following the worker. They stepped into his office.

"Have a seat boy," said the worker. Edward sat down wondering what was going to happen.

The worker then opened a cabinet, he took out some items.

"These belonged to your father," said the worker.

"I think that they should be given to you, I have kept them in here for many years now". The items were placed on the desk, there were some overalls, some boots, a notepad, and a pocket watch. Edward picked up the pocket watch. He opened it to see that it had stopped. Edward put the watch in his pocket, he wanted to get that fixed later. He then picked up the notebook. Edward turned to the last page and in it was a note which said;

"Dear Edward, one day you are going to be alone, I will no longer be around to protect you. I have taught you everything I know. You will be a very strong, loving, and kind man. You have your mothers' heart. Always remember to follow your heart, Edward. I am so proud of you for being the amazing boy that you are. I hope one day you will forgive me for not seeing you turn into the wonderful amazing man that I know you will be. I love you son always and forever".

The note was signed off by your loving father. Edward began to weep, he started to show emotions. He missed his parents so much. To have them taken away at such a young age had haunted Edward for many years. The worker looked at Edward.

"Take the rest of the day off young man, go see your

girl and I shall see you tomorrow". Edward thanked the worker he took the notebook and pocket watch; he left the boots and overalls behind. He then left the office. He went down the stairs and picked up the brush. He swept one more piece of the floor before leaving the factory and heading home.

As he left the factory he stopped. He turned and decided to head towards the sycamore tree instead. He wanted to be alone for a little while. He wanted to think about why his father would take his own life and leave him all alone in the world. Edward arrived at the sycamore tree. He sat down at the base of the tree and opened the notebook. He read the note his father left for him, then he began to read the diary entries that his father had written about his days in the factory.

Edward had finished reading the notebook. He pulled the pocket watch out of his pocket. He opened it up and realised he could get it working by rotating the lever. Edward did this and the watch began to tick. He looked at it closely and realised in the cover of the watch was a picture of his mother. Edward did not have any pictures of his parents. All he had was his memories. He began to cry, his emotions getting the better of him. He put the watch down, placed his head into his knees and cried continuously. Until a soft voice spoke,

"Edward I am here". It was Dorothy.

Dorothy approached Edward; he had heard her voice, but he did not look up. He kept weeping into his hands. She sat down next to him, she shuffled ever so close to him. She touched his arm.

"Edward, it's ok I am here and you can talk to me

about anything," said Dorothy. He remained silent and continued to weep. She placed her arm around his shoulders and pulled him in for a cuddle. Edward then started to relax. He put his arms around Dorothy and cried onto her shoulder. He then started to tell her about what had happened to his parents.

Dorothy sat with Edward and listened to his story. It made Dorothy feel very emotional. She could not imagine a life without her parents. Edward told her how hard it was to live on the streets and have no one to go to. His story started to make Dorothy cry.

"Please don't cry my love," he said.

"I have done enough crying for everyone today". Edward then showed Dorothy the pocket watch and the picture of his mother.

"Wow she is so beautiful," said Dorothy. Edward replied,

"yes, she was". He talked about his mother and how she used to teach Edward how to peel vegetables and how to keep on top of cleaning the house. Dorothy knew that Edward loved his mother. She could tell just by how he was talking about her.

Edward then gave Dorothy the notebook.

"Read the last page," he said to Dorothy. Dorothy opened the notebook and turned to the last page. There she saw the letter that was written to Edward from his father. The letter sent chills down Dorothy's spine. She thought to herself was this written the day his father took his own life? She did not want to ask Edward at this time as she thought it may upset him further. Instead, Dorothy did not say a word. She just held him close and kissed him softly on the cheek. They both sat there in silence for the rest of the evening watching the sun go down over the horizon.

As TIME PROGRESSED FORWARD Edward continued to work in the smelting factory. He had been sweeping the floors for many weeks now and was hoping that a promotion would be on the cards. Dorothy continued to go to school, she now knew what she wanted to be when she was an adult. She wanted to be a nurse. She told Edward that she wanted to look after people and help them. Edward thought this was an amazing idea. He would tell Dorothy that he could never be anything special because he just did not have the intelligence. Dorothy would always tell Edward not to be silly and that he could do anything he wanted if he put his mind to it.

One day Edward was working in the factory, it was getting close to the end of the day.

"Hey, boy come here," called the worker. Edward put down his brush and approached the worker.

"You've been working so hard these last few weeks boy, I feel that its time you did a little something else". Edward's eyes lit up and he started to smile. Was this his big opportunity to prove his worth?

"What do you have in mind sir?" asked Edward.

"Well I need someone to unload the metals, bring them in to the factory and prepare them for smelting," replied the Forman. Edward could not believe he was getting a promotion. He felt that he was finally needed for something.

"Yes, sir I would be honoured," squeaked Edward in delight.

"Good, now tomorrow you start". The worker then handed Edward his wages for the week.

As Edward was leaving the factory, he saw Dorothy waiting for him outside.

"How was your day?" she asked. Edward grabbed Dorothy around her waist and pulled her in close.

"I got a promotion today and it's an extra 2 shillings a week."

"Edward that is fantastic," cried Dorothy. Edward then grabbed Dorothy and pulled her away from the factory.

"Quick, if we have enough time I can take you to the shops, I have just been paid today". Dorothy did not get much chance to reply. She was whisked away to the clothing shop.

THEY ARRIVED AT THE SHOP; Edward wanted to treat Dorothy to a new dress. Dorothy was delighted, no boy had ever taken her shopping before, let alone buy her anything. As they walked around the shop Dorothy noticed a beautiful mustard coloured dress. Her eyes lit up, and she couldn't help but stop and stare at this dress. Edward noticed that Dorothy had found something that she really liked.

"Why don't you try it on my love?" said Edward.

"No Edward it is too expensive I couldn't". Edward

continued to insist that Dorothy try on the dress. After many attempts at persuasion, she took the dress and went to try it on.

"Come here Edward," she called from the changing room. Edward walked toward the dressing room. His jaw dropped when he saw how gorgeous Dorothy looked in the mustard dress. It fit round her waist perfectly, it went down just below her knee. His eyes looking at her body up and down.

"Y.y.y.y.you look so beautiful," he stammered. Dorothy giggled and thanked Edward. Edward just could not believe how a dress could just fit someone so perfectly. He told Dorothy that he was buying her the dress.

Edward then realised that the dress would cost him his entire wages for the week. He did not tell Dorothy this because if he did, she would not let him buy it for her. Edward paid for the dress and told Dorothy that it was a special treat for her. She gave him a big hug and kissed him on the side of his head.

"Thank you so much". She was delighted and felt so loved. They then left the shop and started to head home. They passed the bakery on the way back to the house.

"Edward we should get a loaf of bread to take home for supper tonight," said Dorothy. Edward began to panic; he had no money left and he could not afford a loaf of bread. His mind started to wander. How do I get out of this he thought. He turned to Dorothy and said,

"it's late in the day the bread won't be that fresh now, come on let's just head home". Dorothy shrugged her shoulders, she then took Edward by the hand and walked him into the bakery.

The bakery smelt delicious, the smell of fresh bread and cakes made Dorothy smile. She looked around the bakery at all the fresh loaves of bread and all the delicious cakes that were on display. She could sense that Edward was feeling nervous and something was not quite right.

"What is it Edward?" she asked.

"N.n.nothing," he replied. Dorothy knew that Edward only stuttered when he was feeling nervous or anxious. The baker then appeared out of the back of the shop. As he came into the shop, he looked at Dorothy.

"What can I get you?" he asked. Dorothy replied,

"a fresh loaf of bread sir". As the baker went to take a loaf off the shelf, he noticed Edward in the corner of the shop. The baker then realised who it was.

"It's you! You little thief," he shouted at Edward. Edward started to feel sick the baker had remembered him when he stole the loaf of bread.

"You owe me money boy". Edward looked at the baker and said,

"I am sorry sir, I was hungry and I had no money and I had no home". The baker scowled at Edward and told him that it does not make it right to steal. If he was that hungry all he had to do was ask for some help.

Dorothy remained quiet, she remembered the day when she had first met Edward, she remembered how he looked so skinny and frail. She paused for a moment and said to the baker.

"The day he stole from you is the day I met the love of my life, he has been so lovely, sweet and kind. Please just give him a chance". The baker looked at Dorothy and let out an almighty sigh.

"Ok, its fine," he said. He then handed Dorothy a loaf of bread and told her that there was no charge. Edward could not believe what was happening. Why were so many people being so generous? Why did so many people actually care? He was stunned. They both left the bakery and then headed home in time for supper.

"HI MOTHER," called Dorothy as she came into the kitchen with a fresh loaf of bread.

"This is lovely," replied Anna.

"It's still warm, let me get this prepared for supper". Dorothy wanted to help her mother in the kitchen. They began to prepare the vegetables and Anna sliced the bread ready for the meal. Dorothy felt happy, it was not very often that her and Anna did things together.

"I love you mother," said Dorothy. Anna stopped what she was doing, this was not a conversation that they would normally have. "Anna turned to Dorothy,

"I love you too my sweetheart". The two then embraced in a hug. Dorothy felt that all the difficult times were just a thing of the past and that her and her mother could be close once again.

"So boy, how are you getting on at the factory?" asked George. Edward informed George that he had been given a promotion, to help bring the metals into the factory and prepare them for smelting. He told George that it was an extra 2 shillings a week. George was pleased he told Edward that he could now help out more around the house and help buy the groceries each week. Edward agreed with this as he wanted to help out so much. He wanted to make George feel so proud of him.

"I see that you're maturing nicely boy," said George.

"Thank you, sir," replied Edward. George then looked across to Anna and said

"what do they call this love, coming of age". Anna nodded and told Edward that he was definitely turning into a sweet young man and that they were so happy to have him living with them. Edward felt loved, he felt that he had a family again. He was beginning to feel proud of himself and that he was no longer that homeless little boy. But a young man who was going to go far in life.

It was morning, the time had come for Edward to start in his new job at the factory. He got up very early as he was extremely excited. He waited downstairs for Dorothy to arrive. He sat on the armchair feeling giddy and excited. Then he heard a door, downstairs came Dorothy wearing the beautiful mustard dress that he had bought for her the previous day. She looked as beautiful as ever, her long golden hair was put into a plait. It was hanging over her right shoulder.

"Wow, my lady," he said. Dorothy smiled and said to Edward

"you still approve then". Edward nodded and said to Dorothy

"I am the luckiest person alive". Dorothy giggled and said "well let's get you to work." They both then left the house and Dorothy escorted Edward to the factory. The two embraced with a long passionate kiss, before Edward said he needed to go and they would see each other after he had finished work.

Edward approached the worker. He asked him where he needed to be.

"Okay boy, you need to go out front and help bring in those metals." Edward nodded and went out to the front of the factory. His heart sank when he saw what he would need to lift and bring in. The beams he saw looked heavier than he was. He knew there was no way he could lift these up. Edward did not want to disappoint anyone. He approached one of the beams and bent down to try and lift it.

"What on earth are you trying to do?" said a worker.

"Well, sir I am trying to get the beams inside."

"Well that won't work, it's far too heavy for one person to lift," said the worker. Edward felt relieved he knew then that this would be a teamwork job and that he didn't have to try and do it all alone.

"My name is William," said the worker.

"I.I.I.I'm Edward," stuttered Edward. Edward was nervous. He hadn't had any male friends in a very long time. The worker put his hand forward to gesture a handshake. Edward accepted the handshake and two shook hands. They then started to move the beams together into the factory.

Edward and William spoke all day long about what they liked to do and their interests. Edward would talk about Dorothy a lot. William knew that Edward was in love he could tell by how enthusiastic he was about Dorothy.

"Sounds like you have got a great girl there," said William. Edward laughed and replied,

"she is amazing, she makes me feel so incredible inside". The pair continued to engage in deep conversation for the rest of the day. When the shift came to an end. William said to Edward,

"let's be friends". Edward smiled and said

"certainly". Edward knew now that he had a friend in William and that things were really looking up for him.

Edward and William began to spend a lot of time together. The new-found friendship between the two boys would last many hours after work. They had a unique male bond. Something that neither boy had felt before. Edward felt on top of the world. Not only now did he have a home, a beautiful girlfriend. He also had an amazing new friend in William. Their friendship would only grow over time. Edward didn't care. He was not going to allow things to get in the way of his happiness and his new-found friendship.

3

BLOOD BROTHERS

Brotherly love is a bond, an unspoken bond that is undeniably hard to break. Just because someone is not from your natural bloodline does not mean they are not family.

WEEKS HAD PASSED Edward and William worked together every day at the factory. They would always help one another throughout their shift. They would sit together during their breaks. They would then spend some time after work together, playing marbles together on top of some of the old drum barrels. William was a very talented marble player and was teaching Edward to play. Dorothy would continue to visit Edward after work, hoping that she would be able to spend some quality time with him. Edward had a new friend now, he wanted to spend time with his friend. This could at times make Dorothy feel jealous inside. Dorothy felt that Edward did not care for her anymore. The time that they had spent was becoming less and less as each day went past. At times Dorothy would find herself sat on her mound under the sycamore tree on her own. Hoping that Edward would turn up to visit her. Dorothy felt lost, alone and that her relationship with Edward may be coming to an end. Dorothy was so in love with Edward that this was breaking her heart. However, she just didn't know how to tell him.

"Edward, are we going to spend some time together this week or are you going to be playing your silly game all the time," said Dorothy. Edward looked up and went bright red in the face.

"Y.y.y.yes my lady," replied Edward. He then turned to William and shrugged his shoulders. William did not want to get in the way of the relationship that Edward and Dorothy had.

"Edward it's fine, you spend time with your lady, I will see you tomorrow here at work," said William. Edward nodded towards William and then turned to Dorothy. The two then went for a walk together where they sat down under the sycamore tree.

Dorothy sat there quietly for a few moments.

"Is everything okay my love?" asked Edward. Dorothy looked at Edward and then burst into tears.

"Why, are you not bothering with me anymore?" she asked.

"I.I.I.I am so sorry my love, I did not realise I was upsetting you by spending time with William," replied Edward. Edward then put his arms around Dorothy and told her that he would make more of an effort with her, but he did like having William as his friend. Dorothy was happy that Edward had a friend, but she was so envious that all his time was spent with William and not with her anymore. Dorothy lay into Edward's chest and said,

"promise me, you will spend more time with me". Edward breathed deeply and replied,

"I promise".

———————

THE FOLLOWING MORNING Edward was up bright and early. He had made breakfast for everyone in the house and had made a huge effort to clean up the house. George came downstairs first

"bloody hell boy, well done, who would have expected this?" he said. He then sat at the table and started to tuck in to his breakfast. Shortly after Anna and Dorothy came downstairs together.

"Oh wow," said Anna who was delighted that she did not have to slave away in the kitchen that morning. Dorothy looked around, she smiled at Edward and whispered to him

"thank you". Edward then knew that he had made the effort to make Dorothy feel happy again. They all then sat down and ate breakfast together before it was time to set off for work.

Dorothy accompanied Edward to work, they walked to work hand in hand chatting and laughing it was like the good old days again. Edward knew that he had won Dorothy's heart back and that things between them were stronger than ever. When they arrived at the factory William was stood at the entrance waiting.

"What time do you call this mate?" he said to Edward.

Dorothy snapped

"he's not bloody late you fool". Edward looked at Dorothy in disbelief he couldn't believe that she got so angry for nothing more than a silly joke. William dropped his head down.

"I am sorry, I did not mean to cause you any offence". Dorothy then felt horrible, she apologised to William for being blunt. She then gave Edward a kiss and told him that she would see him later on.

The boys got ready for their shift ahead, they began talking about wanting to work on the smelters. They both wanted to be promoted, but they did not want to stop working together. Edward told William that his father used to be a smelter and when he was younger, he would come in to the factory and help his father out. He learned so much about the smelting through his father and he wanted to follow in his father's footsteps. William listened to Edward tell his stories about how Edward and his father would enjoy the smells of molten metals and how they used to extract the ore from these. William was amazed at how knowledgeable Edward was. He then said to William

"what was your father's name?" Edward replied

"Thomas". William then stopped and paused.

"Thomas was your father?" said William.

"Yes, he was, why?" replied Edward. William then went on to explain that Thomas was not just an ordinary smelter but he was also the reason as to why William works in the factory. Edward was intrigued he wanted to know what had happened, how his father had helped to get William work. William went on to say that he was once homeless too, his family had abandoned him, and he just left to fend for himself. He explained that one night he took refuge in the factory to escape a storm. He thought that the factory was empty and that no one was there. All he wanted to do was get some sleep and feel safe.

William then told Edward that when he was in the factory he was looking around trying to find somewhere to sleep. As he was moving around, he knocked over a shovel which caused a bang. That's when he heard the voice.

"Who's there?" this voice boomed. William said he started to panic, he froze and then out of the shadows came this man looking down on him. William then looked at Edward and said the man said to me

"well who are you and what are you doing in this factory?" William replied with,

"I am sorry sir I don't have anywhere else to go." Thomas then introduced himself to William and told him that he could stay in the factory for one night. That if he needed a place to stay that he could come back in the morning and do some work to help make money to find somewhere to live.

"He looked after me," said William.

"He gave me a job, somewhere to sleep, he was like a father to me, a father that I never had". Edward was stunned this was his father and he had no idea that his father had been helping someone else. Edward then reached into his pocket and pulled out his father's journal. He flicked through some of the pages and there was a diary entry.

"Today I found a young boy in the factory, he told me he was homeless, he had nowhere to go. No money, no food and was scared. I took pity on this boy, I gave him something to

eat, some blankets and offered him a job to start tomorrow. I wonder if he will work here, I hope he does and I hope he is willing to learn lessons in life. Lessons I am prepared to teach him".

Edward showed the diary to William. William was in shock; he had no idea that Thomas had kept a diary.

"So, we are like brothers?" asked William. Edward shrugged his shoulders, he closed his eyes and replied.

"I guess we are". Edward was not sure what to make of the situation. He thought about Dorothy and what she would think of all this. He did not want to risk losing Dorothy. But he knew that as soon as he would see her, he would have to tell her the truth. The two boys continued working until the end of their shift. They both spoke about what Thomas was like and how he basically treated the boys the same, both like his sons. As the horn went to signal the end of the shift Edward said to William,

"I have to go now". William was stunned by this as they played marbles daily after work every single day. He just replied with,

"ok, see you tomorrow".

EDWARD RAN out of the entrance and down the canal, Dorothy was walking towards the factory. He ran straight up to Dorothy and picked her up and spun her round.

"I have missed you so much," he said. Dorothy was smitten she hadn't seen Edward this happy to see her in such a long time. He then put her down, pulled her in and kissed her deeply.

"Oh Edward, that was so beautiful," she said. Edward then told Dorothy that he had learned so much today and that he couldn't wait to tell her what he had found out. He then grabbed her by the wrist and said,

"let's go to the sycamore tree."

Edward asked Dorothy to sit with him. Dorothy was very intrigued as to what Edward was going to tell her. Edward then started to explain about his father, and that there was links to William.

"What do you mean?" asked Dorothy. Edward was speaking so fast that Dorothy was struggling to understand what he was saying. Edward stopped, he slowed down his speech. He then explained that his father had taken William under his wing. Instead of keeping him in the house he kept him in the factory and gave him a job. He then showed Dorothy the diary entries about William. Dorothy read them,

"I am so sorry," she replied. Edward did not expect an apology from Dorothy.

"Why are you sorry?" asked Edward. Dorothy looked into Edward's eyes

"he is your brother and I was jealous that I was going to lose you to a friend". Edward looked deep into Dorothy's eyes.

"It's ok my love you don't need to be sorry, I love you". Dorothy told Edward that she was not going to be jealous anymore and encouraged Edward to start spending time with William as they were basically family now.

Edward was just amazed about how understanding Dorothy was. He couldn't believe that things were going so well for him. Dorothy was deeply in love with Edward, she did not want to see him sad or unhappy. She knew that this was probably the last piece of family that Edward had. She did not want to stop that, nor did she want to get in the way.

"Remember all that time ago when you told me that your mother had said follow your dreams" Dorothy said. Edward nodded, he hugged Dorothy

"I cannot believe you remember that," he replied.

How would I ever forget that?" Dorothy said. Edward giggled and the pair decided to head home.

IT WAS SUNDAY, Edward did not have to go to work. He had arranged to meet up with William. The boys decided to play some football and marbles. They were having lots of fun. William was very talented at games; Edward could not keep up with him. After they had played for a few hours, William grabbed Edward by the hand.

"Want to make it official?" he said.

"Official what do you mean?" replied Edward. William just looked at Edward like he was being stupid.

"Well blood brothers what do you think I mean?" Edward was so confused he did not know what a blood brother was, but he did not want William to know that.

"Of course, I know what you mean," replied Edward.

"Excellent, let's do this then," replied William.

William then reached into his pocket and pulled out his pocket knife.

"W.w.w.w.what are you doing?" stammered Edward. William could see that Edward was very anxious.

"You really don't know what a blood brother is?" asked William.

"No, I don't," replied Edward. William went on to explain that it was just a small cut on the hand and then they would shake hands sharing blood. This making them blood brothers. Edward agreed and William proceeded to cut his own hand. The sight of William's blood made Edward feel dizzy and faint.

"Your turn," said William. Edward couldn't cut himself he was too scared to even attempt this. He then said to William

"you do it to me." William then grabbed Edward's hand and sliced it with the blade. The pair then shook hands. Then embraced in a cuddle. They were officially blood brothers now.

EDWARD COULD NOT WAIT to tell Dorothy the news that he and William were now officially blood brothers. The boys played a game of marbles together before Edward set off back home. When he arrived home, he was greeted by Dorothy. She noticed the blood dripping from his hand.

"Edward what has happened to your hand?" she gasped.

"My love, I have incredible news," replied Edward.

"William and I are officially blood brothers". Dorothy continued to just stare at Edward's hand she was rather shocked that Edward would go to great lengths to feel like he had a brother.

"Edward you did not need to do that," she said.

"I know but this means a lot to me". Dorothy understood that this was maybe the only family Edward had left. She gave him a cuddle and asked him to come and sit down, so she could clean his wound.

Edward sat down on the chair. Dorothy went in the kitchen to get some cotton and some water. George arrived back in; he had been in the pub drinking. He noticed Edward's cut on his hand.

"I remember that," he said.

"Blood brothers now are you boy?" Edward grinned and replied,

"yes sir". George informed Edward he did exactly the same thing when he was younger with his friend.

"Well, where is your friend now?" asked Edward. George huffed and puffed.

"It was Harry," he replied. Edward's heart sunk. He still felt so guilty about the death of Harry from all those months ago. His body language dropped and he fell silent.

"I am so sorry sir," Edward said to George. George let out a huge sigh.

"It was not your fault". George then started to talk about Harry, how they were best friends from a very young age and how they used to love playing marbles together.

"Harry is the reason I met my beautiful wife". Anna smiled at George.

"Yes, my dear," she replied. Dorothy was keen to know how her parents had met. "Father what happened how did you meet mother?" George smiled at Dorothy,

"well me and Harry were in The Crown, it's a pub just outside of town. Harry saw Anna and told me that his friend was here. When I looked over my heart melted. There she was my beautiful wife". Anna just smiled from ear to ear she loved hearing the compliments that her husband would say. Dorothy and Edward smiled. George and Anna were just like they were in the past.

Dorothy came over to Edward and began to tend to his wounds. She knew that her father had caused some upset by mentioning Harry, she couldn't be annoyed at her father as him and Harry had been friends for their entire lives. Edward held out his hand, Dorothy carefully cleaned his wound. She whispered softly to him

"I love you". This made Edward smile. She then applied some cotton to his hand and told him not to take it off until she said so. Edward laughed, he dare not do anything that he has been told not to do. Especially by Dorothy. George piped up,

"I guess we all know who's in charge out of you two then". Dorothy and Edward both giggled, they were both deeply in love with one another.

EDWARD WANTED Dorothy and William to get to know each other better, he would try on so many occasions to get them to talk and to spend time together. However, Dorothy never really wanted to do this. She just wanted to spend time with Edward. One day Edward said to Dorothy,

"I have spent so much time with your family, will you please try a little and spend some time with mine?"

Dorothy sighed she knew that this meant a lot to Edward. She grabbed Edward's hand.

"Ok, for you my darling," she said. Edward felt a huge sigh of relief he wanted the tensions to end between William and Dorothy. Edward then said to Dorothy

"no time like the present." With this he whisked her off and took her to see William. As they walked to the factory hand in hand, Edward noticed that Dorothy was unusually quiet. Edward squeezed her hand softly three times. Dorothy looked up blankly at Edward.

"Do you know what that means?" Edward softly asked Dorothy. Dorothy frowned slightly and looked briefly down at the intertwined hands

"no."

"It means I love you. Any time we are holding hands I want you to feel the love flowing from me to you, and if I squeeze you three times it's an extra affirmation to say

"I LOVE YOU." Dorothy smiled slowly.

"Thank you, Edward, you always know just what I need, I am a little anxious about spending time with you and William together. I kind of feel the odd one, I'm not jealous it's just a strange thing, having to share you." Edward laughed, a low rumble in his throat.

"Thank you Dorothy, don't fret, we will have a wonderful time together." Dorothy and Edward continued their walk to the factory happily, both smiling to themselves.

William was sat down outside the entrance to the factory, drawing a picture when they arrived.

"What are you drawing?" asked Dorothy. William held up an image of the canal.

"I am drawing what I see". Dorothy and Edward were amazed at the drawing that Edward had created out of just a small piece of charcoal.

"William that is remarkable," exclaimed Dorothy.

"Thank you," he replied. Dorothy then sat down with William and the two started to talk. Edward was happy that they were now talking and was very hopeful that things between Dorothy and William would start to get better.

"I will leave you two to talk," said Edward.

"I am just going to pop to the shop and get some eggs". Dorothy looked up at Edward and smiled.

"See you soon my love".

William and Dorothy were alone now, sat on the step entrance to the factory. William continued to draw.

"What else can you draw?" asked Dorothy.

"Anything you like," replied William. Dorothy could see how talented he was as an artist.

"Have you ever thought about selling your artwork?" she asked him.

"Never considered it," he replied. He then stopped drawing and turned to Dorothy. He looked into her eyes and said,

"you have the most beautiful eyes I have ever seen." Dorothy blushed. She started to giggle

"thank you," she replied. William then attempted to grab Dorothy's hand.

"Excuse me, what are you doing?" she screamed. William said to Dorothy,

"he will never need to find out." Dorothy was not impressed.

"I am with Edward do not try and do this again". William then grabbed Dorothy and tried to kiss her. She pushed him away and slapped him hard around the face.

"Never ever put your hands on me again," she shouted.

"I'm sorry, I have never kissed a girl before and I just wanted to see what it was like," replied William. Dorothy felt disgusted. She was torn on what to do. Does she tell Edward what William had just tried to do? She was confused, she did not want to upset Edward.

Shortly after Edward returned carrying some eggs and a loaf of bread. He noticed that William had a red mark on the side of his face and that Dorothy had moved a few feet away from him.

"What has happened here?" he asked. William looked at Edward and said,

"oh nothing I slipped and fell on the step". Edward then turned to Dorothy.

"Is everything ok my love?" he asked. Dorothy looked at Edward and said

"yes, everything is fine darling we are getting on really well". William held his breath and then let out a huge sigh of relief. Dorothy then stood up and gave Edward a very passionate kiss. She made sure that William could see this. She wanted him to know that she was with Edward and that nothing would ever change that.

William stopped drawing.

"Fancy a game of marbles?" he asked Edward. Edward looked at Dorothy she nodded to indicate that this was fine.

"Yes, certainly," Edward replied. The two boys then

started to engage in a game of marbles. Edward could tell that William was feeling tense, he had a funny feeling that something was not quite right.

"You can talk to me," Edward said.

"There is nothing really to talk about, let's play this game," replied William. Edward just nodded and continued to play marbles. Edward had never been able to play at the standard of William, but today he was playing much better. He knew something was not right. But he did not want to upset anyone. When the day ended. William went back into the factory and told Edward that he would see him again tomorrow.

EDWARD WENT HOME WITH DOROTHY. He was very worried about his blood brother. The walk home was very quiet. Dorothy held onto Edward's hand very tight. Something had happened but what? Edward could not get this out of his head. When they arrived home, Dorothy gave Edward a quick, cold kiss and said,

"goodnight my darling, I will see you in the morning". This was very unusual for Dorothy. Edward was very confused this just never happened. He then knew that he had to go and talk to William again to find out the truth.

Edward was lying on the sofa staring up at the ceiling. He could not stop thinking about what had changed. He could not settle nor could he fall asleep. This gave him little choice he needed to know what was going on. He needed to go and speak to William. When the house was quiet and everyone was asleep, Edward left. He went to the factory and went inside. He was looking for William. He has questions that he needed answers to. Edward crept up the metal stairs. They began to grind and then he heard William's voice.

"Who's there?" Edward replied,

"it's me Edward I am here to talk". William asked Edward to come up the stairs. When Edward arrived at the top of the stairs, he noticed that William had a dirty makeshift bed in the corner of the room and that he was still technically homeless. Edward felt so sorry for William as this was him only a few months ago.

"Come and sit down," then asked William. Edward then sat down on the makeshift bed next to William.

"Can you please tell me the truth about what happened today?" asked Edward. William sighed and told Edward that when he left, he and Dorothy got close.

"I really wanted to kiss a girl, I wanted to see what it felt like," said William. Edward was in disbelief his blood brother attempted to kiss his girlfriend.

Edward became angry

"is that why you had a red mark on your face, she hit you".

"Yes, she did," replied William. "How dare you try and kiss my girlfriend," replied Edward. William knew Edward was very angry, and he did not want this to ruin the relationship that they had both built up.

"I am truly sorry brother," William said. Edward stormed off out of the factory. He was angry he felt so betrayed. As he was walking home, he just couldn't let the anger go, but he knew he couldn't be angry forever. Edward stopped and paused. He did not want to lose his friendship with William. After turning things over in his head Edward turned around and headed back to the factory. When Edward arrived at the factory, and he saw William he felt the anger again but he couldn't stop feeling like he had no choice but to forgive William. He shrugged his shoulders and looked around the room.

"I am glad you told me the truth," he replied.

"Never let this happen again or that's it. We are finished," he told William. William started to smile he knew he had been forgiven. The two boys then shook hands.

"Brothers to the end," said William. Edward grinned and replied,

"yes, brothers till the day we die". The bond between the boys was strong. Edward now knew that he would have to tell Dorothy about what had happened.

THE FOLLOWING MORNING Edward was sat downstairs, he had been up for a while, waiting to clear the air and see his beautiful lady. He was ready for his day ahead. He was waiting for Dorothy. Dorothy came downstairs and was startled to see Edward ready so early.

"Are you ok my darling?" she asked.

"We need to talk my love," he replied. Dorothy sat down next to Edward, she started to feel concerned that something terrible was about to happen.

"Last night, when you were asleep I went to speak with William," he said. Dorothy started to panic, her hands were instantly clammy, and she felt sick to her stomach.

"I didn't do anything," she replied to William, her voice shaking with emotion. Edward took both of Dorothy's hand and told her that he knew that and that William had confessed everything to him. That he had tried to kiss her. Dorothy was shocked she couldn't believe that William had actually confessed to Edward about what had happened. Dorothy then said

"what did you do with him?" Edward looked at Dorothy and smiled.

"I forgave him, he is my blood brother and I love him". Dorothy did not say anything she just put her head onto Edward's shoulder and held him close. Edward slowly squeezed her hand three times, smiling.

Dorothy remained very cautious around William for the next few months. She did not want a repeat of what had happened in the past. She would only spend time with William if Edward was around. William would always try and make jokes towards Dorothy to try and ease the tensions between the two. But this would not usually work and Dorothy would continue to snub him throughout the time that the three spent together. Edward knew that this could not happen. He wanted everyone to get along.

"Please both of you, will you just try for my sake?" Dorothy stopped and paused she looked at Edward and then she looked at William.

"Ok she said, I will do this for you my darling". William then joked

"about time". Dorothy just rolled her eyes the two

then started to talk. This is exactly what Edward wanted, everyone to get along. With no tensions, anger or hate.

———

CHRISTMAS WAS COMING, it was a very cold December, there were lots of media reports about the rise of Hitler in Europe. Tensions would start to build. People would be talking in the markets. They were fearful of the unknown and if any tensions would make their way from Europe to Birmingham. People began to panic, the older generation more fearful. Dorothy would overhear people talking about the previous Great War. The unknown was ahead and the people of Birmingham clearly did not like this. Edward and Dorothy were oblivious to this. They were in love they did not have a care about what was happening in countries that were so far away. One morning George was in the kitchen talking to Anna.

"Something big is going to happen," he said. Anna turned to George.

"Don't be so silly this will all blow over after Christmas," she said. George not convinced then left the house. Dorothy asked her mother what was wrong.

"Your father is just worried that war may be coming". Dorothy then said wasn't that all sorted out before I was born.

"Yes, it was, don't worry everything is going to be fine," she said.

Edward was curious he was listening to the conversation. He was intrigued and wanted to know more. He went to the market and purchased a newspaper and he read the cover about the rise of Hitler and the Nazi party. When Edward saw that this was in Germany he relaxed, he did not need to think or worry about something that was happening so many miles away in a faraway land. As he walked through the market, he saw William.

"Hey William," called Edward. William ran over to Edward and said,

"have you been reading the news?" Edward then showed William the newspaper that he had just bought.

"Maybe we should look about signing up to the army," William said very excitedly. Edward just laughed at William.

"We are not old enough yet". William grinned

"but when we are, we should". Edward grinned and agreed and said yes when they were old enough.

"We are blood brothers and we stand together no matter what," said William. Edward agreed and said if they were going to join the army, they would do it at the right age and when the time was right.

IT WAS CHRISTMAS 1937; Edward had invited William over to the house. Dorothy was not overly keen on the idea, but she knew inside her heart that it was the right thing to do. Everyone was sat around the living room fire. It was warm and cosy, a stark contrast to the impersonal, draughty factory that William called home. William was so grateful to be invited over, to feel like he belongs somewhere during the festive period, even if it is for a few hours. He handed Edward a bag, somewhat shyly. Edward took the bag from William and opened it. In the bag was a pen knife.

"William you shouldn't have, but thank you so very much," replied Edward.

"Well boy that will come in useful," laughed George. Dorothy giggled her father was such a joker. Dorothy then handed Edward a present. Edward opened it and inside was a brand-new flat cap.

"It's incredible, I absolutely love it," he said. Dorothy was so happy that Edward enjoyed her gift.

It was then Edward's turn. He handed Dorothy a gift. It was in a small intricate, feminine box. Dorothy was very interested in opening this box to see what was inside. She carefully lifted the lid to the box and inside was a beautiful heart-shaped necklace.

"Edward this is absolutely breathtaking," she cried.

"It opens up Dorothy. If you look inside we could have a photograph done, and we could be together inside your pendant". Dorothy became very emotional, tears started to stream down her face. Tears of joy. Everyone in the room gasped, they were so happy that Edward could make Dorothy feel so loved and cared for. When Edward tore his eyes way from Dorothy's happy face, he saw George smiling at his loving wife.

All the gifts had been exchanged and it was time for dinner. The smell of the fresh vegetables and the meats was incredible. Everyone was so hungry and could not wait to tuck into their meals. George turned to William.

"So boy, what do you want to do with your life?" William looked straight at George and did not hesitate.

"I want to be a soldier". George clapped and was

pleased with this. Edward looked across and said to George,

"I will also sign up to become a soldier, of course when I am old enough". George looked at the boys.

"Good, we need more great soldiers for this fine country". Dorothy called out,

"you promised no more fighting". Edward looked at Dorothy.

"It's ok my love it's very unlikely that we will have to do any fighting." Dorothy's response

"you never know".

George went on to tell everyone around the table that representing your country is a very proud moment, even if there is no fighting. Everyone should do their part. Dorothy was not convinced but then Anna spoke out

"the last war was the reason that me and your father met". Anna went on to explain that George was a soldier and had served in the battle of the Somme. He took some shrapnel damage and when he returned home and was seen in the hospital. That's where Harry introduced us." George remained quiet. He had never spoken about the war or the battles he had faced on the battlefield. He then looked up and said to everyone,

"one day I will share my story". Everyone then continued with their meals. Edward and William would continue to talk about the army and how they would always have each other's backs as they were blood brothers.

4

TENSIONS ARISE

The fear of not knowing what the future holds can raise anxiety and tension in one's self. Tension can spread very quickly and consume entire communities.

SIX MONTHS HAD PASSED, it was now June 1938. Edward and Dorothy were now both 15 years old. The tensions in Europe had only increased. Everyday there was a new headline on the front paper either about Hitler, or something that prime minister Neville Chamberlain would quote to try and ease the tensions and fear inside the communities. There was a heavy promotion of for people to join the military. There would be leaflets everywhere. George knew what was coming. He remembered the battle of the Somme, something that he had never spoken about. George knew that Dorothy would not like what was coming if Edward chose to go down the army route.

Edward still worked at the smelting factory with William. Neither of them had been promoted. The days got longer and Edward and William were both dog tired at the end of the day. Dorothy was still studying hard in school, her dreams of being a nurse her main goal.

Edward and Dorothy were sat at home. They could hear George being very loud upstairs with Anna.

"What is going on?" asked Edward.

"I don't know," replied Dorothy. Dorothy was keen to know what was making her father feel so on edge. She crept up the stairs to listen to the conversation. She could hear George speaking about Germany.

"The Germans have already annexed Austria," George shouted to Anna. Dorothy didn't quite know what this meant. But she knew it didn't sound very good.

"George my darling, please don't worry. I am sure this will all blow over and no war will happen," Anna replied in a soft calming voice. Dorothy gasped the sound of war made her feel sick to her stomach. She crept back down the stairs to Edward and told him what she had heard.

"So, this is what all the commotion I hear in the factory and down the market is all about," he said.

"Edward do you think there is going to be trouble?" she shrieked.

"Honestly, my love, I don't know," replied Edward.

"But please my love let's not worry about that now and let's go out and enjoy ourselves". Dorothy nodded and agreed. They both got up and left the house to head towards the market.

As they arrived at the market, they saw William.

Dorothy rolled her eyes and thought to herself.

"Here we go, what is he going to do now?" Edward called to William. William looked over and started to walk over towards Edward. As he approached Edward, he noticed a girl sat on a wooden box crying. She was wearing a long grey dress. She had deep red hair. William couldn't see the girls face properly but he was so curious as to why she was so upset. William paused, he looked at Edward and then looked at the girl. Edward then noticed what William was looking at. Edward nodded at William to indicate that he should go and talk to this girl. William did not hesitate, he slowly walked over to the girl and sat down on the wooden box next to her.

"Excuse me, are you ok?" he asked. The girl continued to cry in her hands not appearing to notice William talking to her. William waited a minute.

"Hello miss. I am William," he said. The girl remained sobbing, she then said

"Clara" in a soft snuffly voice. William had got a response. He was happy. Yet he was still very intrigued as to why Clara was so upset.

Edward and Dorothy continued to watch. Dorothy wanted to help the girl. She asked Edward if she should go over and try and help. Edward turned to Dorothy.

"Why my love, let William try if he cannot help then yes go and help her". Dorothy rolled her eyes again at Edward.

"My love will you please stop doing that?" he said.

"Ok, but this is really silly now," she replied. They then noticed that William had managed to get this girl to look up. William then said to the girl.

"Please tell me what's wrong I want to help you". Clara looked into William's eyes. William looked into Clara's. William's heart begun to pound. He couldn't believe her gorgeous curly red hair and her amazing brown eyes.

"Wow, you are so beautiful". Clara looked at William in disbelief.

"I don't feel beautiful," she replied. Clara then started to sob uncontrollably again. William was dumbfounded he just didn't know what was wrong. William did not want to give up. He wanted to persevere to try and help Clara.

He sat next to Clara and waited, whilst Dorothy and Edward stood watching. Clara then stood up abruptly. She turned to William and said,

"my father lost his job, now I am worried about how we are going to survive." William did not like to hear this. He gave Clara some shillings and told her that he would help her if she needed that. Clara smiled; she wrapped her arms around William squeezing him tight.

"Thank you, William," she said in a very soft quiet voice. William embraced the hug. With this Dorothy and Edward approached slowly.

"Clara, I would like you to meet my very special friends Dorothy and Edward". Clara looked at Dorothy.

"You are so pretty," Clara said in a small hoarse voice. Dorothy giggled. She thanked Clara for the lovely compliment. Edward reached out to shake Clara's hand. She accepted the handshake. William was grinning and Edward could see this. He felt happy that William was able to help someone out in need. Dorothy felt as if the world had been lifted off her shoulders. She could not be happier if William had a female friend as the attention wouldn't be on her anymore.

"Clara, would you like to spend some time together?" William asked. Clara stayed silent. She was not sure what to do. She did not think that her father would like her spending time alone with a boy.

"Sure, but how about just the 4 of us for now?" she replied. William felt a bit gutted. He wanted to spend time with Clara alone. But he also knew he had to respect her wishes.

"Yes Clara of course the 4 of us. If that is okay with you two?" he said to Dorothy and Edward. Edward did not want to make the decision on behalf of Dorothy, they had only just met this girl. He whispered into Dorothy's ear

"what do you think?" Dorothy spoke out to everyone.

"Yes, let's all go and have some fun". Dorothy did not mind having another girl around. In her mind she thought this could be good, a female companion. Someone she could enjoy spending time with. Whilst the boys went about their business playing their games.

As the four of them went to go for a walk, there was a very loud bellowing voice

"Clara let's go". Clara froze she looked at Dorothy,

"it's my father I have to go now." William's face dropped he had only just met this beautiful girl, and he wanted to spend some time with her, to get to know her.

"Clara, when I say let's go I mean let's go," boomed the voice.

"I am so sorry I have to go, maybe see you around?" she said to everyone. Clara then ran off down the market to her father. William looked defeated Edward could see this.

"It's ok, we shall see her again," Edward said to William. William rubbed his hands together and shrugged his shoulders.

"I, guess so," he replied. "Come on William, let's go play some games," said Edward.

"No, not today. I think I'm gonna hang around here for a bit," replied William. Dorothy felt her spirits lift. She had Edward all to herself, and she knew exactly what to do.

As WILLIAM WALKED off into the market Dorothy grabbed Edward's hand.

"Let's go and get a picnic," she said. Edward was fizzled,

"a picnic?" he replied. Dorothy giggled,

"yes, silly you'll see". She then took him by the hand and took him over to the greengrocer. She grabbed some strawberries and some apples. Edward was confused as to what was going on, but he did not mind. He was spending time with Dorothy. They continued to buy bread and some biscuits. Dorothy then said,

"let's go". Edward then had a hunch about what was going to happen. They walked down to the canal. Dorothy carrying a basket with one hand and Edward holding her other hand. As they walked down the canal Edward would squeeze Dorothy's hand three times. This would always make Dorothy smile. She loved it when Edward expressed his love for her. Together they walked up to their favourite place, the sycamore tree. Dorothy laid down a blanket that she had brought with her. Edward thought to himself

"was this her plan all along?" They both sat down on the blanket and Dorothy started to organise the fresh fruit and the savories.

Dorothy looked into Edward's eyes,

"I have been waiting for a moment like this for a very long time." Edward smiled. He gazed lovingly into Dorothy's deep blue eyes. The pair started to munch on the strawberries and had some biscuits after. Edward then took Dorothy's hand, he squeezed it again three times. Dorothy then asked Edward

"why do you squeeze my hand three times? Is there a story behind it"? Edward nodded,

"yes, my love. When I was young my mother used to squeeze my hand three times. She did this so I knew I was loved, I was protected and I was safe". Dorothy's heart sank. Edward barely spoke of his mother.

"What was your mother like Edward?" she asked. Edward's eyes welled up, a tear from each eye rolling down his face.

"M.m.m.my mother was amazing, she used to read stories to me, she used to hold me in her arms and tell me how much she loved me". Dorothy knew then that Edward missed his mother deeply.

"What happened to your mother?" she asked. Tears continued to stream Edward's face. Edward paused he wiped away his tears.

"She got sick, it happened so fast. She died holding my hand, the last thing she said to me was always follow your dreams." Edward then leaned into Dorothy's shoulder. She placed her hand on his head and begun to stroke his hair.

"I love you," she said to Edward. The pair just sat there together and held onto one another until the sun went down.

As THE SUN rose the following day Edward woke. He woke to the thundering footsteps of George upstairs. He was clearly getting ready for the day. Anna came downstairs first and started to prepare breakfast for everyone. Then the thundering footsteps of George came down the stairs. He was huffing and puffing. His towering presence darkened the room. He sat down at the table and just stared into empty space. Edward was unsure of what was wrong with George, however, he remained very curious. Dorothy came downstairs shortly after, she came to the dining table and sat down next to her father. She looked up at him. She knew something was wrong. Edward then joined them at the table as breakfast was being served by Anna.

"What is wrong father?" asked Dorothy. George cleared his throat, and quietly he said,

"I'm scared". Edward was dumbfounded what could this giant of a man be afraid of.

"What is scaring you father?" asked Dorothy. George then put his head in his hands and softly said

"war". Edward was so curious as to why George would be so scared of war.

"It's ok sir," he said.

"I will be a soldier and I will help protect everyone". George then raised his head and stared straight through Edward.

"You don't understand boy, you have no idea what it's like. The pain the suffering, the things you see". Dorothy placed her hand on her father's.

"Share it with us," she pleaded. George nodded. He knew it was time to tell his tale.

George held onto Dorothy's hand he looked at Anna, he then looked at Edward. He held his breath and then said,

"It was September 1916, I was 19 years old at the time. We were sent to the Somme in France, it started off as a normal day, but hell was all around me when we reached the front.

The blood-curling screams of men dying all around me. The soldiers rushing to carry the wounded away, to save the sick and the dying. Air was thick with the smell of death, rotten flesh and the smell of ammunition.

Every time I rushed forward with the others I was scared of what I would see, they were dropping like dominoes. The sight was horrific. Men dying and dead next to me. The sight of a river of blood flowing freely not stopping. Ever-flowing and never ceasing to stop.

I could feel the thud of my heart pounding with every step I took. Edging closer to the battlefield was exciting and scary in equal measure, my adrenaline pumping through my veins. I was scared and excited to be part of the bloody battle. The Somme wasn't what I had imagined; a landscape with a few soldiers battling. It was a scene of carnage and of immense suffering and horror.

I didn't expect the wave of sadness, the horror of war to hit me, to realise I could be one of the soldier's dead, with no grave for the fallen. Unmarked, a life wasted for what? The horror of the Somme is the stuff of nightmares. The unspeakable blood, terror and a living nightmare.

I was sent to be a solider to protect our country and be a hero. I knew I had a job to do to protect and serve, but at what cost? One life, hundreds, thousands or millions? I lost count of the soldiers next to me that became the fallen. The ground turning to red as they fell, the sound of the others shouting for the stretcher bearer. I remember shouting for Arthur the unit stretcher bearer as Jack fell, he had been with me from the training camp. He was only a kid he had lied about his age. Arthur did indeed come to collect him, but as he approached, he shouted to say he was a goner. I didn't look back to see if he had been retrieved, I was scared to look in the face of death".

Everyone who was sat round the table was sat there in absolute shock. Dorothy continued to hold her father's hand. Anna began to weep. Edward just could not believe the horror's that George had faced. He had never heard anyone speak of the war before. All he had heard was that soldiers have fun and travel around the world. This story was about death, suffering and immense loss. Edward wanted to speak, but he just did not know what to say. Dorothy softly said,

"father I am so sorry for what you have been through". She then leaned into her father's chest engaging in a hug. After a few moments George stood up.

"I am going out for a while," he said. Edward looked at George and said

"I need to get to work".

"Father can I come with you?" asked Dorothy quietly.

"No, I need some time alone," George replied. Dorothy then turned to Edward and indicated that she would walk with him to work.

AS THEY WALKED TOGETHER to the factory Edward would continuously squeeze Dorothy's hand three times. Dorothy would smile every time and squeeze his hand back gently three times. Edward knew that Dorothy was very upset he wanted to try and cheer her up.

"My love, I know you're worried about your father, but he will be ok," said Edward. Dorothy squeezed Edward's hand really tight, tears brimming in her eyes

"I have never seen father like this before," she replied, her thoughts churned with her father's unusual disposition.

"We will be there for him," replied Edward. This made Dorothy smile, she loved the fact that Edward was going to be there to help her father through his difficult days. As they approached the factory, they saw William, he was talking to someone who was wearing a long black coat. As they got closer, they realised it was Clara.

"What is she doing here?" Edward whispered to Dorothy.

"Dorothy shrugged her shoulders,

"how would I know?" she replied. As they approached William they were greeted with,

"hey guys, look who's here". Clara turned and smiled at the pair. She then said

"I had to come and see William, I had to say thank you to him for the help he gave me the other day".

William was smiling, a huge grinning smile, he clearly liked talking to Clara. She had an aura about her. A powerful sense of independence. She was beautiful like a piece of fine art in a museum. He could not take his eyes off her.

"Would you like to do something together one day miss?" William asked Clara. Clara smiled

"I would love to, but I cannot let my father find out, he would not like it at all!" she replied to William. William did not care; he had never had a girlfriend before. He just wanted to spend some time with a girl, especially one as beautiful as Clara. Clara looked at William,

"I shall see you when you finish work then," she said. William grinned.

"Certainly miss," he replied. Dorothy was watching on. This made her skin crawl, she remembered when William had tried to come onto her and was worried he would try this again with Clara. She wanted to warn Clara, but for Edward's sake, she didn't. Dorothy walked ahead of the group now, lost in thought. Edward picked up his pace to catch up. As Edward caught up, he shouted over his shoulder to William,

"hurry up we don't want to be late".

Edward walked into the factory; come on William we have got work too. A love-struck William kissed Clara's hand and then reluctantly followed Edward into the factory. Edward was quiet that morning. He could not get the image of a weakened George out of his mind.

"What's wrong brother?" asked William.

"Oh nothing, I just have a lot on my mind," replied Edward. William clearly knew that something was bothering Edward.

"Is it Dorothy?" he asked.

"No not at all, let's just get our work done William please," Edward snapped back. William was not happy about how Edward spoke to him. He stormed off in anger and went outside to get some fresh air. Edward paused he knew he had overreacted, he knew it was not William's fault that he felt the way he did. Edward went outside to meet William, and as he came round the corner he spotted William, leaning against a wall. He looked exhausted.

"I am sorry," Edward said. "I am really worried about George". William did not like George at all, he was intimidated by his presence this huge dominating mountain of a man. William was terrified of George and did not want to keep hearing about him, his response was curt,

"well he is a big man he will be fine". Edward just shrugged this off and carried on working, whistling away to a song that he had heard on the wireless.

―――――――――

It was the end of the day, as promised Clara was waiting outside the factory for William. Dorothy was also waiting for Edward. The two girls were having what appeared to be a long discussion about the boys. William started to panic. He did not want Clara to know about his past with Dorothy. He started to rub his hands together and his bottom lip was twitching. As soon as Dorothy saw Edward come out, she stepped forward,

"Come on Edward we should get back now," called Dorothy. Dorothy held out her hand to Edward, and he noticed that it was trembling slightly.

"Are you ok, my lady?" he asked quietly, taking her hand. Dorothy nodded and squeezed his hand three times. Edward grinned. Dorothy sighed gently as they began to walk home.

"I'm just a little anxious about my father that's all." Edward stopped and pulled her in close. He stroked her hair, and she leaned heavily into him for a moment.

"It means a lot to me that you are with me Edward, my father likes you too, I just need to know he is ok." Edward pulled her in tighter and murmured into her hair,

"don't worry beautiful, your father will be fine, come on quick, let's get home, everything will be ok I promise." Edward tugged at Dorothy's hand, and they continued their walk home together. Edward smiled as they walked,

'Dorothy needs me' he thought. He felt happy. He had a purpose to protect and care for Dorothy. He loved her with all of his heart, and he wanted to make sure that he was there for her as she had been for him all that time ago.

William and Clara were alone now and William liked this, he had a huge smirk on his face at the prospect of having Clara all to himself.

"Would you like to come for a walk with me miss?" William asked Clara.

"Yes of course," replied Clara in a very confident tone. She was not fearful of anyone. She was very strong-willed. She had a soft spot for William, she thought he was handsome if not a bit skinny. William was smiling he was feeling good about himself. He took Clara down a narrow, stony path leading to a canal towards the woodland.

"Would you like to go through the woods?" he asked Clara. Clara was unsure she didn't think it would be safe, but she didn't want William to think little of her.

"Ok, let's go," she said. The pair walked into the woods. The trees were towering over the path. The bushes were overgrown. You could smell the damp leaves. It was dark, sun blocked out by the towering trees that were covered in leaves. The temperature felt cool. It was shaded and isolated. Clara rubbed her shoulders,

"it's a bit cold in here," she said to William.

"It's cold in the factory every night," he replied. The ground soon became stodgy, the path had turned into mud.

"William my feet keep slipping in this," Clara wailed.

"It's ok, it will all settle down let's just keep walking," he replied. After they passed the blackberry bush and the rhododendrons with their gnarled and knotted roots, William started to look around. He was checking behind him and in front of him. Clara was too busy navigating her way through the slippery terrain to notice William. William knew the coast was clear, he put his arm around Clara.

"What are you doing?" she asked.

"I was just going to give you a hug," he responded in a cool, quiet voice. Clara was now feeling on edge she knew this was way too soon. She was getting very tense, but she allowed William to keep his arm around her. As they got deeper into the woods William moved to slide his hand down on Clara's breast. As he was sliding his hand towards her breast she moved away, quickly. She screamed

"no," and then pushed William away. He walked purposefully towards her, towering over her. Clara turned to face him, she was angry and fuelled with rage that this person would touch her the way he did. She threw a punch and caught William on the end of his nose. Sending him crashing onto the muddy floor. Clara then approached William she stood over him.

"I did not give you permission to touch me like that". Clara turned and walked back down the path, carefully through the trees and bushes. Only when she got out of the trees, did she hold her hand up and watch it tremble. She was shocked to see that her hand was not only trembling, it was covered in blood, William's blood.

William continued to lay there on the floor, he felt humiliated. However, he was glad that there was no one around to see him getting knocked down by a girl. He thought to himself that he blew his chances with Clara, he started to punish himself in his head. Why am I so stupid? Why can I not treat girls the way Edward does. As he started to stand up, he noticed the blood dripping from his face. He pulled out his handkerchief wiped his nose and realised that Clara had caused him to have a nose bleed. He ran down the path hoping to catch Clara. When he got out of the woods, he looked around. He noticed her sat on the edge of the canal sobbing. He thought to himself "what have I done?" He approached the sobbing Clara. As he got closer, she stood up.

"Stay away from me," she said.

"I am so sorry miss, I don't know what came over me," he replied. \

"If you come any closer I'll put you in this canal," she said to William. William started to sob. He fell to his knees and started to cry out that he had nothing, no family no home, nothing. Clara started to feel sorry for William. She walked over to him and placed her hand on his head. He sobbed and sobbed.

"I am deeply sorry miss," he kept repeating. Clara just could not stay angry at this poor sobbing boy. He had already helped her so much.

"Never ever do that again," she said. She then put her arm around William and gave him a cuddle.

Dorothy and Edward arrived back home. As they came in the door, they saw George sat with Anna.

"Father is everything ok?" asked Dorothy. George smiled at Dorothy.

"Yes, I feel much better now. Opening up and talking about many experiences have made me come to terms with things a little better," he replied. Dorothy felt so relieved that her father was feeling better in himself. Edward was somewhat more skeptical. He thought that this was an act from George and that there is no way that anyone who had been through what George had been through would be ok after just talking about it once. However, Edward did not want to create a scene and went along with Dorothy to comfort her father. Edward sat next to George; Dorothy sat the other side. They each took one of George's hands. Edward could not believe the size of George's hand. It swallowed his whole. They just sat there with George in silence. Reassuring him that they were there for him.

OVER THE NEXT FEW DAYS, William would spend a lot of time with Clara. He knew he had to behave himself. Clara was not a person for messing about or putting up with him being foolish. He would talk to Edward all day about Clara. Edward was pleased, he was happy that his blood brother had met someone and that things were looking up for him.

"I tell you Edward, she is very strong-willed," William said to Edward.

"Well that is good then isn't it," replied Edward. William then went on to tell Edward about the incident where he had tried to touch Clara. "So that's how you got those black eyes then," joked Edward.

"Yes, I did not really fall over, I was just embarrassed to tell anyone that I got knocked down by a girl". Edward laughed,

"well she is a fiery red-head, everyone knows not to mess with those girls". William started to laugh loudly this had really amused him. As the day was coming to an end the boys were getting excited that they would see the girls.

After work as per usual, there was Dorothy and Clara waiting for them.

"Do you mind if I just go with Clara," asked William.

"Not at all," replied Edward. Dorothy loved this. She

loved being alone with Edward, being able to be herself around him and not worrying what William was getting up to. Clara and William then walked down the canal towards the market. William reached for Clara's hand; she was initially hesitant but accepted his hand. As they walked into the market there was a huge bellowing voice from behind them.

"What is all this about?" Clara froze she knew who the voice was. William had noticed that she was scared. They turned around and stood behind them was a very angry looking man.

"Sorry father," Clara murmured.

"Who are you and what are you doing holding my daughters' hand?" shouted Clara's father. William started to panic. Sweat beads started to appear on his head and his voice became hoarse.

"I am William, sir and I am a friend of Clara's," he said.

"I don't think so," bellowed Clara's father.

"You stay away from my little girl; do you hear me boy or else I will bury you alive". William started to feel violently sick. He let go of Clara's hand. His knees were trembling, and he was trying to stop himself from bursting into tears. Clara became very upset,

"father, how could you?" she cried. He then turned away from her father and ran through the market crying out. Clara's father looked even more angry. Then pushed William out of the way and told him to stay away. He then proceeded to follow Clara through the market.

William was stunned at what had just happened. He really liked Clara and now he was told he could not see her anymore and that he had to stay away from her. He wondered what he could do to be able to see her again. He left the market and headed back to the factory where he sat on his makeshift bed and cried himself to sleep. Meanwhile, Dorothy and Edward were sat in their favourite spot under the sycamore tree. Dorothy was holding Edward's hand.

"Edward do you still want to be a soldier?" she asked.

"I don't know my love, what George has told me has made me think very carefully about what I want to be," he replied.

"Well I still want to be a nurse, I want to help people who are sick, injured and need care," she told Edward. Edward smiled; he loved the fact that Dorothy wanted to help others in need. He felt so proud of her and knew that one day she would make the most amazing nurse.

"Of course, you will be a nurse, and you'll be the greatest nurse in the country," replied Edward. Dorothy started to giggle she gave Edward a soft kiss. Edward then squeezed Dorothy's hand three times. She looked deep into Edward's eyes.

"I am so in love with you," she said softly.

WILLIAM WOKE the following morning to see Edward standing over him.

"Come on, it's time to get ready for work." Edward could see that William had been crying, he knew something was wrong.

"What is going on?" he asked. William looked at

Edward and started to weep,

"Clara's father does not approve," he said. Edward took William's hand and pulled him up.

"You need to give him some time to come round," replied Edward. Edward nodded he agreed that he would have to allow time. But he was so worried that he was not going to see Clara again. He waited in hope that one day she would return to the factory to see him again. The boys started work, shifting the metals into the factory for smelting.

Every day when the boys finished work William would remain hopeful that Clara would turn up. 3 months passed and it was September 1938. There was still no sign of Clara. Every day this would break William's heart. He had found the perfect girl for him. One that could keep him in line and one that he had strong feelings for. Dorothy would become annoyed at times as Edward and William would spend long periods playing marbles after work. All Edward wanted to do was cheer William up. But Dorothy didn't see this. She would go to the sycamore tree and sit underneath it on her own. Thinking about her relationship with Edward and that he just does not spend the time with her once again. Dorothy could not continue like this. She wanted Edward back, she had to do something. She sat under the tree and realised she needed to find Clara.

Dorothy spent two weeks searching the market and the surrounding areas in the hope that she would find Clara. She started to lose hope until one afternoon she saw the red curly locks stood at the fruit stall right in front of her. She slowly approached and knew it was Clara. As she walked towards the stall, she stood directly next to Clara. She picked up an apple and said,

"hello Clara". Clara froze, turned, and looked to her left. There she saw Dorothy stood next to her.

"Hello Dorothy," she replied.

"Can we please talk?" asked Dorothy. Clara let out a huge sigh, she knew what was coming.

"Is this about William?" she asked.

"Yes, it is. He really misses you and he is hurting". Clara paused for a minute.

"I miss him too, but my father does not approve". Dorothy thought to herself that she was not going to get anywhere with this conversation.

"Could we go somewhere and talk?" Dorothy asked. Clara nodded,

"where should we go?" Dorothy stopped to think. She did not want to go to her sacred place, but then an idea popped into her head.

"Let's go and sit by the canal," she replied. Clara agreed and the pair left the market and headed to the canal. As they were leaving the market Dorothy noticed that Clara was appearing on edge. She kept looking around as if she was worried she was being followed.

"What's wrong?" asked Dorothy.

"I am worried about my father following me," replied Clara. Dorothy linked arms with Clara and said,

"don't worry I am a girl I'm sure he won't mind," Clara smiled. They continued their walk arms linked to the canal.

The pair sat down on a bench. Dorothy explained to Clara that William felt heartbroken every single day and that he hoped every day that she would be waiting at the entrance of the factory when it was the end of the shift. Clara really missed the time she had spent with William. Clara then said to Dorothy,

"the first time we were alone he was not nice, he tried to touch me so I hit him". Dorothy just rolled her eyes. Clara was confused.

"Are you not surprised then?" asked Clara.

"No," replied Dorothy.

"He tried to kiss me once a long time ago". Clara went bright red, she became angry.

"What a dirty boy," she said. Dorothy nodded in agreement, but she went on to explain about William's troubled upbringing and that he had not tried anything with her since that day.

"He only tried it the once, but I put him in his place, he was so sweet, kind and caring after that so there is good in him," said Clara. Dorothy was starting to feel relieved. She knew that this could work and that Clara may come back into William's life even without her father's approval. After talking for an hour Clara agreed to walk with Dorothy to the factory to see the boys.

When they arrived at the factory Edward and William were playing dominos on the step to the factory.

"Hello William," said this soft voice. William dropped his domino, his hand started to shake. He knew this voice. He looked up and saw the beauty stood in front of him.

"You're here," he shrieked. He jumped up and approached Clara. He went to give her a hug. Clara put her arms out in front of her.

"Slow down, not here, I cannot risk father finding

out". William stopped and put his hands in his pocket.

"Of course, miss," he replied. He was smiling and looked happy again. Dorothy grabbed Edward's hand this time she squeezed it three times. Edward looked to Dorothy and kissed her on the cheek and told her,

"I love you too". Everyone was happy again. Finally, things were looking up for the four of them.

As THE MONTHS passed Edward and Dorothy would visit the tree many times a week, enjoying picnics and spending their alone time together. William and Clara would go on secret walks when Clara knew her father was not around. The news around the market was all about Hitler and the potential risks that he posed. There was so much tension in the market place. The traders were worried about stocks and trades. Uncertainty was in the air. George was quiet again. He needed a lot of care and attention from Anna, Dorothy, and Edward. Every day Edward would find a newspaper at home, one that George had bought. He would read the headlines. He sometimes thought to himself that George was right all that time ago and that war is coming. Dorothy was very concerned about her father. She was not concerned about war. Dorothy felt that this was not going to happen. But she hated seeing her father look so weak. She wanted to ease his pain, his tension. She needed to be there to support him. As George came home, he looked pale. The only words to come out of his mouth,

"it's coming".

5

IT'S COMING

Knowing what is coming can lead to the fear of your nightmares becoming reality.

MAY 1939 Birmingham was bristling with life. It was so busy, yet there was still panic in the air. People were running around frantically. News reports stated that Hitler had mobilised the German army. People were scared they knew something big was about to happen. Neville Chamberlain had announced in March that if Poland or Britain were invaded then they would come to each other's aid. People were fearful of Hitler. The power and control that he seemed to have over Europe and the fear factor that he introduced. Not everyone was scared, William and Clara remained a secret couple. Oblivious to what was going on in the world around them. Dorothy and Edward were stronger than ever, their love growing stronger each and every single day. George remained withdrawn; he was suffering. His anxieties only getting worse day by day. He would wake in the night in cold sweats. He would often drop down to the floor if he heard a loud bang. This started to worry Anna, who did not want Dorothy to know what was truly going on with George.

It was approaching Dorothy's 16th birthday. Edward had previously turned 16 a few months ago. He wanted to do something special for Dorothy. He went out and bought lots of lovely food for a picnic. He also found a stunning new dress for her. It was a red velvet dress. It was beautiful, he knew it would fit her perfectly. He bought the dress and couldn't wait to spoil Dorothy on her big day. He met up with Edward and Clara.

"We need to throw a surprise for her at the house," he said. William was up for it; Clara was a bit reserved.

"What if I am seen by father?" she said. Edward had a think,

"I know, we could get you a hat and try and disguise you so we can sneak you in the house."

"That's a brilliant idea," replied William,

"I'll go now and get this sorted out," said William. With this William ran down towards the marketplace in search of a hat for Clara. Edward returned to the house. George and Anna were in the kitchen, Dorothy was upstairs in her bedroom. He approached Anna and asked if they could do something at home for Dorothy. Anna smiled

"what a lovely thoughtful idea," she said.

"I shall get started on the preparations". Edward then approached George who sat quietly reading a newspaper.

"Sir, I would love to do a surprise for Dorothy at home". George lowered the newspaper.

"I don't think this is the time to be celebrating," he

said. Edward knew that George was concerned about the future.

"Sir, you are only 16 once. Please do this for Dorothy". George did not want to upset his daughter.

"Do what you need to do boy," he replied. Edward was so happy he ran upstairs to Dorothy. He jumped onto her bed and gave her a kiss.

"I shall be back later my love". Dorothy was reading a story she giggled at Edward and told him she will see him later.

Edward was so happy he could not wait to surprise Dorothy on her big day. He met back up with William at the factory. William had purchased a very discreet small black hat that could hold Clara's hair if it was bunched up. Clara was sat with William; she was concerned about being seen by her father. She put her hair up and put her hat on. She then put on a large grey sheet over her clothes.

"What do you think?" she asked. William nodded and said

"no one would recognise you like not even me". Clara smiled she had a plan. She was looking forward to surprising Dorothy on her big day. Edward was so excited everything was going to plan. They were all ready to surprise Dorothy on her 16th birthday.

———

TWO DAYS PASSED and it was time for Edward to give Dorothy the best day of her life. He was so excited. He had bought himself a new three-piece outfit. It was very smart. New grey trousers, a white shirt, and a matching waistcoat. George looked at Edward,

"well boy, you can look like a gentleman. I have to go out now, but I will be home later for the celebrations." George then left the house with Anna to go shopping for the celebrations later that day. Edward really wanted to impress Dorothy. As Dorothy came downstairs she saw Edward and her jaw dropped.

"Edward you look so handsome," she said in a startled tone. Edward ginned,

"thank you my lady". He then approached Dorothy, put his arms around her and whispered in her ear,

"happy birthday". Dorothy chuckled. Edward then handed her a package wrapped in brown paper with a pink ribbon and rose attached. Dorothy smiled. She was so intrigued to see what was in the package, she carefully took the ribbon off. She then took off the rose and placed it in her golden hair.

"How do I look?" she said to Edward.

"Beautiful," he replied. Dorothy then continued to remove the paper. As she opened it her eyes started to swell. She saw this beautiful red velvet dress. She grabbed Edward.

"Thank you, I love it". Edward was happy that Dorothy was pleased with her gift.

"Why don't you put it on?" he asked. With that Dorothy ran upstairs to try on her new dress.

Edward waited patiently downstairs for Dorothy, it seemed like she was gone an eternity. Then he heard the sound of her bedroom door. There she was at the top of the stairs. Wearing the bright yellow dress, with a pink rose in her hair. Edward was speechless he started to stutter again

"m.m.m.my lady, y.y.you look so beautiful." Dorothy had a huge smile on her face. As she approached Edward, she took his hands and kissed him softly on the lips. Edward was still at a loss for words.

"Are you ok Edward?" asked Dorothy.

"Yes, I am just so lucky to have you," he replied. Edward then whispered in Dorothy's ear,

"Let's go out I have a surprise". Edward then took Dorothy by the hand and the pair walked through the market. Everyone was staring at Dorothy they were amazed by this beauty walking before them. They arrived at the canal. Dorothy begun to smile more; she knew where they were going. Their sacred place. When they arrived at the sycamore tree the sun was shining, the birds were whistling in the trees. It was just bliss. Edward pulled down a basket from the tree. He laid out the blankets and started to set up an early morning picnic for them. Dorothy was so happy, her heart beating rapidly. She knew how much effort Edward had put in for her birthday and she just felt so incredibly loved. She grabbed Edward's hand and placed her head on his shoulder. Edward then squeezed Dorothy's hand three times. She smiled and just lay into him feeling safe, secure and happy.

As THE MORNING turned into afternoon, Edward started to look at his father's pocket watch. He had to meet William and Clara at 2pm. Time was getting on, and he could tell how content Dorothy was, but the day was not over, and he wanted to make sure everything was going to plan for the celebrations.

"My, love I need to go to the factory for a little while". Dorothy sat up,

"why Edward, can't we just sit here all day?" Edward was a little stunned he did not want to lie to Dorothy, but he wanted the surprise to remain a surprise.

"I have to give the boss something, I won't be long". Dorothy nodded

"ok, shall I wait here for you?" Edward felt relieved.

"Yes, my love please wait here I won't be long". Edward stood up and ran across the field towards the canal. He ran as fast as he could to the factory. True to their word, Clara and William were there waiting.

"Is everything ready?" gasped Edward in his exhausted voice.

"We are good to go," replied William. Clara was disguised ready to be hidden.

"Go to the house and help George and Anna get everything set up," Edward asked.

"Come on then William, I don't want to be wearing this all day," Clara said. William then linked Clara's arm and walked off down the canal towards the market to head to the house. Edward then ran as fast as he could back to the sycamore tree. Where he saw Dorothy sat on her mound waiting.

"Is it all sorted now Edward?" asked Dorothy. Edward was so out of breath; he had run so fast he struggled to reply,

"y.y.yes my lady".

"Sit down Edward, catch your breath," she told him. Edward sat down next to Dorothy, he wrapped his arms around her and the pair cuddled for a short while.

"I think we should head back to the house now," said Edward. Dorothy looked at Edward, she stood up.

"Come on then let's go, it is getting rather late," she replied. Edward then took Dorothy's hand and pulled himself to his feet. He packed up the items in the basket and placed them back on the branch of the tree. They then walked hand in hand back towards the house. As they approached the market the whistling towards Dorothy became noticeable. Dorothy would smile, she loved the fact that so many people thought she was beautiful. Edward, on the other hand, was a bit annoyed. He would grimace from time to time when the men would start whistling. Dorothy would notice this; it made her giggle. She loved how protective Edward was of her.

They arrived at the door of the house. Edward was nervous, he was hoping that everything was in place. He slowly opened the door and held it open for Dorothy. As she walked in everyone shouted surprise. She paused she did not expect this, she went as red as her velvet dress.

"Dorothy you look so much like your mother," called George. Dorothy started to smile. She was still bright red; her heart was racing. She couldn't believe that everyone would go through the trouble to be there for her on her birthday. Clara came over to Dorothy,

"happy birthday". Clara then Dorothy a hug. William was stood in the room with his hands in his pockets.

"Happy birthday Dorothy," he called. Dorothy

thanked everyone for the lovely surprise. Anna looked at Dorothy.

"My beautiful baby, just look at how you have turned out, I am so proud of you," she said. The table was set beautifully. A new table cloth had been placed on the table and the decorations around the table were beautiful. Dorothy was so happy. Edward was smiling, he had pulled it off and gave Dorothy the best day she could ever have possibly hoped for.

As they sat around the table George put on the radio, the first music to be played was a beautiful song by Judy Garland called

"over the rainbow". Everyone went silent the music was beautiful. This incredible voice that they could hear. No one had ever heard such beauty in a voice before. The harmonic connection between the sounds of the music and everyone sat around brought them all closer together. As the song came to a close, they all sat down to have some food. The beautiful aroma of the fresh chicken made everyone feel so happy. Clara took off her gown and hat to reveal a beautiful canary yellow dress.

"What a beautiful dress Clara," said Dorothy. Clara smiled at Dorothy

"thank you." They started to talk about the beautiful song that they had heard on the radio. George said,

"I may be wrong but I think it's a feature song from that moving picture, but I cannot remember the name, but I don't think it's out until November this year". Edward then had an idea, what a brilliant idea, they could go and see a moving picture sometime. He thought Dorothy would love this. Dorothy was sat there also thinking about this moving picture. She was so desperate to see a moving picture. However, she did not want to keep asking Edward for things all the time.

Suddenly everyone heard a small rumble, Edward stood up and looked outside. It had started to rain. Edward came away from the window and told everyone that it was just a bit of rain. He sat back down at the table. Everyone continued to laugh and joke, things were going well until there was a huge boom of thunder. George immediately jumped off his chair and crawled under the table.

"Father what are you doing?" asked Dorothy.

"Take cover, they are incoming," he shouted. Dorothy started to panic; she didn't know what to do. She looked at her mother. Anna was just sat there in shock. She had never seen George like this before. George remained under the table. Edward told everyone to come away from the table and to give George some space. Something was clearly wrong with George. Edward thought that it was the newspapers about the issues in Europe and what could be coming this way. Dorothy had to do something. She crawled down under the table.

"Father it's just thunder, nothing is coming". George was trembling, sweat pouring off his face. Dorothy reached for her father's hand. George was very disorientated he looked frightened.

"Father please take my hand". George then reached out and took Dorothy's hand. Dorothy sat under the table with George.

"It's ok father you are safe now, it's just bad weather".

Dorothy managed to convince George to come out from under the table.

George was still trembling. Everyone in the room could not believe that this giant of a man would be so fearful of thunder. Clara and William were both frightened.

"We are going to go now," said William. Edward agreed.

"I think it's best of you both get off, we shall meet up again soon," said Edward. Dorothy was still stood by her father's side.

"Mother will you help me take father up to bed?" she asked. Anna came over and took George's other hand. They both walked George upstairs into his room. He kept repeating

"It's not over". Dorothy was so worried about what was happening to her father. She lay down next to him on the bed with Anna lying on the other side, comforting him until he finally managed to fall asleep.

Edward remained downstairs, he wanted to know what was causing George to become so scared and so afraid. He remembered the story that George had said about the Somme. But he didn't know who the people were that George was close to. He had no real idea about the sights that George had seen. Edward looked around to see if he could find anything that may help. He couldn't find anything. He thought to himself, is George right? War is coming?

Dorothy stayed with her father throughout the night. The following morning, she came downstairs, she looked exhausted. Her eyes were bloodshot red, there were huge bags under her eyes.

"My love I am truly sorry," said Edward. Dorothy just sat down next to Edward and lay her head in his lap.

"I am so worried about father," she muttered. Edward knew that George needed some sort of help. He clearly was not well and that he needed to see a doctor.

"My love, we need to take your father to see a doctor, something is very wrong with him". Dorothy nodded in agreement.

"Let me talk to mother to see what we can do," she replied. Dorothy then went upstairs and found Anna stood in the bathroom brushing her hair.

"Mother, father needs more than what we can give him. I think he needs to see a doctor". Anna let out a huge sigh. She stopped brushing her hair, she placed her hands on her hips and turned to Dorothy.

"I know he does, but he will not go," she replied. Dorothy knew how stubborn her father could be, and she knew that he would just not do as he was told. She then had an excellent idea.

"Mother we will bring the doctor to him them". Anna smiled

"that's very smart, get to it then," she told Dorothy. Dorothy went back to her room to get herself changed for the day.

DOROTHY DID NOT TAKE her time getting ready, she threw on an old black dress and did not even bother doing her hair. As she came downstairs Edward was a bit stunned to see Dorothy's hair all messy.

"Would you like to wear a hat?" he asked her. Dorothy scowled at Edward, no time for that. We need to go and get a doctor to come and see father. Dorothy was clearly in a hurry; she was dragging Edward by his hand through the market at some speed. Edward noticed William and Clara, he called to them. Dorothy said we cannot stop now we will talk to them after.

"Hey Edward, is everything ok?" shouted William.

"Can't stop now," shouted Edward back as they continued running to the medical centre. As they arrived at the medical centre Dorothy rushed in. The sound of soft classical music playing in the background, it was a very white room but it was also very calming. Edward let Dorothy run up to the reception, whilst he stood admiring the paintings on the wall.

"Excuse me I need a doctor," she shouted. A nurse heard Dorothy's plea.

"What is wrong, can I help?" Dorothy was out of breath, struggling to get her words out.

"Take your time," continued the nurse.

"It's my father, he's really unwell. Something is wrong with him. Can you get a doctor to come and see him"? The nurse saw how visibly upset and distressed Dorothy was. Dorothy was stood with her head hanging low, her arms were shaking and her whole body was twitching.

"I will see when the doctor can come over, please wait here and I will be right back". Edward walked over to Dorothy. He took her hand,

"come and sit down whilst we wait," he said. Dorothy

walked with Edward and sat on a chair with Edward in the waiting room. Edward would squeeze Dorothy's hand three times. This started to relax Dorothy. Edward could feel the tension leaving her hands.

A door opened, then the sound of footsteps were heard coming down the hallway. It was the nurse. She approached Dorothy and placed her hand on her shoulder.

"The doctor will come and see your father tonight once he has finished here".

"What time is that?" she asked. The nurse replied about

"6pm". Dorothy was so thankful she could not stop thanking the nurse. She gave the nurse her address and thanked her again for the help.

"I have to get back to work now," said the nurse who proceeded to leave.

"I really love this music, it's so calming," said Edward. Dorothy rolled her eyes,

"is that all you have been thinking about Edward"? she replied. "Not at all, it's just nice," he said. The pair then left the doctor's surgery and headed back to the market to see if they could find William and Clara.

DOROTHY WAS MUCH MORE SETTLED NOW; she knew help was coming for her father. As they came into the market, they saw Clara and William sat down on a stool cuddling up to one another.

"How sweet is that?" Dorothy told Edward.

"Yes, my love, this is us every day". Dorothy giggled they approached William and Clara and started to converse.

"How is your father"? asked Clara.

"He is going to see a doctor today," replied Dorothy. William spoke out and said

"that is good news I hope he is going to be ok". Dorothy thanked William and Clara for their compassion and kind words about her father. Edward wanted to do something together,

"shall we all go for a nice walk and catch up"? Clara liked the idea, she wanted to get out of the market, but William would always insist on meeting there. Everyone agreed and the four of them left the market.

"Sorry your birthday did not end so well," Clara said to Dorothy.

"It's ok, father is poorly and I was happy to stay with him for the night," replied Dorothy. Dorothy and Clara talked and talked all the way down the canal. Edward and William were talking about how happy they were that they were both in love and things were going so well for them.

As they walked about a mile down the canal, William asked to stop. Everyone sat down on the edge of the canal. William sat with Clara; Dorothy sat with Edward. The two couples proceeded to cuddle into one another. Then

"what the hell is this," shouted this huge booming voice. Clara immediately let go of William and jumped up.

"Father it's nothing," she replied.

"This does not look like nothing to me," shouted Clara's father. William's heart was beating faster than a hummingbird's. He was panicking he turned around and could see the rage on Clara's father's face.

"What did I tell you boy"? William did not say a word. Dorothy jumped up and stood in front of William.

"Please do not hurt him," she pleaded.

"Move out of the way girl," he screamed. Dorothy was now scared, this large menacing man stood in front of her salivating. She could smell his breath and feel the heat on her face. Edward grabbed her and pulled her out the way to protect her. This gave Clara's father easy access to William. William spoke out

"please sir, please don't".

William's pleas were not listened to. Clara's father grabbed him by his collar and picked him up off the ground. He pulled William up to his face,

"I warned you boy". William was shaking with fear, the spit from this angry man covering William's face when he spoke.

"Father please let him go," begged Clara. Her father not taking any notice threw William down on to the floor. William crashed onto the floor landing on his back. He let out a whimper. He tried to get up only to be punched in the side of the head by Clara's father. The force of the punch knocked William out. He was motionless on the floor. Edward ran out to his brother,

"William are you ok, William"? There was no response.

"You bastard," shouted Edward at Clara's father. Clara was so upset; she fell to the floor in floods of tears.

"What did you call me boy"? said her father.

"He called you a bastard," shouted Dorothy. Clara's

father filled with even more intense rage, he charged towards Dorothy, he was menacing. Dorothy was so scared she closed her eyes she did not know what to expect. She waited for the imminent pain she was about to feel, but nothing happened. She opened one eye and noticed Clara stood in front of her.

"I HATE YOU," screamed Clara at her father.

"You have hurt my love, you have threatened my friends, I hate you, I don't ever want to see you again". His tone then changed. Such hateful words coming out of Clara's mouth made her father look weaker. He looked at Clara

"I am only trying to protect you". She screamed at him

"well, don't I am finally happy and all you are doing is trying to ruin my life," she screamed.

"I don't want you here leave us alone". Clara's father looked as if he was going to cry. He started to rub his eyes. He turned around without saying a word and walked off into the distance.

Everyone then tended to William, he was starting to come round.

"My head really hurts," he said.

"I am not surprised; you took one hell of a knock," replied Edward. Clara and Edward helped William get to his feet.

"Are you going to be able to walk"? asked Clara.

"Your father is so dangerous," William said to Clara.

"I am so sorry I never meant for that to happen," she replied. Edward and Clara walked William to the factory, Dorothy followed Monday's behind, keeping a lookout in case Clara's father was nearby waiting to strike again. As they arrived at the factory Clara told Edward that she would take it from there. Clara then thanked everyone for their support today and that she would look after William throughout the night.

"Edward what time is it"? asked Dorothy". Edward pulled out the old pocket watch.

"It's time we get back to see the doctor".

THE PAIR RAN and ran as fast they could to get back to the house. They had to be there for George. The air started to fill with mist, which began to dampen their clothes. As they arrived back to the house both Dorothy and Edward felt damp and dirty. They went inside, Edward checked his pocket watch it was 5:35pm they still had time to get changed. Dorothy ran up the stairs and slammed her bedroom door shut. Edward gathered some belongings from his bag and took them into the washroom. The pair got changed very quickly. They both met up in the living room, sat in anticipation waiting for the doctor to arrive. George and Anna were sat down. George was reading his newspaper and Anna was knitting. Edward sat there with Dorothy staring at his pocket watch. George had no idea that he was about to have a visit from a doctor.

Dead on time, there was a loud knock on the door.

"Who could that be?" murmured George.

"I'll get it, father," said Dorothy. She jumped up off the chair and ran to the door. She opened it slowly to see a small man wearing spectacles, he was wearing a long white coat. He had smart trousers, shiny shoes and was carrying a satchel.

"Hello miss, I am Dr Bennett, I am here to see your father. Is that correct?". Dorothy smiled; she was pleased that the doctor had arrived to help.

"Yes, Dr Bennett please do come in," said Dorothy in a soft pleasant tone. As Dr Bennett stepped inside George looked at the man, he suddenly became agitated, he began to shout.....

"I'm not going with you! You can go away; I'm not going to that place again." He kicked the dining room chair over and began to raise his fist.

"I won't let you take me away and lock me up."

Dorothy had never seen her father act this way before, he was usually a very calm yet moral man. He stood up for his beliefs and his values in a composed manner. She thought to herself what had he seen? Where had he been taken to?

George continued to become angrier he moved to the kitchen where he picked up a knife, he repeated again,

"I'm not going back there, you won't take me alive. I'd rather be dead than go back THERE!". Dorothy began to sing the song she had heard, somewhere over the rainbow, she knew her father liked it. His mood changed, he dropped the knife and dropped into a chair. He started to sob uncontrollably. Dorothy walked and cradled her father in her arms, he started apologising.

The doctor slowly moved to sit with George, in a calm and caring tone, he asked George why he is crying. George kept repeating

"it's coming." He then appeared to look straight

through the doctor, then he begins to tell him about the 'Bloody battle of the Somme" of the loss of life and the fields of death.

"I'm sorry I got so angry I don't know what came over me, ALL this talk of war has made the events come back to me. I didn't see our visitor. I saw Dr Emerald who was the field doctor. He tried in vain to save so many. He could heal some of the physical wounds, he cared for the dying and eased their pain. He was trained for the stuff that messes with your head. He couldn't cure my nightmares that happened in the day and the night, the ringing in my ears of the shells, the blood-curdling screams. The smell of death that I sense."

"Instead, Doctor Emerald decided who was "fit for service", those who were "discharged from service" and those that needed time to rest! I went into the battlefields a few times, but the flash backs started when I need to get across to take a message from one unit to another..... I became a liability. They thought I needed time away to rest. The mind is not easy to fix, mine was shattered into several pieces. Not literally but I was always on heightened alert."

"Sorry when I saw you Doctor, I thought you were sending me back or taking me to the 'other place'. Then I was transported back to the field and I could see the men running, the shells firing and the blood-curdling screams".

"George, I need you to listen to me, you aren't going mad, you are suffering from a condition called Shell shock. It's a result in part of the repetitive shelling, you see the symptoms vary from man to man. For some it made then a gibbering wreck for others it makes them cry or others aggressive." Dorothy was relieved to hear what this was, but she was scared as well, where did her father think he was going back to? Was it the trenches or somewhere else?

The doctor got out his papers and began to read out loud,

"I can see that at one point you were brought back and placed in the hospital." George then began to look past them again, as he recalled where he was sent.

"It was a big ward, in a hospital in the middle of nowhere. The ward had about 20-25 people. Some were cradling themselves and rocked, silent, making no noise. Others were looking for a fight and then there was me I cried and just wanted to go home. I felt like I was there for a life time." George became silent again lost in the past.

Anna and Dorothy offered Doctor Bennett a pot of tea. Anna went and boiled the water on the stove, whilst Dorothy took the tea leaves out. They waited for the tea leaves to brew; the teapot kept warm by its tea cozy. The best china cups and saucers were used and the tray was taken to the parlour reserved for guests. The dollies were on the sofas and the smell of freshly brewed tea permeated the air. George, Dorothy, and Anna sat on the sofas. Anna strained the tea as it followed freely through the strainer. The golden top milk added later.

George by now had settled again and he had made a fire, the open fire glowing brightly. Doctor Bennet explained that shell shock was a disease caused by man, that its effects were life-changing and that he was here to support George and not to take him away. Dorothy was so relieved as were Edward and Anna. They could keep George at home, but they knew that he needed a lot of care. Dr Bennet then explained that electric shocks may help.

"No," said Anna. No one is shocking my husband. Dr Bennett also explained about isolation and restricted diet.

"I do not want my father locked away on his own," said Dorothy in a concerned voice. Edward then finally spoke out

"what about a restricted diet"? he asked. Dr Bennett explained that the diet consisted of bully beef, jam, cheese, and bread.

"That does not sound appetizing," said Edward.

"The idea of this diet is to kickstart the metabolism, which we hope will help alleviate some of the symptoms George is having," replied Dr Bennett.

George remained sat on the sofa. He nodded and said "let's give it a try". Dr Bennett thanked George and everyone for their time. He shook George's and Edward's hand and Dorothy let him out. Everyone sat back down in the living room. They continued to have cups of tea. George was still very quiet. But he was much more relaxed than he was before.

"Well we best get some shopping in the morning" Edward said. Dorothy looked at Edward and smiled. They knew they had to get the right things to help George. They did not want to see him in the confused state he was in before. They did not want him to be taken away and nobody wanted to see George being electrocuted.

Three months had passed since George had seen Dr Bennett. It was now August 1939 and tensions in Europe were sky-high. Hitler had stated that Germany had become more powerful than the allied forces and that he would reign supreme. The official treaty between Great Britain, France and Poland had been signed. Fear was consuming the market place. At the smelting factory, there would be days where many of the workforce would not show up. George had been using his diet for the last three months and was feeling much better in himself. Until a late august morning when he picked up a newspaper from the market. He went straight home where Dorothy, Edward, and Anna were sat at the table drinking tea. George approached the table, he threw down the newspaper and said,

"I told you, it's coming".

6

THE POWER OF FEAR

Fear is so powerful; it can spread faster than wildfire. Fear can consume a person and take over their lives.

IT WAS AUGUST 31ST 1939, Edward was in the market. There was a lot less going on than usual. It was unusually quiet. Many of the stalls had not been opened. The sky was cloudy and there was a lot of damp in the air. He walked around the market trying to find out what was happening. No one appeared to want to talk. Until he approached the fishmonger.

"Excuse me sir, why is it so quiet? What is going on?" The fishmonger let out a huge sigh,

"have you not seen the newspaper's boy?" he exclaimed. Edward had not had chance to look at a newspaper.

"No, sir I haven't". The fishmonger then picked up his newspaper and showed Edward the front-page news. Edward held his breath and his heart started to race.

"See boy, the German army has mobilised and there

are reports that there is a very large presence on the Polish border." Edward knew that if the German's moved into Poland then Britain would go to War.

"Thank you, sir," he shouted at the fishmonger. Edward ran to the newspaper vendor and bought a newspaper. He ran as fast as he could out the market back home. As soon as he came running in the door everyone was sat drinking a pot of tea.

"Look, look everyone!" he screamed, as he threw the newspaper on the table.

"Well what is the problem?" asked Dorothy. George picked up the newspaper and simply said to everyone.

"It's time".

The room fell silent. Was George right all this time. Maybe the memories of the Great War had given him signs that something was on its way. Edward turned to Dorothy.

"I think we need to go and inform William and Clara," he said in a very panicked tone.

"Father, mother we have to go and tell our friends we need to warn them". The pair raced out the house, through the empty market which was now like a ghost town. They ran down the canal and towards the factory. It was very early morning and no staff on duty. As they arrived at the factory Edward proceeded to enter. Dorothy stood at the bottom of the steps.

"I cannot go in there," she said.

"Of course, you can, no one is here yet," replied Edward. Edward went back down the stairs and took Dorothy by the hand. He walked her inside. They went up the stairs to see William, he was asleep on his makeshift bed cuddled into Clara.

"William wake up," shouted Edward. Edward jumped up startled with such force that he caused Clara to fall onto the floor.

"What is this"? shouted Clara.

"War is coming, George was right," shouted Edward. William continued to rub his eyes. He was still half asleep. He then said

"that's fine we will be soldiers". Dorothy became angry.

"You stupid fool, you do not understand what it is like. My father is suffering because of war in his past". Dorothy then stormed off down the stairs.

"My lady, wait," called Edward.

"Go after her," said Clara. Edward did not hesitate and ran down the stairs after Dorothy.

As he got to the entrance of the factory, he looked around. He could not see Dorothy anywhere. He could start to feel raindrops on the back of his neck. He decided to head to the sycamore tree. He knew it would be dry under the tree and that Dorothy may have gone there for sanctuary. As he arrived at the opening to the field, he could see the silhouette of Dorothy sat on her mound in the distance. Edward slowly walked over the tree. He didn't say a word and just sat down next to Dorothy. He took her hand and squeezed it three times. She smiled,

"I love you too." Edward held onto Dorothy's hand, she then let out an almighty sigh.

"I really hate William, he is such a fool, and he does not understand what could happen to you both if you go to war." Edward was shocked, he knew that Dorothy was not overly keen on Edward, but he did not know that she hated him.

"I understand why you are worried my lady, but we are too young to go war, nothing has even happened yet. I guess I caused us all to panic. It still might blow over." Dorothy leaned into Edward's shoulder.

"I really hope you are right," she replied. The rain became more intense, the tree providing them both with the shelter that they needed at that time.

When the rain stopped Edward and Dorothy proceeded to head back to the factory. Edward was now late for work. They had tried to warn their friends that potential danger would be coming their way. As they arrived at the factory the lead worker was waiting at the door.

"WHAT TIME DO YOU CALL THIS"? he said to Edward.

"I.I.I.I am really sorry," replied Edward.

"Get to work," Edward was told. He said goodbye to Dorothy and headed to work. William was already hard at work shifting some metals.

"Where has Clara gone"? asked Edward.

"She can't stay here whilst I am working, she goes off and does what she wants," replied William. Edward nodded in agreement and the pair continued their duties. William was very quiet with Edward for the start of the day, angry at what Dorothy had called him.

"I am not foolish, nor am I stupid," he told Edward.

"I never said you were," replied Edward. William let out a grunt, he was still frustrated that no one would take him being a soldier seriously.

"I want to be a soldier; I want to stand up for what is right," said William. Edward stared directly at William and told him

"if you want to be a soldier and a real man then start acting like one." William stopped work, his shoulders dropped, and he dropped his head, he knew that he had not been behaving in the way he should. He knew if he wanted to impress, he would have to start acting more like a man and not like a silly foolish boy.

William apologised to Edward,

"I promise I will make you proud of me brother." Edward smiled, he was pleased that William had made a promise to not let him down and do better for himself. As they day drew to a close Edward headed downstairs.

"Are you coming, Clara might be here"? he said to William.

"Sure," William replied. The boys headed downstairs to meet the girls. Who on time were there waiting, both having a long gossip about their outfits. As the boys approached the girls, they both gave them hugs. William then turned to Dorothy,

"I am sorry for what I have done to you in the past, I will now better myself and be the good decent man that I should be". He then turned to Clara,

"you mean so much to me and I never want to hurt you again". Clara wrapped her arms around William and gave him a kiss.

"If you ever try to hurt me you will be very sorry," she

joked. William laughed. Dorothy looked towards William

"I forgive, but I don't forget". She didn't need to say anymore. She took Edward's hand

"let's go home." Edward and Dorothy headed off home. William and Clara headed back in the factory. It had been a very long day and everyone was tired, and they all needed some well-earned rest.

As Edward and Dorothy arrived at home, they realised it was very dark. They went into the house and noticed that George and Anna were not about.

"Wait here," Dorothy said to Edward. She creeped up the stairs very slowly to see if George and Anna were asleep. As she got to the top of the stairs, she could hear her father snoring. Dorothy crept back down the stairs, she grabbed Edward's hand and led him up to her bedroom.

"Please Edward, stay with me tonight". Edward was scared, he knew this wasn't allowed.

"You, know I can't my lady," he replied to Dorothy.

"I need you to hold me, please". Edward really wanted to spend the night with Dorothy, but he was so scared if anyone found out. He did not want to be thrown out, not after all this time and everything they had all been together through. Dorothy stared into Edward's eyes; his heart began to melt. He then followed her very slowly upstairs to her bedroom. Dorothy turned the doorknob so very gentle, trying not to make a sound. As they went into her room. She started to get undressed. Edward turned around; he did not want to make Dorothy feel uncomfortable.

"I am ready Edward," she called. Edward turned around to see Dorothy lying in her bed.

"Come and hold me Edward," she asked softly. Edward did not want to undress too much. He removed his jacket, shoes and trousers. He then got into the bed next to Dorothy, he wrapped his arms around her and kissed her neck softly.

"I love you," she said. "Edward smiled and squeezed Dorothy's forearm three times. Dorothy closed her eyes, she felt safe and secure. Edward on the other hand felt more tense, he was overthinking about what would happen if someone came in the room. Shortly after they were both fast asleep in each other's arms.

IN THE EARLY hours of the morning, Edward woke. Something in his mind had triggered, something was wrong, but he did not quite know what it was. He could hear screaming and shouting in his head, as if thousands of people were suffering. He quietly got out of Dorothy's bed. He got dressed and checked his pocket watch it was 5:20am. He went downstairs and made himself a cup of tea. A few hours later, Dorothy emerged.

"Is everything ok"? she asked. Edward looked at Dorothy,

"I had unimaginable dreams, of pain and suffering". Dorothy sat down next to Edward and gave him a cuddle. She lit a candle and told him that everything was going to be ok. Then there were the thunderous footsteps of George coming down the stairs. He walked into the living room, and he turned on the wireless. Everyone then just stood in silence, the news report that Germany had started an invasion of Poland blared through the speakers. George's eyes started to fill up. He had known it was inevitable. Edward quietly whispered to Dorothy

"my dreams". She took his hand and squeezed it three times. Anna came into the room; she saw the look on everyone's face. She leaned into George

"You were right". It was now September 1st 1939. They all knew now that war was coming.

Edward still shocked by his thoughts and what had actually happened needed to tell William, he had to warn him.

"Dorothy, we need to tell William and Clara about this". Dorothy agreed.

"Mother, father, I will go with Edward to the factory, I will be back very shortly," she said. George did not say a word. Anna nodded at Dorothy and the pair then left the house. They ran down the lane towards the market. As they got into the market, it was a ghost town. Hardly anyone was there. It was like they all were at home listening to the news broadcast. The pair continued down the canal and towards the factory. When they arrived at the factory William was saying his goodbye's to Clara to start work.

"William have you heard the news"? shouted Edward.

"What news"? called William. Dorothy approached Clara and informed her of the news on the radio.

"I need to warn my father," said Clara. Clara then turned and headed off to go and find her father to tell him of the news. Edward now out of breath started to stutter.

"G.G.G.Germany has started to I.I.I.Invade Poland," he wailed. William looked in disbelief.

"So, this means, we are going to war," he replied. Dorothy butted in

"no it does not, that has not been said by anyone on the wireless". They all knew though that if Poland were to be invaded by another European country that Britain would intervene.

THE FACTORY WAS UNUSUALLY QUIET. Many of the workers had chosen not to come into work that day, perhaps due to the events surrounding them. The boys continued with their duties as per normal until lunchtime. When the lead worker approached them,

"there is not much point today boys, I just don't have the workforce. Go home and take the rest of the day off". William and Edward looked at each other. They stopped what they were doing and raced out of the factory. They ran back to the house, where Dorothy was sat with her parents. Talking about what might actually happen next. Everyone sat down around the table. William and Edward were concerned that George may have to go to war. They did not tell Dorothy their concerns, but they both knew that this was worrying Anna too.

"I best go and sort out some lunch for us all," said Anna.

"I shall help you mother," said Dorothy. The pair then headed into the kitchen. George looked at the boys,

"Do not, lie about your age. You won't go to war until

you're both 18". George was calm and quiet when he said this, it was not his usual deep powerful voice. Edward looked at William and he looked at George.

"Yes, sir," he replied. William nodded at George to indicate that he also agreed. The girls then came in with some tomato soup and bread. No one was overly hungry. William was worried about Clara. Dorothy was worried about her father. The power of fear was consuming everyone.

Shortly after lunch William left the house, he needed to find Clara to see if she was ok. He walked around the ghostly market for an hour. Hoping to find her. He was about to give up and in the distance, he noticed her long wavy red hair. But she was not alone. She was with her father. William started to panic; he knew that the last time he met her father things did not go well. As they got closer to William he began to tremble more, he thought do I run away or do I stand my ground. William wanted to run, but his legs would just not let him. He stood there and as they approached, he heard Clara.

"Hello William".

"Hello Clara," he replied. By now Clara's father was stood only a few feet away from William. He was towering over William. William looked up, the huge bushy beard dripping with sweat in front of him. William knew he was about to get another beating. He closed his eyes and was waiting for the inevitable. A few seconds passed, William opened one eye and saw that Clara's father was just looking at him.

"Listen boy, I don't like you. I don't have to like you.

But I need to thank you for taking care of my little girl". William then let out a huge sigh of relief.

"It was my pleasure sir," he said in a very squeaky voice.

"Don't you have somewhere to be boy"? said Clara's father. William nodded and turned around and walked away out of the market. He knew that Clara was safe, and he had a good feeling he did not need to worry about her father anymore.

BACK AT THE HOUSE, there was a knock on the door. George opened the door to be greeted by a member of the military.

"We are evacuating sir, are there any children here that we can evacuate to safety?"

"Get out of here," shouted George. Dorothy came running to the door,

"how old are you"? asked the solider. As Dorothy looked out onto the street, she could see many children being taken onto buses. She knew that they were evacuating. She did not hesitate, and she lied about her age telling the soldier that she was 18.

"Good day to you all," replied the soldier. George slammed the door shut.

"It's starting already," he said.

"They are evacuating the cities and moving the children into the countryside. We are preparing for war," he said. Edward was shocked at Dorothy and shouted "why did you not go with them; you need to keep yourself safe my lady". Dorothy shouted back at Edward,

"I am not leaving my parents, here we stick together". Edward shocked at how Dorothy responded placed his hands in his pockets and sat down. He knew this was an argument he would not win. Everyone stayed in the house for the rest of the day. Whilst soldiers knocked on all the doors to try and evacuate as many children as they could.

Two days had passed and no one had left the house. They turned on the wireless to get the latest news update. The news came directly from Neville Chamberlain himself.

"Great Britain and France have declared war on Germany". Fear started to kick in at the house. George started breathing very heavily his eyes swelling up. This is what he had feared for so long and now the reality was here. George knew that bombs would fall, people would become homeless and die. He knew the harsh reality of war; he knew what it was like to be on the battlefield watching your friends fall all around you. The fear that was running through his mind could be seen by everyone in the house. Seeing George so fearful brought the fear and reality to Dorothy and Edward. They now understood that what was about to happen, was going to change the lives of everyone around them forever.

Dorothy needed to get out of the house, she grabbed Edward and dragged him to the door.

"It may not be safe my lady," said Edward. Dorothy did not care she did not feel safe in the house but knew somewhere where she could feel safe.

"Edward I need this," she shrieked. Edward and

Dorothy then left the house. The presence of soldiers in Birmingham was high. Dorothy and Edward had not seen so much military before. The market was closed, the canal was isolated. There were no signs of the small children that would play by the edge of the canal. It was ghostly as they got to the factory it was closed. William was sat on the steps talking to Clara. Dorothy and Edward did not stop. They carried on toward the sycamore tree. As Dorothy sat down on her mound she burst into tears.

"My lady we are going to be ok," said Edward. Dorothy couldn't speak her emotions getting the better of her. Edward pulled Dorothy in close and begun to stroke her hair. He was trying to relax her. Trying to make her feel safe and secure in their sacred space.

"Hey Edward," was heard in the distance. Edward looked up as did Dorothy, who knew about their sacred place? They looked around to see William and Clara headed toward them. Dorothy was furious,

"how did they find out about our place"? she asked Edward.

"I.I.I don't know my lady," he murmured. As William and Clara got closer all came to light. Clara said

"we tried to call you both, we saw you walk past the factory but you did not hear us, so we thought we would follow on". Dorothy was still annoyed. This spot was for her and Edward. William and Clara sat down.

"So, you have not been evacuated"? asked William.

"NO," said Dorothy.

"Did you also lie about your ages"? asked Clara. Dorothy then smirked at least she was not the only person who lied, so they didn't have to be dragged away and be at risk of being split up.

Dorothy still irritated that William and Clara had come to her and Edward's spot, spoke out.

"Clara, William, could you please give myself and Edward some peace. We came here to be alone and to talk to each other". Clara understood what Dorothy was talking about,

"of course," she replied. William, on the other hand, was not so impressed.

"I have not spent much time with Edward lately," he said in a harsh tone.

"William I will talk to you later, please allow me and my lady some time alone," Edward said in a very conservative manner. William then realised that this was not the time or place to be arguing.

"Come on William, let's go for a walk," said Clara. William and Clara then stood up and walked back across the field towards the canal.

Edward and Dorothy were alone again.

"What do you think is going to happen with this war?" Dorothy asked.

"I don't know my lady," replied Edward. He then went on to explain to Dorothy that nothing had happened yet and that everything was going to be fine.

"Come here my lady." As Edward pulled Dorothy in close he squeezed her tight.

"I will not let anything happen to you," he said. Dorothy smiled and closed her eyes, she felt safe, warm and content. She trusted Edward with her life and knew that he would always stick to his word and that he would never let anything happen to her.

"Come on Dorothy, let's go home." It was late and it was becoming dark. Dorothy and Edward started to head home together. The town was eerie, there was a mist descending from the canal. Dorothy held onto Edward's hand really tight, she said to him

"there is a storm coming isn't there"? Edward nodded his head in agreement and simply said

"the storm will pass".

AS THEY GOT HOME, George was pacing up and down in the living room. Dorothy had a concerned look on her face.

"Mother what is wrong with father"? Anna looked at Dorothy and shook her head,

"he is worried that he will be called up to fight again". Dorothy looked stunned,

"but isn't father too old now to be called up"? she replied.

"Yes, he is but that does not mean they won't change that rule," replied Anna. Dorothy was very concerned she ran over to her father and wrapped her arms around him. George stopped pacing he placed his arms around Dorothy and kissed her on the top of her head.

"My beautiful angel, no matter what happens I love you," said George. Dorothy's eyes started to swell up, a teardrop falling from each eye. Edward came over and joined in the cuddle. The three of them embracing not knowing what the future was going to hold.

———

OVER THE NEXT FEW MONTHS, fear was surrounding the town, people were being brought back from war with horrific injuries. Stories of people that Dorothy and Edward knew being killed in action. It was very solemn and everyone was starting to worry who was next. If they were going to get a knock on the door saying that one of their loved ones had been killed in battle. George had not been called up to fight. This was a blessing to Dorothy, Anna, and Edward. Patrols were still heavy in the town. Food and supplies were starting to become difficult to get hold of. It was now January 8th 1940. That morning George turned on the wireless. The news announcement that rationing food and products was to come into force. That getting supplies in from Europe and other countries was proving to be difficult due to the ongoing war and the battles in the British waters.

"I will go to the market and see what I can get," said Edward.

"I will come with you," replied Dorothy. The pair left the house to go to the market.

The market was very busy it had not been this busy in months. People were panicking not knowing if they were going to be able to buy any food. Worrying about where their next meal would come from. The atmosphere was so tense that you could cut it with a knife. People were trying to barge their way to the front of the queues just to try

UNDER THE SYCAMORE TREE

and get some vegetables. Edward and Dorothy stared at the carnage around them. They could not believe how serious this had become. People we trying to steal the food. They saw a man steal two large fish. The fishmonger unable to do anything about this due to the demand at his stool. The power of fear was immense. The war and the news were bringing out the worst in people and their good nature seemed to have diminished.

"Look there's William and Clara," shouted Dorothy.

"William, Clara over here," shouted William.

"Look William, its Edward and Dorothy," said Clara. William and Clara headed over to Dorothy. William was carrying a small satchel.

"Did you manage to get anything?" asked Edward.

"Yes, but hardly anything they are only allowed to sell small amounts," replied William. Edward and Dorothy knew they needed to act fast, everyone was going crazy shouting and barging their way past to just get some food.

"William where is the best place to go?" pleaded Edward.

"Follow me," replied William. He took Edward through the market and out down a back alley. The girls struggling behind to keep up pace with the boys. As they got further down the street Edward noticed a shop. It was empty no one was there; everyone was at the market trying to get all their fresh produce.

"This shop sells things that can last a little longer than the fresh food," said Edward. William looked at Dorothy and smiled. They entered the shop where they were greeted by the shopkeeper.

"Things have gone up in price, hope you understand,"

said the shopkeeper. William smiled at the shopkeeper and looked around the shop. The prices had indeed gone through the roof, but they needed food to survive. Dorothy picked up some potatoes and bread. William grabbed some tinned salmon, soups, and casseroles. They paid for the food and headed back outside.

"Did you get what you needed"? asked William.

"Yes, thank you," said Dorothy.

"William we should go and tell my father about what's going on," said Clara. William and Clara then headed off down the street and out of sight. Edward and Dorothy proceeded to head home to show George and Anna what food they managed to get. They walked down the narrow street towards the market. It had only got busier and people were now getting violent and fighting over what they could purchase. Panic buying was all around them. As they proceeded through the market there was a man lying on the floor. There was blood surrounding his head, yet nobody around him seemed to care. Dorothy stopped Edward.

"We can't just leave him like this". Edward looked around and shouted for help. There were so many people but nobody came to their support. Dorothy screamed,

"will somebody please help this man"? A few people stopped and looked at Dorothy. They looked at the man on the floor, but then looked away and proceeded to carry on trying to panic buy. Dorothy always wanted to be a nurse, she always wanted to help people.

"Edward help me get him to his feet, he needs a doctor".

"Certainly, my lady, but it won't be easy, if he cannot

walk," replied Edward. The pair then dragged the man up to his feet. He was unable to weight bare; he was still unaware of his surroundings. They then knew they needed to carry him through the market to the doctors.

"I HAVE AN IDEA," said Edward.

"What is it"? asked Dorothy. Edward pointed to an empty wheel barrow that was only a few feet away.

"Brilliant," called Dorothy. Edward ran over and grabbed the wheelbarrow. The pair then managed to carefully put the man into it. Edward pushed the wheelbarrow with Dorothy stood in front to navigate. They managed to get to the doctor's office. Dorothy started to bang on the door, after a few seconds the door was opened by the kind nurse that she had spoken to about her father in the past.

"Please, this man needs your help" pleaded Dorothy. The nurse looked at the man,

"bring him in urgently. I will get Dr Bennett." Edward struggled to get the wheelbarrow up the step. He pushed and pushed but to no avail.

"Dorothy grab the front I can't get this inside". Dorothy grabbed the front of the wheelbarrow and together they got the man inside. As they got inside Dr Bennett came running out of his office. He looked at the man,

"he clearly has a head injury". Dr Bennett asked Dorothy and Edward to bring him to his treatment room. When they arrived in the room all four lifted the man onto the bed. He checked the man over and his nurse started to clean his wound. "Here, hold this and keep pressure," the nurse said to Dorothy.

"I..um..ok," said Dorothy. She held a pressure pad to the man's head to try and stop the bleeding. After a few minutes Dorothy was asked to let go, the bleeding had stopped.

"Thank you, we shall take it from here," said Dr Bennett. Dorothy and Edward then left the treatment room still shaken from their ordeal.

"Edward I cannot go home; I need to know that he will be fine". Edward knew there was no way that Dorothy would leave until she had seen the nurse or Dr Bennett for an update.

"I understand my lady, let's sit down and wait," replied Edward. Edward and Dorothy sat down in the waiting room. Edward held onto Dorothy's hand and would squeeze it every now and then three times. Each time he did this Dorothy would smile. He wanted to keep her calm, he did not want Dorothy to become distressed or upset. An hour later, the nurse came out of the room. Dorothy jumped up off her seat and asked what was going on.

"Today young lady, you have helped save a man's life". Dorothy was startled, amazed she had helped someone in need. She hugged the nurse and thanked her for her kind words.

"You can go in and see him if you wish." Dorothy walked slowly towards the treatment room, Edward stood up and followed her. As they arrived in the room the man was lying on a bed. He had a bandage around his head and his arm. He was awake, he moved his eyes towards the door where he saw Dorothy standing with Edward behind her. He softly said,

"thank you for saving my life". Dorothy was so happy, she wanted to hug the man, but yet she didn't want to hurt him. She slowly approached the bed, she took his hand,

"it was my pleasure sir," she said. Dorothy then spent some time just sat with the man. After he fell asleep, she walked towards Edward.

"Shall we go home now"? he asked Dorothy.

"Yes, it's been a long day let's go home".

When they arrived back at the house they were greeted by George,

"where did you two go to... London? You been gone for hours". Dorothy burst into tears, the day had completely drained her, and she was exhausted.

"Look what you have done George," scowled Anna.

"No, it's not you George, it's been a tough day. The market was chaos I have never seen anything like that before. People were fighting, stealing. Everyone was panicking, it was mayhem. Then there was an injured man who needed help, we had to put him in a wheelbarrow to get him to the doctors." George and Anna stood there in disbelief. Their daughter was a hero, she helped get a man to the doctors. Edward continued

"if it was not for Dorothy, that man may have died.

She saved his life." George approached Dorothy and gave her an enormous cuddle.

"I am so proud of you; you will make an excellent nurse," he said. Dorothy continued to weep, she just wanted to rest now. George took her over to the sofa and sat her down. He then asked everyone else to sit down.

"After the Somme, I returned home in November 1916, I was wounded after taking shrapnel damage to my leg. I was no longer fit to fight in the Great War. I remember when it was January 1918, they started to ration sugar, food was being sent abroad to help feed the soldiers in the war. Supplies were difficult to get in this country due to attacks from the Germans at sea. Initially, it was just sugar, it was not that much of a hardship, however, panic started to happen a lot more in April, when butter, cheese and margarine were added to the list. They created a ration card for everyone. Even King George and Queen Mary had a ration card. It started to cause panic, people were scared they did not know when they would eat, what food they could get. Everything was in such short supply. It was scary seeing even the most placid of people becoming aggressive over food. The rationing didn't stop until 1920, two years after the war had ended. That is the power of fear, war brings fear, suffering and even death to people that are not even fighting in it. Things are not going to get better fast; this is something that we need to prepare for. The fear will consume your thoughts, it will make you feel weak and helpless. But it can be beaten. Do not let the power of fear consume you."

Everyone remained in silence, George had spoken out about more of his troubles. He was right before about the war coming and everyone knew he was right again.

Dorothy headed upstairs to bed. Edward settled himself down on the sofa, he was unable to sleep that night. He was turning 17 soon and in 1 year he would be conscripted to join the army if the war hadn't ended. He could not get this off his mind. He was scared, but he knew what George had told him was right. He could not let the power of fear consume him. He needed to be strong for himself and Dorothy. He would continuously go over this in his head. His thoughts consumed by the chaos he had seen today. Was this just the first day of many days like this ahead?

7

SHATTERED HEARTS

For many a shattered heart can never be repaired. The love and admiration that we may have for others can never be replaced by another.

IT WAS NOW late January 1940, the beautiful song that they would continue to hear on the wireless 'Over the rainbow' was from a moving picture called the 'Wizard of Oz.' Dorothy really wanted to see this. Edward, Dorothy, William and Clara were all sat on the steps of the factory talking about this.

"Shall we go?" asked Edward. Dorothy smiled

"I have been hoping you would say that all day". Clara giggled,

"never got the hint Edward". William started to laugh.

"Come on let's go and see it then," said Edward softly.

"What now?" replied William. "Well no time like present," joked Clara. Dorothy started to giggle.

"Come on then let's go," said William. The four of them took the long walk towards the theatre. When they arrived, the queue was long. A lot of people wanted to see the magic behind the beautiful song that would be played almost every single day. They all waited so patiently, it seemed to take forever but they soon arrived at the ticket booth.

"Four tickets for the Wizard of Oz," asked Edward.

"Certainly sir," replied the attendant. William took the tickets. He could see the excitement on Dorothy's face. None of them had seen a moving picture before this was to be a new experience for everyone.

When they arrived in the theatre, they couldn't believe what they were seeing. Popcorn, ice cream. The sweet smell of popcorn overpowering their minds.

"I must get some popcorn," shrieked Clara.

"I think we all should," said Edward. They queued up for their popcorn. They had never even tasted this before. They couldn't believe the taste. It was magical melting in their mouths. They proceeded into the theatre now. In front of them an enormous red curtain. They all sat down in their seats. William sat next to Clara with Edward sat next to Dorothy. This was it, the moment that Dorothy had been waiting for. The red curtains started to open. Behind this enormous white screen which soon came to life. Here they were seeing this amazing experience for the first time.

As the moving picture began to play Dorothy grabbed Edward's hand, she was so excited, and she squeezed his hand three times. Edward smiled he held onto Dorothy's hand and looked over to see William and Clara cuddling into each other. Edward smiled; everyone was happy. It made him feel good about life for the first time in a long time. Dorothy was so engrossed by what she was seeing, she whispered to Edward

"we have the same name, she is called Dorothy too". Edward smiled; he loved that Dorothy was happy. The film played on and on. Everyone deeply engrossed by the moving images projected onto the screen in front of them. As the film came to an end everyone in the theatre stood up and applauded the cinematic masterpiece that was before them. Dorothy was smiling, her dreams of seeing a moving picture finally coming true.

"That was outstanding," exclaimed Dorothy, she had a huge smile across her face. She linked Edward's arm, and they walked out the cinema with Clara and William following behind. As they left Dorothy would hum the theme to 'over the rainbow' continuously. The music, the vibrant colours and the incredible atmosphere of the cinema flowing through her mind. She could not wait to go home and tell her parents about her amazing experience. As they walked down the long road from the theatre Clara started to sing 'over the rainbow' her voice was majestic and beautiful. Everyone stopped walking, Clara then stopped singing

"what is wrong why have we stopped?" she asked.

"That was beautiful," said Dorothy. Edward and William were shocked they looked at each other and then looked back at Clara.

"You have the voice of an angel," said William.

"Oh, don't be so silly," she replied.

"Clara, you're very talented," remarked Edward. Clara started to smile.

"Let's keep walking," she said. As they walked down

the road Clara continued to sing in the most beautiful voice they have ever heard. People were stopping as they walked past to stare in amazement at how the beautiful vocal sounds of Clara were ringing around the street.

As they got back to the market Clara noticed her father. He was wearing a military uniform. Confused and not knowing what was going on Clara approached her father.

"Father, why are you in uniform?" Clara's father dropped his head down,

"I have to go war," he said softly. Clara's eyes swelled up, her cheeks went bright red, her lips begun to tremble.

"Please father you do not have to go. Tell them no," she wailed. A tear fell from Clara's father's face as he softly said

"I cannot do that, I have to do my service". William came running over to see what was going on followed by Dorothy and Edward. As they got to Clara a bus arrived carrying more men in military uniforms.

"This is my bus Clara," said her father. Clara burst into tears, she did not want her father to go to war.

"Look after my girl," he said to William.

"Yes, sir you have my word," replied William. Clara continued to plead with her father not to go. She wrapped her arms around him.

"Take me with you father".

"Clara please don't make this any harder," he replied. Clara held onto her father tears streaming down her face.

"It is time now Clara". As Clara let her father go, he opened the door of the bus and stepped on.

"I love you Clara," he said softly. Clara with tears streaming down her face

"I love you father, come home safe". He then closed the door to the bus and the bus drove off. Clara fell down to her knees and began to cry and scream uncontrollably. Her heart was shattered, her father had now gone to war. In her heart, she did not know if she would ever see him again.

William sat down on the floor next to Clara, he tried to reach for her hands. Clara initially pulled away.

"No, leave me alone," she screamed. William did not take no for an answer. He managed to get hold of Clara's hands he then placed them on his shoulders and looked her in the eye.

"Everything is going to be fine, I can feel it". Clara cuddled into William,

"He's gone," she cried. Dorothy and Edward then sat down with Clara, the four of them then embraced in a friendly group hug.

"We will not leave you Clara," said Dorothy.

"Yes, Clara we will all be here for you". Clara all sniffly thanked everyone for being so kind to her. William and Dorothy helped Clara back up to her feet.

"I am tired," said Clara.

"Let's get you back for some rest," replied William.

"Good idea," said Dorothy.

"Do you need any help?" asked Edward.

"No, we will be fine, we will talk soon brother," replied

William. William and Clara then headed off back to the factory so Clara could rest and settle.

EDWARD AND DOROTHY continued to head home. Dorothy was very concerned about Clara. She knew what her father had been through when he had been sharing his stories and was worried that the same thing may end up happening to her father. Edward knew something was bothering Dorothy he could see the concerned look on her face. Edward held onto Dorothy's hand and squeezed it three times. Dorothy would smirk from time to time, but Edward knew something was still not right.

"My lady, are you worried about Clara and her father"? he asked.

"Yes, Edward I am. What if the same thing happens to Clara's father like it did mine or even worse". Edward paused he stopped walking with Dorothy and took both of her hands.

"Please do not think the worst, things may work out. Everything could be fine and you know what, it will be fine because I feel what William felt too". Dorothy started to smile, she loved how positive Edward could be even in very difficult situations. She started to feel calm, more relaxed and reserved about the future for Clara and her father. For the rest of the journey home, Dorothy would continue to hum 'over the rainbow'.

When they arrived back home, there was George and Anna sat down talking about the war.

"Nothing has happened George, it has been quiet so far," Anna said to George.

"Early days," replied George to Anna. Dorothy was so excited to tell her parents about the moving picture that she had seen today.

"Father you know that beautiful song on the wireless, well we saw the moving picture for that film today". George did not say anything he just puffed, he then stood up

"that is good Dorothy, please tell me if you plan on going to any busy places again, they may not be safe," said George. Dorothy was dumbfounded, what was not safe about the theatre she just did not understand her father's concerns. Edward knew, he whispered into Dorothy's ear

"War, busy areas are targets." Dorothy then understood

"oh, yes father of course I will inform you next time. My apologies," she replied.

"Let me tell you a story about the Great War, please everyone sit down," George asked.

THE TEA WAS BREWING in the teapot as they all sat with George at the table, he had that glazed look on his face as he began to tell them of the Great War.

"The first time I encountered the German airship ...... I forget what it was called......... ah now I remember, it was a zeppelin. It was on the night of 31st May 1915, the zeppelin appeared over north London where I'd been for a visit. The zeppelin would come out of the dark - you couldn't see them. It began dropping its deadly cargo on the darkened streets

below. It was the first time London had been bombed from the air. The aim of the zeppelin was to break morale at home and force us, to abandon things further afield and to get the government to get our troops to return home. The target line was keeping to a line east of the Tower of London.

The people didn't react with panic but got on with the job of clearing up. They weren't fazed, but for some this led to a feeling of fear, impending doom, and a realisation that the war was coming home to us. War that I didn't want or need. I hadn't realised that I'd become a target simply by being in London. You think you're safer in a large number, but in war time in the capital you're a moving target. I thought I'd visit your Uncle Alfie before I was stationed abroad, as I knew I'd get my orders pretty soon. I didn't see your Uncle Alfie as he was in the fire brigade. He had been called to 16, Alkham Road, the home of Robert Lovell and his family. The zeppelin had started a fire in the upper floor of his house. Needless to say, Uncle Alfie was busy........ me I'd had my first experience of war and the mighty zeppelin. Little did I know that a year later I'd be embroiled in the 'bloody' battle of the Somme."

Everyone was silent, amazed by George's story. It gave Edward and Dorothy an insight into what war looks like when it comes home.

"Father, do you think there will be bombings here again in England"? asked Dorothy. George sighed

"it's inevitable, it's not if. It's when," he replied. Edward took Dorothy's hand he knew she was frightened at the prospect of further bombings. He squeezed her hand three times; he knew this would always make her smile. As Edward held Dorothy's hand he looked to Anna and asked "what were your experiences in the Great War?"

Anna poured everyone a cup of tea from the teapot,

"My story is very different to George's. I did not see much in terms of bombings, casualties or deaths. I was living in the country during most of the Great War, what I did see was the aftermath, the destruction that the bombs had caused. People were made homeless, their livelihoods destroyed. It took some time to rebuild, but we did. One thing I have learned about war. No matter how hard we are hit, we always come back stronger. We rebuild, and we reunite into a much stronger nation".

Edward and Dorothy were in awe of what they were hearing. They both sat there thinking what could happen? When it could happen and how it could happen? Edward whispered to Dorothy

"perhaps they see themselves in us?" Dorothy whispered back

"I do not think so Edward, I think they are both scared about what could happen to us". Edward glanced into Dorothy's eyes and smiled. He knew she made a lot of sense with her words of wisdom. He promised to ensure that he would take care of Dorothy no matter what, these were words in his heart that he knew he would stick to in this life and the afterlife.

BACK AT THE FACTORY, William was consoling a distraught Clara. Her heart broken over her father going off to fight in the war. William was holding her as much as he could. Clara would at times push William away, not wanting any sympathy. She wanted her father.

"Miss please try and get some sleep," William said in a very calm soft tone. Clara would continue to just scream and wail she was exhausted but in no mood for a conversation. William was at the end of his tether he did not know what to do to help Clara. He walked downstairs to the factory entrance. He saw another man having a cigarette.

"Excuse me sir, could I please have one of those"? he asked.

"Sure thing," said the man. He handed William a cigarette and lit it with a match. William took a puff on the cigarette and immediately started to cough.

"First time," said the man.

"Yeah," replied William. Not wanting to look weak he continued to smoke the cigarette.

After he finished the cigarette, he turned around to head back into the factory. He felt light-headed and dizzy.

"What on earth is going on he thought to himself". After a minute of staggering around William managed to find his bearings. He felt a lot calmer and headed back up to Clara. He now had a plan. As he got to the top of the stairs, he noticed it was unusually quiet. He turned the corner to notice that Clara was fast asleep. He chuckled to himself and smiled. He did not need to do anything at all to console her anymore. He went over to the bed and put a blanket over Clara. He then gave her a kiss on the head and sat down on his stool. He opened up his sketch book and proceeded to draw an image of Clara soundly like an angel.

A FEW WEEKS HAD PASSED, more and more news was coming in regarding British forces being mortally wounded in battle in the war.

"Boy, get your friend, we have work to do," George said to Edward one morning.

"Yes, sir. But may I ask what this is for"? replied Edward. George became increasingly agitated with Edward.

"Go and get your friend," he shouted. Edward knew George meant business and ran out of the house without even saying bye to a stunned Dorothy who was just sat on the sofa. Edward ran as fast as he could to the factory where William was talking to Clara outside.

"William let's go we have work to do, George has asked for your help." William glanced at Edward. He then looked back at Clara

"Let's finish this later". Clara gave William a cuddle and said softly

"we will continue later". William then ran off with Edward back to the house to help George with his task.

When the boys arrived at the house they went inside.

"Father is in the garden," said Dorothy. The boys walked to the back of the house and went outside. There was George with large metal panels. They went outside,

"what is this sir?" asked Edward.

"Boys, this is a shelter, it will protect us from the bombs from the sky". Edward and William had not heard of or seen any bombs drop from the sky.

"Is this necessary sir"? asked William. George became irate

"Yes you fools this will save your lives you wait and see". The boys felt very intimidated, they started to help George build the shelter after a few hours of fitting the panels together the shelter was complete. Dorothy came into the garden, she saw this large metal structure,

"that's an air raid shelter," she said shocked.

"Father do you think it's going to happen". George walked over to Dorothy he put his hands on her shoulders and softly said

"nothing can stop it".

Edward knew that having this shelter was a sense of security for George. All he wanted to do was to protect his family. Something that any loving husband and father would do.

"How many people can we fit in there"? asked Edward.

"As many as we can," said George. Everyone smiled, they knew that if the worst was to happen then this could help save as many people as they needed it to.

"I should tell Clara," said William. Anna came outside and saw the shelter,

"yes we should tell the others who don't have this security," she said. As everyone looked at the shelter before them a voice in Edward's head was telling him that hopefully this was never needed.

10TH MAY 1940 Winston Churchill was now sworn in as

the Prime Minister of Great Britain, the speech he gave in the House of Commons being shared on the wireless everyone was listening and his words of

"blood, toil, tears and sweat" reignited belief to George. There was a fearless leader and someone who would give everything to help Great Britain become victorious. The market had started to bristle with life. People were feeling confident and safe. They had motivation. The speeches from Churchill giving them hope and inspiration that Britain would become victorious. Edward felt proud he was now 17 and if the war was to continue, he knew that in a year's time he would be called upon for his services. Now feeling more confident and seeing George looking less fearful he believed things were going to start looking up.

MANY MONTHS PASSED, there had been small bombings in the city of Birmingham and many people were wounded. Dorothy was helping out with the doctors assisting with treating patients. Her dreams of becoming a nurse were turning into a reality. The air raid sirens would continuously go off throughout the months of August, September and October. St Philip's Cathedral was hit hard by an incendiary causing significant fire damage. Birmingham university suffered damage along with the town hall and art gallery. George would always ensure that he kept everyone in the shelter at the first sound of a siren. William and Clara were now living in the house with Edward, Dorothy, Anna, and George. George felt a great responsibility to keep everyone in the house safe from the war going on around them. Dorothy would come home late after helping out, tired and exhausted. Edward would spend a lot of time with Dorothy sat in her room, supporting her.

"I love helping people Edward," she said.

"I know you do my lady; you're going to be an amazing nurse," said Edward. Clara and William would stay downstairs with Edward. The house was a tight squeeze, but it was cozy and everyone was together which made them all feel more safe and secure.

IT WAS the 19th November 1940, it was a very chilly morning and the sun had just risen. The amount of air raids that had been before them had caused major disruption in the city centre. The house and the surrounding areas where Edward and Dorothy lived remained intact. Suddenly there was the sound of thunder, the siren started to sound. George jumped out of bed.

"Everyone wake up, get in the shelter now." Everyone grabbed some belongings and blankets whilst George and Anna grabbed some food and water. Everyone piled into the shelter and George bolted the door shut. They all sat down waiting for the inevitable to come. They could hear the aircraft above, the sounds of the propellers. Then what followed. There were heavy explosions,

"that sounds very close," said Edward.

"Far too close," replied George. Clara cradled into William; he knew that she was very frightened. The sounds of explosions all around them. Everyone got very close to one another. They all held hands and started to pray, pray for hope that the bombs would stop.

George decided that everyone should stay in the shelter for at least 1 day after the last sound of an explosion. Not everyone was happy with this. Clara turned to William

"how can we stay in here so long? You know I hate feeling trapped." William rolled his eyes,

"Clara, it is not safe out there, we have to be safe. I promised your father that I would take care of you". Clara still not overly happy about having to stay in the shelter crossed her arms and begun to sulk.

"My lady, perhaps you should go and have a talk with her," said Edward. Dorothy agreed with Edward and went over to Clara and sat with her,

"Clara you are safe with us here, we will all look after you. Please do not be afraid". Clara put her arms around Dorothy,

"thank you," she replied. George then pulled out some dominoes from his bag.

"Shall we have a game; help keep us busy". Everyone thought this would be a great idea. They all played dominoes into the night, everyone was laughing and joking. They were all having so much fun that they managed to drown the sounds of the explosions out around them.

Over the next 5 days, the explosions and the sounds of aircraft continued to unsettle everyone.

"Is there any end to this"? asked Edward.

"I don't think so," replied William. "It's just relentless it's like every so many hours more bombs get dropped."

"Yes, sometimes the bombs sound so close and yet sometimes so far away," said Dorothy. Anna remained quiet she had noticed that the supplies with the food were running low. She whispered to George

"we have one day's worth of food left". George stood up

"I have to go into the house," he said.

"No father, it's not safe," Dorothy was pleading with her father not to go out there.

"If I don't go, we won't survive anyway". George then forced the door open of the shelter. He stepped outside; the area had remained intact. He ran into the house, and grabbed a much as he could carry before running back into the shelter. He bolted the door.

"I am ok," he said to everyone. Dorothy and Anna both grabbed George and hung onto him. Edward smiled he was glad that George was ok.

It was now the tenth day. The bombs had started to slow down between blasts. Clara was increasingly agitated spending long periods sat with her head between her knees rocking backwards and forwards.

"I don't know how much more she can take," said William.

"Just do what you can," asked Edward. William would spend long periods consoling Clara, he would even try and encourage her to sing. Which she would do from time to time.

"I will sit with her," said Dorothy.

"Why don't you go and sit with Edward and my

father"? she asked William. William thanked Dorothy for her help, and he went to sit with Edward and George. Dorothy put her arms around Clara and started to hum to her rocking back and forth in the motion Clara was. George held open his hands,

"boys take a hand." Edward and William both took one of George's hands each.

"Do you still want to be soldiers"? asked George.

"Yes sir," replied William. Edward did not think he would get a say in what happened and expected to be forced to be a soldier, so he simply replied with

"yes". George let out a huge sigh and started to tell the boys another story.

"To be a hard working-class man is easy you go to work and you protect your family. The hardest part is when trouble strikes you .... here you need the strength of ten steel girders, you can't be weak. Your strength is the thing that protects you and your family. It's the thing that matters as it fuels your actions. In war and peacetime 'love' can lead to trouble; the heart is easily led. You need strength of heart and courage to resolve to be together in the good and the rough times.

The thing is that no one tells you that life is made of a series of chapters and these can be good, bad, something to live for and sometimes to grieve for.

I know I'm a changed man as a result of the bloody Great War, its messed with the wiring in my brain....... I see and hear the ghosts of the men I've lost, the pals and their grieving widows.

I just want you to both know that I'm a proud man and I'm proud of the way your lives are shaping. You are both brave and energetic but with compassion. I know that you will be good husbands and eventually fathers. I only hope that if this 'bloody' war continues that you continue to be compassionate that you don't grow weak in mind or spirit, because your girls need you as you are."

Both Edward and William smiled, they felt that George was so proud of them. They both sat back and relaxed. George lay down on the floor and closed his eyes. All of a sudden Clara jumped up,

"I need air, I need to get out," she screamed. She ran towards the door and forced it open. She ran out of the shelter. William jumped up as he went to leave the shelter he was grabbed by George.

"No boy, it is not safe out there". William started to thrash about

"I have to protect her, I PROMISED". William was in distress. George then flung him to the back of the shelter.

"You cannot go out there, I will go and get her," said George.

"Father no, you cannot risk this. Do not go out there," pleaded Dorothy.

"I can't leave her out there," replied George. Dorothy grabbed her father and squeezed him tight

"come back safe," she said. William shook George's hand and thanked him.

"Do you need my help sir"? asked Edward.

"No boy, you are now in charge you have to protect everyone," replied George. George then stepped outside the shelter and closed the door.

George moved round the side of the house and walked onto the Main Street. The smell of burning buildings was thick in the air. The black smoke was surrounding him, difficult to see and breathe he made his way towards the market, wrapping his jacket around his face to prevent smoke fumes from consuming him. When George turned the corner into the market, he could not believe the destruction before his eyes. Building's destroyed. Rubble falling off of damaged buildings. The fires, bodies littered all over the floor with people trying to help their loved ones. It was carnage. George had seen this all before, but he had never seen it this close to home. Having to step over the bodies on the floor around him he made his way through the market. Through the smoke he could see a young lady.

"Clara come back," shouted George it's not safe. Clara turned and looked to George she was clearly in shock at the sight of all the death and destruction around her. George knew that she was frozen unable to move. He made his way through the rubble, fire, and smoke.

As he got closer to Clara, he could hear the sound of planes from above. George looked up to see small specs in the sky. He knew now he had to move fast. He ran over to Clara

"hold on," he picked her up and started running. There was a huge explosion behind him which caused the bakery to explode into flames. The blast caused George to drop to his knees. He closed his eyes and he could see the Somme, the mines exploding all around him. His friend's falling before him from the intense gunfire around him.

"Fall back," he could hear from the commanding officer. In his flashback an explosion caused him to fall down.

"Get up soldier and fall back," he could see his

commanding officer stood over him. George then shook his head and as he opened his eyes, he regained his focus. He forced himself to his feet.

"I have got you and we are going to get out of here," he said to Clara. He pushed himself to walk as fast as he could, stepping carefully over the bodies and the debris around him with Clara held tight in his arms back towards the shelter.

———

BACK IN THE SHELTER, Dorothy was sat holding Edward's hand. She was worried about him. Anna was sat with William making sure he was ok. All of a sudden there was a huge bang. The entire shelter shook violently.

"What was that"? asked Dorothy.

"That was too close," said Edward. The blast was so powerful that it knocked Anna down on to the floor. Dorothy's heart started to race. She wanted to know that her father was ok. As time passed there was no sign of George. It had been many hours since the last blast.

"I am going out there," said Dorothy.

"No, my lady remember what George said," replied Edward.

"Yes, we need to go out there I need to find Clara," said William. Edward looked to Anna,

"What do we do?" he asked. Anna stood up and walked to the door she opened the door and said

"we go and find them". They all stepped outside the smoke was so strong the smell of burning was intense. The devastation around them was unreal.

"So, this is the apocalypse," said Edward.

As they walked onto the main road, the heat from the fires would cause sweat to pour off Edward. Dorothy held onto him tightly, she was terrified. There was so much smoke, so much heat that it was hard to see. When they arrived at the market. They could see the true devastating effects of the blast. The bodies littered all over the market caused Anna to fall to her knees in tears. Dorothy turned into Edward and started to cry. William ran into the market shouting

"Clara." He started to tug at the bodies in hope he would find her. Edward then noticed something, He saw a man and what looked like a small woman under some rubble.

"Edward, over here," he called.

"Listen to me my lady, stay with your mother". Dorothy wiped her tears away and went to sit with her mother. As William got closer to Edward, he also saw the male and female bodies under the rubble. William's heart sank he did not want this to be Clara. The boys frantically started to remove the rubble as fast as they could. Brick by brick they took them off. They turned the male body over. Edward gasped. William fell to the floor in tears, screaming at the top of his voice in anger. Dorothy and Anna come running over, everyone started to cry. There was George motionless with his eyes wide open. Dorothy jumped down onto the floor and started to do chest compressions. Edward grabbed Dorothy,

"stop there is nothing you can do". Dorothy started to scream and wail uncontrollably.

"Father please, wake up father". She then turned to

Clara's lifeless body on the floor. Dorothy saw nothing but rage for Clara. She began to hit her with both of her hands ferociously hard on her chest.

"How could you, you killed my father with your selfishness," she screamed. William pulled Dorothy off Clara

"leave her alone, she has suffered too," he cried. Edward then wrapped his arms around Dorothy,

"I am angry too, but this solves nothing," he said to Dorothy.

William then sat on the floor next to Clara she was covered in blood, he took out his handkerchief and wiped her face clean. He then closed her eyes and cradled her body into his arms.

"I am so sorry, I failed you I could not keep you safe." Clara was still no life flowing through her body. William cried as he held her close sobbing at the loss of the girl that he loved. Dorothy pushed Edward away

"I need time with my father," she said with tears pouring out of her eyes. She then collapsed onto her father's chest. Edward knelt down by her side, he could not leave her, he put his arms around her shoulders. Whilst she lay on her father's chest emotionally distressed. Anna stood back the entire time she was frozen and unable to move, seeing her beloved husband lay there with no expression on his face. She was angry at Clara and devastated at the same time. She did not know what to feel or how to feel. She hated Clara for what she had done, but she could not express these emotions, the shock overpowering her body as she saw George and Clara both lifeless, silent and still.

SOON AFTER MANY SOLDIERS ARRIVED, they started to clear up the bodies and found that some people were still alive. They came over to where Dorothy, Edward, William, and Anna were. They looked at George and Clara,

"We are truly sorry, they did not make it". Dorothy was still lying on her father's chest.

"I am so sorry father," she said as she kissed him on the head softly.

"We need to move the bodies miss," said a soldier. Dorothy would not leave her father. The soldiers becoming increasingly agitated.

"Miss, we have work to do," the soldier said. Edward knew he had to step in. He put his arms around Dorothy's chest and lifted her off George. She began to start screaming very loudly, kicking out

"let me go, that's my father." Edward knew he could not do that. He had to take Dorothy away. As he pulled her away, he let her go. She turned around and slapped him around his face,

"that's my father, do not take him away from me." Edward reached out and grabbed Dorothy pulling her in.

"I am here," he said. He held her tight, and she sobbed uncontrollably into his shoulder. As she cried Anna came over, she touched Edward on the shoulder

"leave her with me, you need to go and help". Edward then slowly took Dorothy's hands and placed them onto her mother's shoulders. Dorothy and Anna were locked together, holding onto each other both in floods of tears, yet supporting one another through the loss of George.

Edward and William helped the soldiers move the bodies of Clara and George for them to be taken to the morgue. An inconsolable Dorothy wept into her mother's arms. William was angry continuously shouting that he will have his revenge. Edward was sick, he could not help the vomiting, he couldn't believe what had happened. All of their hearts were shattered by the tragic events that fell before them. They knew they couldn't stay around; they were asked to move on by the soldiers. They knew they had no choice, no real chance to grieve, to say goodbye.

"We need to go," said Edward. Nobody else said a word all that could be heard was the high pitched cries from Dorothy. They all started to walk slowly away from the market. As they walked Edward thought about what George had said, he knew he was now the protector of the family.

8

THROUGH THE HEARTACHE

Heartache will affect us all at least once in our lifetime.
Fighting through the heartache to see that there is still hope is
an important aspect of recovery.

BIRMINGHAM WAS A MESS; it was hit hard by the intense blitz that had lasted for the last 10 days. The destroyed market and surrounding buildings were met with mourners, many of who had lost loved ones. The house was unscathed, still intact. The atmosphere in the house was very emotional. A distressed Dorothy refusing to come out of her bedroom. William had helped himself to George's drinking cabinet and was drinking large volumes of alcohol. Anna still in shock had not spoken a word. Edward confused and lost without George, unable to understand what he had to do to help Dorothy. William was rocking in the chair,

"I failed her," he said to Edward.

"No, you did not," replied Edward. William was still full of anger,

"I will have my revenge," he said. Anna sat at the dining table staring into an empty teacup and had not moved for hours. Edward had an idea. He went into the kitchen and made a pot of tea. He then poured four cups out. He then turned his attention to the staircase, he needed to see Dorothy.

He went up the stairs, creeping slowly. He did not want to cause any loud noises. As he got to the top of the stairs, he knocked on her bedroom door. There was no response, he placed his ear to the door and could hear Dorothy's cries. He turned the door handle and walked carefully into the bedroom. Dorothy was lying on her bed face down crying and sobbing. Edward walked over to the bed and sat down next to Dorothy.

"My lady, I am here". Dorothy turned her head to look at Edward. Her eyes deep red with huge bags underneath them. Red marks running down her face from where the tears had been flowing.

"I can't believe he is gone," she said in a trembling tone. Edward did not want to upset Dorothy, he was unsure of what to say. Instead, he grabbed her hand and squeezed it three times. Dorothy moved over slightly and placed her head on his lap. Edward began to stroke her hair.

"I miss him so much," she said.

"I miss him too," replied Edward softly. It did not take long after this for Dorothy to fall asleep. Edward carefully lifted her head back onto her pillow. He gave her a soft gentle kiss on her head and left her bedroom. He went back downstairs to speak to a drunk William.

"Let's go we need to see what's happened out there," said Edward.

"Why, what is the point. Everyone is dead," replied William.

"Not everyone, now let's go," said Edward in a strong powerful voice. William put down his drink and stood up. He then followed Edward out of the house.

As THEY GOT off the street and towards the market, the trail of destruction was now visible. As the smoke had now settled and the fires had been extinguished the devastation was truly horrifying for the boys. The bodies had all been removed, but the bloodstains were still there on the floor. Buildings were heavily damaged, many without the roofs some completely destroyed. There was a heavy presence of soldiers and civilians all helping to clear the ruins around them. The boys carefully walked through the market. The mood was low, people were crying in the streets. Many now homeless, widowed or without parents. The boys managed to find their way to the canal. They wanted to check on the factory. As they got close, they could see that the factory had damage. The side entrance completely torn away. They walked around the building to the main entrance which was intact. The factory was empty, no signs of life. The boys both knew that business was now closed.

"Brother, we must sign up to the army. We must have our revenge". Edward let out a huge sigh,

"now is not the time, it is time to grieve. When we are

18, we will have no choice but to join." William not convinced walked back down the steps

"what have we got left"? he asked Edward.

"Dorothy, she needs me," replied Edward.

"Well I have nothing; she was taken from me. What have I got left"? shouted William. Edward stared deep into William's eyes and just said

"you have me." William then realised he still had his blood brother, that they were still united. He shook Edwards hand and said "brothers until the end".

Two DAYS PASSED, Dorothy still hiding away in her bedroom, barely coming out. Anna pottering around the house but being very quiet. She was clearly mourning the loss of her husband. Edward was playing dominos with William at the table when there was a quiet knock on the door. Edward looked to William

"who could that be". William shrugged his shoulders. Edward stood up and came to the door. He opened it slowly to be treated by a man in military uniform.

"Hello sir, we have reason to believe that the occupants of this house might be able to formally identify two bodies." Edward paused and looked to Anna; she came to the door.

"Yes, I should be able to help. My husband was killed a few days ago in the bombings." Dorothy could overhear the conversation. She came running down the stairs.

"I need to go to. I need to see father". William jumped up, he came running to the door and asked them

JAMES KEITH

"is there a girl there, red hair long and wavy". The soldier informed everyone that he could not discuss individuals, and they would need to come to the morgue to identify the bodies.

Everyone followed the man out of the house and made their way to the morgue. Dorothy could not believe the amount of people who were sat on the streets, their homes destroyed. She thought she was the only one who had suffered at the hands of the bombing. But the realisation that this had affected nearly everyone around her made her feel more inspired to help.

"Mother we need to help these people, we have a home, we can offer support". Anna looked towards Dorothy,

"we just don't have the room. I would love to help people; we can invite them in the shelter if we need to". Dorothy was not keen on leaving people out in the cold. But she knew her mother was right. A few minutes later they all arrived at the morgue.

As they entered the front entrance the realism kicked into everyone. There were bodies everywhere. The amount of people killed in the blasts was unreal. Nobody expected to see hundreds of bodies laid out throughout the entire morgue. Tears started to stream down Dorothy's face at all these people who sadly lost their lives. People like her now without mothers, fathers, and siblings. She grabbed onto Edward's arm.

"This way," shouted the man. They followed him down the corridor passing body after body. When they turned the corner, they all froze. The man pulled back a

164

cover to reveal Clara, all the wounds had been cleaned away. William stepped forward,

"she looks asleep," he said softly. That is Clara, she looked so peaceful. Her hair had been cleaned up and her eyes were closed. He placed his hand on his head.

"Oh, she's so cold," he was shocked he did not expect it. He slowly placed his hand back on Clara's head. He then leaned forward and softly kissed her on her lips.

"Sleep well my angel," he said as tears started to roll down his cheeks. He gently covered her back up and walked down the corridor to the entrance of the morgue.

The man then proceeded to the next body. As he raised the sheet, Dorothy gripped Edward's arm really hard. When the sheet was lowered there he was.

"That's my husband," cried Anna as she burst into tears. Dorothy stepped forward, her heart was racing and her eyes were swelling up. She saw her father looking so peaceful.

"May I hold his hand"? she asked the man.

"Yes," the man replied. Dorothy softly placed her hand on her father's. She was shocked at how stiff it was. As she stood there holding his hand, she softly whispered into his ear

"the angels will look after you father, one day I will see you again". She kissed him on his head, she was fighting her emotions. All she wanted to do was cry and scream. She turned to her mother and took her hand.

"Mother please". Anna stood with Dorothy, and they both placed their heads on his chest. Embracing him one final time. Edward stood back and allowed them both the space they needed. Dorothy kissed her father one last time

"I love you father always and forever". Her and Anna then turned away from George and walked towards the man. Edward then slowly approached George. He held George's hand; the cold feeling gave Edward shivers down his spine. He took a deep breath closed his eyes tight and said

"thank you sir, thank you for taking care of me. Thank you for making the man that I have become.

"I won't ever disappoint you. I give you my word." Edward then opened his eyes to see Dorothy stood by his side.

"Thank you, Edward," she said softly before kissing him on the cheek. The man thanked them for their help identifying the bodies, before telling them they would be able to bury them soon. They all then started to walk down the corridor to catch up with William. Who was waiting outside smoking a cigarette.

William was quiet, his mood was low. Things had started to look up for him, yet there he was feeling all alone in the world once more. Edward put his arm around William's shoulder and softly whispered into his ear

"I will never leave you". William started to weep, with small teardrops rolling down his cheeks. He turned to Edward and embraced him in a brotherly cuddle. The two boys both hurt and struggling to handle their emotions following the deaths of George and Clara. Dorothy stood watching the boys embrace, she was linking her mother's arm, wondering how herself and her mother would manage to cope now that her father was no longer with them anymore. Everyone then headed back to the house, there was no talking on the way back. Everyone remained silent trying to gather their thoughts now that the reality had hit them. There was nothing any of them could do to bring them back. They were deep in thought at a loss with their own grief.

DOROTHY DID NOT LEAVE the house until the day arrived for George's funeral. She barely spoke and spent long periods in her bedroom crying herself to sleep. She deeply missed her father, and she deeply missed his passion that he had for her. That morning Anna put the kettle on the oven to make a warming pot of tea. Edward stood and watched Anna move about the kitchen, thinking to himself how much she was hurting inside. She did not look like she was in pain, as she continued to do her daily tasks like any other day. Her face told a different story her eyes were distant thinking of her loss. However, he knew that the loss of someone you love is like the heart being ripped out, leaving nothing but an empty whole. He remembered how he felt when he lost his parents and how much it affected him and still does. Edward then shook his head and approached Anna

"is there anything I can do to help you ma'am"? he asked. Anna smiled at Edward,

"no young man, thank you for asking". Edward left the kitchen and went into the lounge where William was finishing off putting on his tie.

"Almost ready?" asked Edward. William nodded he was still hurting and feeling the pain of losing Clara. Suddenly there was a click from upstairs. It was Dorothy coming out of her bedroom. As she got to the top of the stairs Edward gasped. She was wearing a long black dress, a black hat and a black face veil which covered her face. She slowly walked down the stairs, as she got to the bottom Anna was placing the tea pot on the table. Dorothy walked straight past William, without even giving him a glance. She took Edward's hand and lifted her veil. She kissed him on the cheek then sat down at the table with her mother for a cup of tea, the silence was eerie and sent a shiver down Edward's spine.

After everyone had a cup of tea there was a knock at the door. It was the undertaker.

"Are we ready?" he asked everyone. Anna stood up and replied,

"yes, we are ready". As they all left the house their eyes opened extremely wide. There were 2 beautiful horse-drawn carriages carrying both the coffins of George and Clara. George's carriage was lined with flowers, it was beautiful. Clara's was empty only a simple single wreath lying on top of the coffin. The horses were immaculately dressed as were the undertakers. No one had expected such beauty in front of them. The sun was shining down on everyone and there wasn't a cloud in the sky. It was like the heavens were showing their respect for George and Clara. They all then held hands and started to walk slowly towards the carriages. William climbed inside Clara's carriage whilst Edward, Dorothy and Anna climbed in George's carriage. As soon as they were safely in the carriages the horses were given the order to walk. As they slowly moved through the town people would stop. The men would take off their hats, in respect for the loss of

George and Clara. The women would bow their heads. Edward watched as so many people lined the streets to stop to look and pay their respects.

There was complete silence all the way to the graveyard. No one spoke, not even a word, yet Dorothy, Anna, and Edward were all linked holding hands together. The ride was bumpy at times over the cobbles. The bumping was causing them to move around the carriage. Edward was holding onto Dorothy tight, he continued to squeeze her hand three times. Every time he did this she would smirk almost smiling. After a few minutes, they arrived at the graveyard where Clara and George would be laid to rest. When the carriages stopped Dorothy let out a sigh. She knew this was time now where she would have to say her final goodbyes to her father. The carriage door was opened and Edward stepped out, meeting William who had previously stepped out of Clara's carriage. The boys embraced in a hug before Edward turned around to help Anna out of the carriage. Edward then looked back inside the carriage. Dorothy was sat staring blankly in front of her.

"My lady, it's time," said Edward. Dorothy turned her head towards Edward, she showed no emotion and took his hand. She then stepped out of the carriage and onto the path. Edward took Dorothy's hand and placed it on Anna's.

"I need to help now," said Edward as he made his way to back of the carriage. William turned and made his way to the back of Clara's carriage.

Edward helped the undertakers carry the casket of George whilst Dorothy and Anna walked behind. William could not help, he wanted to aid in the carrying of the casket for Clara. He thought it was very important that someone was there for Clara, as her father was away fighting in the war. The two caskets were carried through to their resting place and placed in the ground. The holes had already been dug and as they were lowered Dorothy could not control her emotions. She burst into tears

"Father, I love you so much. Please don't leave me I need you". Edward held on to Dorothy keeping her close and tight to his body, so she could feel his heartbeat for her to try and relax. After a few minutes, she began to settle down. She took her place stood over her father's grave barely managing to hold back the tears. Fighting every ounce of emotion in her body. She could not believe that her father was gone. She was hoping that it was all just a bad dream, a nightmare and that she would have woken already.

Many people had turned up to see George and pay their final respects. Clara on the other hand only had William stood there. No one else turning up to pay their respects to the loss of the beautiful girl with an angel's voice. William felt hurt and lost that no one would show up to pay their respects. The minister approached William and asked if he would like to say anything. William shook his head; he did not know what to say. He placed a single red rose onto Clara's casket and then threw some dirt on top.

"I love you," he said to Clara as he walked away to head towards George's service.

The crowd was large, there were veterans from George's brigade, from when he had served in the army.

Edward was astounded at the turnout; he had no idea that this many people knew who George was. The service started and the minister read out some prayers, music followed by a brass band and then it was time for the speeches. The first to step up was a former soldier who had served with George in the Great War.

"What can I say about this great man? George was an incredible man. Not only did he try and save this young lady's life, he also saved my life. During the Great War, we were in the Somme together. It was bloody, it was noisy and it was a living hell. It was everyone's worst nightmare. One particular day things became very bad there was shelling all around us. We felt trapped, it did not seem that there was a way for us to escape. I froze and thought that was it I was about to meet my maker God almighty, I called for my mother in despair. That's when George grabbed me, he carried me out of there and over an embankment to safety, where I was able to retreat. But George did not retreat. He ran straight back into danger to save others. He was not only my friend; he is my hero. He died doing what he loved, helping others and fighting for his country. He was a proud man".

Dorothy and Anna started to weep, they did not know, how brave George actually was and that he would always put his life in danger to help others feel safe and free. At the same time, Dorothy felt so proud of her father and his selfless acts of bravery to ensure the security of others. The minister then approached the front again and said a further prayer. Before calling up the final speaker, Edward. Dorothy looked at Edward, she had no idea that he had prepared a speech for her father's funeral.

"My lady, I owe it to him". Dorothy smiled at Edward

she felt so proud that he would do such an amazing thing for her beloved father. Edward stood up and made his way to the front. He had never spoken in front of people; he was nervous, yet he felt confident. He took his place and looked around. There were so many people, a sea of voices looking at him. He took his focus to Dorothy to try and help with the anxiety. He then started to give his speech.

"My father left me when I was 10 years old. My mother had died shortly before. I had no one, nothing. I lived alone on the streets until I was 13. For three years, I was starving, cold, filthy. I moved from place to place trying to find ways to survive. People may call what happened next fate, destiny or just plain luck. Four years ago, I was starving and I had not eaten for several days. I stole a loaf of bread from the bakery and I ran as fast as I could to get away from the baker. Not looking at where I was going, I ended up bumping into Dorothy. Dorothy was so kind to me and took me to her home. I was not expecting anything, however, George took me in. He gave me clothes, food, warmth, and shelter. He provided me with an occupation. He taught me how to be a man. How to treat people with respect. How to take care of others. His amazing qualities have clearly been passed on to Dorothy. I owe George everything, all the stories he has told me. All the advice he has given me, he has made me become the best man that I could ever have hoped to become. I promise you I shall take care of Dorothy for the rest of my life and beyond. You truly are an inspirational man, a man with a heart of pure gold who would sacrifice his own life for others. I love you George, thank you".

As Edward finished his speech there was a large round of applause from everyone at the funeral. The brass band continued to play music following the speech. This was not the end for George, but now a celebration of his life and who the amazing man was who helped save so many people over the years. As Edward sat down next to Dorothy, she wrapped her arms around him and gave him a kiss.

"That was so beautiful Edward, my father would be very proud of you". Edward smiled. George was an incredible father figure to him and had given him so much hope for his future. As the proceedings came to an end the caskets were buried and covered. Dorothy then laid down some flowers at her father's grave. She turned to William and took his hand. She walked him over to Clara's grave.

"These are for Clara," she said to William. William smiled; this was the first person other than himself to lay flowers down for Clara. Dorothy placed the flowers on Clara's grave and softly said,

"I forgive you, rest in peace".

After the service Edward looked for the soldier that George had saved, he wanted to shake his hand. Edward looked around the crowds of people and found the soldier. He approached the man.

"Great speech young man," said the soldier. Edward smiled,

"yours was fantastic," he replied. He offered his hand and the two shook hands.

"George truly was an incredible man," said the soldier.

"He was, he was my hero too," replied Edward. Dorothy then came over. The soldier took off his hat and bowed down in front of Dorothy.

"It's an honour to meet the daughter of George," he

said. As the soldier stood up Dorothy took his hand

"the honour is all mine sir," she replied. Dorothy then looked at Edward she gave him a kiss on the cheek and then took his hand and lead him away.

"Let's go home," she asked. Edward nodded and the two then walked home. Dorothy was tired, and she wanted to get out of the dress and relax for the rest of the day. As they got home Dorothy went straight to her room to get changed into her nightwear. Anna made everyone a pot of tea. Which was drank very quickly. Dorothy came back down the stairs and spoke to her mother in the kitchen whilst William and Edward sat down at the table and decided to play a game of dominoes to see the day out.

IT WAS NOW MID-1941. William, Edward and Dorothy were now 18. The boys knew that it would not be long before they were called up to go to war. The war was still raging and further bombs had been dropped by the Germans over Britain. Dorothy was terrified, she did not want Edward to be called up to go and fight in Europe. She still missed her father, but always remembered his wise words of wisdom. Dorothy had been working at the doctors helping with the nursing and had just started her training to become a nurse. It was something she had wanted to become since she was very young. Edward and William had helped repair the damage to the factory and continued to work at the smelting factory. Dorothy and Anna would visit George's grave every day. William would visit Clara's with Edward once a week. Edward wanted Anna and Dorothy to have their own time talking to George. However, this would not stop him from visiting George from time-to-time to seek advice.

It was a beautiful sunny Sunday morning. Edward did not have to go to work and Dorothy had a free day. She wanted to surprise Edward and packed up a picnic basket and some blankets. Everything was ready and everything was going to be perfect.

"Edward let's go for a picnic," she asked. Edward had not seen Dorothy this enthusiastic about going out since before George had passed away. He could not resist and agreed. The two then went for a long walk hand in hand. The birds were singing and the sun was beating down. It was beautiful, warm and very relaxing.

"It's been a long time Edward; I think we should go to the sycamore tree". Edward's face lit up they had not visited the sycamore tree since before George passed away. But he was worried, what if it had been destroyed by the bombs and it wasn't there anymore. It crossed his mind all the way down the canal. As they got to the clearing his anxieties eased. There it was standing tall the beautiful sycamore tree in all its glory.

As they arrived at the tree Dorothy placed a blanket on the floor.

"Edward come sit next to me," she asked. Edward sat down next to Dorothy, and they began to eat the strawberries that she had prepared. Dorothy then placed her hand on Edward's face and started to kiss him passionately. Edward's heart started to race. He had never seen this side of Dorothy before. Dorothy could feel the butterflies floating around in her stomach, she knew this was right. She could feel the magic inside her. She then leaned into him pushing him down onto his back. Edward was startled this was different, but he liked it. His heart began to beat harder, Dorothy sprawled over him her hair trailing over her face, touching his body. He could see the sparkle and emotion in her eyes. He wanted to please Dorothy so badly. He started to lean forward, proceeding to kiss Dorothy's neck. He then placed his hands on Dorothy's breasts, she started to grin. Edward wanted to take control, he wanted Dorothy to feel the passion that he had for her. He grabbed her by the hips and then tuned her over onto her back and looked down at her. They were gazing deeply into each other's eyes. The timing was perfect and the location was magical.

Edward then lowered his head and started to kiss her neck softly. Her head started to tip back, and she started to groan with pleasure. He slid his hands down her face and towards her breasts then he slowly started to unbutton her blouse one button at a time. Dorothy was nervous, her breathing heavy. But she was also excited she had wanted to make love to Edward for so long. She then started to reach forward. She started to undo the buttons on Edward's shirt. As they were undoing each other's buttons they continued to lock lips. After a few seconds' Edward managed to remove Dorothy's blouse. He then started to kiss her body slowly making his way down to her breasts where he kissed them ever so softly. The tension was high. The magic was incredible, the two were embracing in ways that they had never embraced in before.

Dorothy pulled off Edward's shirt, then she

immediately started to remove his belt. Edward's heart continued to pound, in his head he did not know what to do, he was starting to panic thinking what if she does not like it. Dorothy could tell there was something on his mind, so she pulled him towards her. She kissed him with fire, passion and in such a way that Edward thought he felt the world move around him. Edward loved this side of Dorothy; he knew she wanted to make love. He wanted Dorothy so much that he pulled down on her skirt removing it from her body. He then slid down Dorothy's body he pulled her legs and placed them over his shoulder before kissing the inside of her thighs. Her whole body was twitching, she had never felt feelings like this before. She felt like she was flying with the angels. Dorothy was extremely aroused; she managed to remove Edward's belt and removed his trousers very quickly. They were now both naked lying together under the sycamore tree. They gazed into each other's eyes.

"I love you," said Dorothy.

"I love you too my lady," replied Edward. They kissed each other softly. Edward then laid his body on top of Dorothy's and they started making passionate love to one another. They were groaning with pleasure. The passion, the romance, the intimacy was all new for both of them. All new feelings which none of them had ever experienced. They would pause to gaze into each other's eyes. To tell one another that they love each other, they did not pause for long as they continued to kiss and make love.

Their love was now connected in a new way, a way that none of them ever had imagined happening before. The pleasure and the seduction from them both made them feel so much more in love. As they came to an end of making love, they embraced into a cuddle lying underneath the tree their bodies locked together. Their skin touching one another's, the feel of skin to skin contact made them both shiver down their spines.

"I love you Edward," said Dorothy. Edward smiled he felt on top of the world.

"I love you too my lady," he replied. They were together in their favourite place, making love for the first time. Nothing could have got better. They continued to lay there until the stars came out at night. Where they both decided to make love to one another again. The magic of the stars made them both feel in heaven. The pleasure and the sensation and feelings of being locked together made them both sparkle. After they began to cuddle again there was bright lights flying across the night sky it was a shooting star.

"Edward, did you see that"? asked Dorothy.

"Yes, I did," he replied.

"Well, make a wish Edward," said Dorothy.

"I already did," smiled Edward. As they both lay there together thoughts would come into Edward's head. Thoughts such as being called up to fight in the war. He would lie there and think to himself that maybe he should just sign up. Save the trouble of being called up. He did not want to mention any of this to Dorothy. He did not want to upset her nor did he want to ruin the magic that they had both experienced together. Instead, he just decided to hold her close, feeling her skin touch his. Soon they both fell into a deep sleep and did not wake until the sun rose the following morning.

9

THE ART OF WAR

To act in war, you must first learn about war. War is not mindless fighting; it is an art. One that has to be played very carefully if you are to become victorious.

WILLIAM AND EDWARD were at the factory. They had been working for a few hours. "Edward, we are both 18 now. We need to sign up and do our part for our country," said William. Edward stopped what he was doing and put his hands on his hips. He really did not want to go to war, but he knew he may have no choice.

"William my brother, I cannot leave Dorothy. She needs me," replied Edward.

"Listen brother, we may have to do this, to honour Clara and George". Edward knew William was right. He knew he had to sign up for the army. But how could he tell Dorothy? He knew that this would really cause her a lot of upset and distress. He looked at his father's old notebook. Hoping to find something he had written that could help him, tell Dorothy that this was something he needed to do. There was nothing there, just memoirs of days in the factory and the letter that was written to Edward so long ago.

"Edward, when we finish work, we need to go and sign up," said William. Edward looked at William and gave him a single nod. The boys then continued their shift until the horn signalled the end of the day.

As they were preparing to leave work, they heard Dorothy call.

"Edward, I am here". Edward knew that Dorothy would not just let him sign up.

"William, what do we do? I cannot sign up with Dorothy around, she will not let me". William laughed,

"come on let's get out of here". As the boys made their way to the entrance and down the steps, they greeted Dorothy. Dorothy swung her arms around Edward, she still had that magical sparkle in her eye that he saw when they made love under the sycamore tree.

"Dorothy, we are going to sign up to join the army and to help fight in the war," said William with a huge grin on his face. Edward scowled

"why brother, now is not the time," he said. Dorothy went extremely pale

"tell me this is not true Edward; please tell me you are not considering joining the army". Edward lowered his head and softly said to Dorothy

"I may not have any choice; I am 18 now. They can call me up anytime. I have to do this for George, for Clara. I have to honour them". Dorothy's eyes started to fill; teardrops started to roll down her cheeks dropping onto the floor in front of her.

"Please Edward, you could be killed, please my father would not want anything to happen to you". Edward pulled Dorothy in and gave her a cuddle. He then softly whispered into her ear

"I will never leave you; I will always be in your heart. But this is something that I have to do". Dorothy held tightly onto Edward. She softly replied,

"I love you".

"Time is running out Edward, we need to get moving if we are going to sign up," shouted William. Dorothy pulled away from Edward, she looked deeply into his eyes

"I'm coming with you," she said softly.

"Well see that was not so bad, just tell the truth, and she understood," gloated William. Edward turned to William and gave him a very deep glare; William knew then that Edward was annoyed and that maybe he had overstepped the mark. That he should have allowed Edward to tell Dorothy himself when he was ready. Dorothy linked onto Edward, she held him very tightly as they walked down the canal towards the market. As they walked slowly Dorothy's mind would wander, all she could vision was when her father would have his breakdowns, due to the shell shock and the things he had seen when he fought in the Great War. She did not want Edward to go through the same thing. She wanted to protect her Edward. She loved him more than life, and she knew that he loved her more than life also. As they reached the end of the canal and turned into the market, the realisation of what was to come, started to hit everyone hard. There were soldiers parading around the streets and the damage to some of the buildings from the blitz a year previous was still evident.

As they walked through the market Dorothy spoke out "please, will you not do this?". Edward sighed, he knew he had no choice, but to do this. He did not want to break Dorothy's heart either, but duty called. Edward stopped walking and took both of her hands. He smiled at her and said, "My lady, I love you so much, you are my world, my everything and no matter what happens our love is eternal". Dorothy smiled she gave Edward a kiss on the cheek. Then continued their walk to the recruitment station. As the boys arrived at the station they were greeted by a tall slim officer

"what can I do for you boys?" said the officer.

"We are here to sign up to fight for our country," said William very proudly. The solider looked at the boys,

"you're both skinny, what use for us will you have"? laughed the officer. William was left speechless by the arrogance of the soldier, Edward looked at Dorothy not knowing what to say. Then Dorothy spoke out

"these boys are hero's they helped my father through his shell shock, they stood tall and helped carry the bodies of two people killed in the blitz. These are real men; they are not boys and they will do anything to protect their country." The officer looked at Dorothy and then looked at the boys.

"This girl has got some balls boys, maybe we should let her sign up and fight". Edward now had enough

"excuse me sir, but we are devoted to helping fight in the war, we want freedom and justice for the ones we have lost. We are not afraid of what we are going to face, we both have stared death and evil in the face many times in our lives. Give us a chance we will do you proud". The officer smiled,

"Good speech boy," he then shook Edward and William's hands and welcomed them to the army. The boys were smiling. Dorothy felt worried and very sick, she knew that they had no idea what they would be facing in the future. As the boys were recruited and paperwork was signed out Dorothy remained very silent. Thinking about what she would do without Edward when they would be away fighting in the war.

AFTER EVERYTHING HAD BEEN DONE, everyone headed home. As they arrived back at the house, Anna had already prepared the evening meal.

"Come sit, dinner is ready," she said to everyone. As they all sat around the table and started to feast Anna asked,

"how was your day?". Without hesitation William blurted out

"Edward and I have joined the army". Anna paused, she sipped her cup of tea and then placed it back on the saucer. Then she spoke

"Good, I am proud of you both". Dorothy was startled she snapped

"mother, how could you be happy about this". Anna sipped some more tea, she looked deep into Dorothy's eyes

"If your father was here, he would want this. He always believed in discipline and respect, he always told me that he learned about these traits in the army". Dorothy was stunned, would her father really be happy that Edward would be going to fight in the war? She did not reply to her mother and started to struggle to eat her meal. She felt sick and all she wanted to do was get into bed and cry herself to sleep.

BOTH EDWARD and William passed all the medical checks with flying colours. It was official now they were ready for the next step. It did not take long before they were to be sent to an army training camp just outside Birmingham. There was only a matter of days left. The situation was now very real, Dorothy was extremely concerned that she would never see Edward again. She could not leave his side and did not want to lose any more time with him. Even though most mornings she would find herself feeling nauseous and being sick, she did not let this stop her from seeing Edward. They were like peas in a pod inseparable. William was excited, he could now wait to get trained up and sent into war. This was his dream to be a soldier fighting against the enemy. Edward was nervous, he knew that he would not see his beloved Dorothy for some time. He loved spending the time with her, they went and sat under the sycamore tree every day. Enjoying the very little time that they had left, before he would be called away.

It was now the final day, the last day before Edward and William would travel outside of Birmingham and into the training camp. It was early morning and Edward could hear Dorothy upstairs being sick, he was concerned as this had been happening most mornings. After a few minutes, Dorothy came downstairs. She looked pale in colour her hair was very wavy, her eyes bloodshot.

"Edward, I'm sorry I'm so unwell, I just don't know what is wrong with me". Edward wrapped his arms around her,

"My lady, I am sure that it's just you being worried about me".

"Perhaps," she replied. Edward made Dorothy a cup of tea, and they sat down together. Edward could see the fear in Dorothy's eyes. Was he really doing the right thing? He did not want to see Dorothy looking so unwell. Yet he did not want to ask too much of her, he did not want to let her down the day before he was due to go away. Before he could speak, she asked

"can we go to our place today?". Edward smiled; this is exactly what he wanted to ask Dorothy.

"Yes, my lady, why don't you go and freshen up, and we shall go together". Dorothy finished up her cup of tea and headed up the stairs to get ready.

AFTER WHAT FELT LIKE HOURS, she came back downstairs. She was dressed in a beautiful yellow dress that almost matched her long golden hair.

"My lady, you are so beautiful," said Edward. Dorothy giggled. She took Edward's hand and squeezed it three times, before leading him out the front door. They walked slowly, holding each other's hands all the way to the sycamore tree. When they arrived, Dorothy sat down and patted on the floor for Edward to sit down. Edward slowly sat down, and Dorothy leaned into him placing her head onto his shoulder.

"Promise me, Edward, promise me you will be ok," she said in a sniffly voice. Edward knew he had to sound confident. He had to make Dorothy believe that he was going to be fine and that nothing would happen to him.

"Yes, I promise," he replied. Edward then reached into his pocket and pulled out his father's pocket watch.

"Dorothy, I want you to look after this for me whilst I am away". He handed the watch to Dorothy, hesitantly took the watch. She then softly said

"I can't Edward, this was your father's, won't you need it". Edward took Dorothy's hand and helped her open up the watch. Inside there was a drawing of Edward. Dorothy gasped it was such an amazing drawing that it looked so real.

"I had William draw that of me, so whenever you wanted to see me you just need to open the watch". Dorothy started to weep; she loved the thought that Edward had put into this. She wrapped her arms around him and kissed with passion.

"I'll cherish this Edward; I will make sure I give it back to you when you return". Edward smiled; he felt a lot more reserved in himself now that Dorothy had more confidence. They embraced throughout the rest of the day, talking about what they would do together in the future.

It was now late evening; the stars were out and the moon wall illuminating the night sky. Edward knew that this was the perfect romantic opportunity, so he stood up.

"My lady please stand with me," he asked. Dorothy

did not think anything of this and decided to stand up. As she got into a full standing position Edward dropped down onto one knee. Dorothy's heart raced, she gasped and placed her hands on her chest. Edward pulled a small ring from out of his pocket,

"My lady, will you marry me?" he asked. Dorothy was shocked, startled and did not expect this. She stayed silent for a few seconds before screaming

"yes" at the top of her voice. Edward placed the ring on Dorothy's finger. He then jumped up grabbed her and spun her round. They then kissed deeply. They stared into each other's eyes.

"When I get back, we will have our wedding," said Edward. Dorothy smiled, she had hope. She was going to get married when he returned.

"I cannot wait to tell mother", she bellowed. She was so excited that she could not stop hugging and kissing Edward. They were going to be husband and wife. It was a dream come true.

THE FOLLOWING DAY it was time for Edward and William to catch the bus to the training camp. They were both packed and ready to go. A nervous Dorothy was pacing up and down the living room.

"My lady, please sit down," asked Edward. Dorothy stopped turned around and started to bite down hard on her fingernails.

"Edward, how can I relax, I am worried about you. I am even worried about William. What if something bad happens to you both?" William smirked, he found it amusing that Dorothy was concerned about his welfare. Edward walked over to Dorothy and took her hand. He squeezed it three times which made Dorothy smile.

"It's going to be ok my lady," he said in a soft calm voice. He held onto Dorothy's hand and walked her out the front door whilst grabbing his bag. William picked up his bag and slung it over his shoulder as they were walking down the road William was whistling away. Dorothy was trembling throughout her entire body and Edward could feel this, and every time he felt her hand shudder, he would squeeze her hand three times. Before long, they arrived at the bus stop. This was it now, Edward was going away and Dorothy was struggling to hold herself together. As the bus pulled up, William jumped on. He turned around to Edward

"come on let's go we cannot stay here all day". Dorothy grabbed Edward by his arm and wrapped her arms around him squeezing him tight. She would not let him go. She couldn't he was the love of her life. Edward embraced Dorothy and held on to her tight.

"Hurry up," shouted the bus driver. Edward pulled away and gazed deeply into Dorothy's magical blue eyes.

"I love you," he said as he softly kissed her on the lips.

"I love you too," she replied. As Edward started to pull away Dorothy could feel him slipping from her fingers. He stepped up on to the bus, before turning around and blowing her another kiss. As the door to the bus closed Dorothy burst into tears. Her heart pounding with emotion as she did not know if this was the last time she would see her beloved Edward.

Edward solemnly followed William down the aisle of the bus until they found an empty seat to sit in. They both sat down, William with a beaming smile on his face, Whilst Edward was teary-eyed, looking at the window at his beloved Dorothy who was crouched down on the floor in floods of tears. As the bus pulled away Edward could not take his eyes off Dorothy, he gave her a wave to which Dorothy was far too upset to wave back.

"Brother, she is going to be just fine, as are we," said William. Edward lowered his head and looked at his bag,

"yes, everything is going to be just fine," he said very quietly. The bus ride was bumpy and very noisy. It was filled with young men on their way to army training to be prepared for the war. The smell was musky like a cheap cologne used to perhaps hide the fear of what was coming head. Edward could hear people talking that they had been called up and sent their papers. That they had no choice and that they were scared, and they wanted to go home. Edward was not scared about what was coming, he was scared about Dorothy and how she would cope with him gone.

"EDWARD, WOULD YOU LOOK AT THAT," said William. Edward peered out the window of the bus, in between the trees they could see where they were going to be. It was a very muddy field and small blocks of building. As the bus turned up the long drive and the camp became closer, the noise on the bus become very quiet. People were in shock at the conditions of the training camp in front of them. As the bus came to a stop the door was opened. On stepped a very tall slim man in an army uniform.

"Get up get your gear and get off this bus, we have got work today," he said in a very strong powerful voice. William gulped in fear,

"William, don't be afraid he will not hurt us," said Edward. William looked at Edward and smiled

"I am not scared of him, I will be fine," he replied. They got their gear and followed the other men off the bus. When they stepped outside everyone was standing in a straight line.

"Fall in," shouted the tall menacing man. Everyone stood perfectly still, whilst he walked up and down eyeballing everyone he passed. The tension was very high this man was highly intimidatingly had a real presence about him.

"I am your commanding officer my name is Sergeant Peters, but you will all call me sir," he shouted. Everyone stood still and shouted

"yes sir".

After both Edward and William had felt intimidated by sergeant Peters, they finally were allowed to attend the barracks where they could put their possessions. They were both handed uniforms to wear and were given some basic necessities; a bar of soap and some towels. Edward and William stepped into the barracks, the smell of sweat and urine was unfathomable. The stench was high and the conditions basic at best. Edward just stared at the skinny little beds up and down each wall. It reminded him of a hospital. The floor was cold and very hard, it was dirty full of muddy footprints. As they made their way over to their beds Sergeant Peters stepped into the room, his footsteps from his heavy boots echoing around the empty barracks. He paced up and down watching everyone

"Brother what is this guy's problem"? William whispered into Edward's ear.

"Quiet," replied Edward. The footsteps got much louder and closer, William started to sweat, Edward could see the sweat beads developing on his forehead.

"My problem is that I have to deal with stupid fools such as yourself," shouted Sergeant Peters to William. William was at a loss for words he did not know what to say, his head barely went up to the Sergeant's chest. Edward remained quiet; he did not say anything. He knew this was not the time or the place to play hero to William.

"All of you outside now," shouted Sergeant Peters.

"Except you," as he stared down at William. Edward followed the others outside. He was worried what was going to happen to William. They had only just arrived, and he was already getting himself in trouble. As they waited outside William was handed a brush, a very small handheld brush and was given his orders to scrub the entire floor of the barracks as punishment for what he had said. Shortly after William was handed his punishment the Sergeant arrived outside. It was exercise time. He ordered all of the boys to run and keep up with him. Edward did not mind running; he was used to running away from trouble in his earlier life. He ran following directly behind the sergeant. The ground was very slippery and his feet were sinking in the mud. It was awful terrain, and he would think to himself, that perhaps this terrain is made this way as it may be similar to what to expect when engaging with the enemy in war. He never spoke to the sergeant throughout the run, but he managed to complete the task without losing too much breath.

As Edward went back into the barracks, he could see William on his hands and knees scrubbing the floor as he was instructed to do. Everyone else soon followed in afterwards wearing their muddy boots. Which trampled mud all over the parts of the floor that William had cleaned. William looked up and then threw the brush on the floor.

"Come on, this is not fair, I have been told to make sure this floor is clean and you've all made a mess of it". Everyone just laughed at William and ignored his pleas. Sergeant Peters soon followed in

"why is this floor still a mess"? he bellowed at William.

"Sorry Sir, I will get it all cleaned," cried William in a crackled voice. William had started the day feeling so confident, now he felt broken, weak and scared. It was now Edward who seemed more confident, who was getting on well with the others and being able to complete all the tasks. As the lights were turned out for the end of the night and Edward and all the other trainees were getting into bed to sleep William was still left scrubbing the floor which he did until the early hours of the morning.

THE FOLLOWING MORNING daylight had not even broken. The lights came on and so did an awful horn. Sergeant Peters came stomping into the barracks shouting at everyone to get up, get dressed and to get outside. William had barely managed to get in to bed and get some sleep. He was exhausted and Edward could see this. He hoped that today William would simply keep his mouth closed and do as he was told for his own sake. As they all got ready and headed outside, they realised how awfully cold it was. None of them were used to being up this early in the day. They could see their own breath in front of them. Again, the first order was simple run and keep up with the sergeant. Edward again had no issue with this, but every time he turned to see William struggling and holding onto his chest. He knew that William was struggling, as they came to an end of the run. William said to Edward

"why did you not run with me"? Edward looked at William and told him that they have to give their best, or they could be punished. William did not like the word punished; it gave him visions of being back on that floor all night long scrubbing the mud off of it. The thought made him feel really sick, and he looked back at Edward and said

"Yes brother, I will give it my everything now".

William started to put his heart and soul into the training. He gave everything that he had, he wasn't as athletic as the others, especially Edward so was standing out as the best of the best in the group of trainees. William honestly could not believe how physically fit Edward was. The obstacle courses were particularly difficult for William, but he spurred himself on. He wanted to impress Sergeant Peters he did not want to let his squad down. He knew that if he kept falling behind that this could be life or death for him. Edward would often help William. He would encourage, run behind and give him all the motivation that he would need.

The training became more intense over the weeks, the runs were getting longer and over different terrains some were flat, others muddy and the worst were through the rivers as it made them all feel cold and wet. One particular day was especially hard, the siren went off early it appeared to be the middle of the night. Edward and William were both shattered and fighting to keep awake. They were told to be ready in two minutes. They were shipped out to a different location, given a map with the rest of the unit and told to get to point B on the map. Then the sergeant Peters said,

"good luck and god speed". Then he was gone.

The unit all set off and ran together, the terrain at first was smooth and dirt track, but then they went off-road. It was getting harder and harder to run as the ground below them became dislodged. William was trying to keep with the unit but his stamina and balance were not as good or impressive as Edward's he was beginning to fall behind. Edward tried to encourage him and linked him when he could. He was beginning to see him as a problem. Edward knew the unit had to come first. Although every man was essential, the unit had to come first If the war was to be won.

Edward ran ahead as he needed to double-check how far the checkpoint was, he told William not to worry and stay at a steady pace. William was not too far behind, it was dark still he misjudged where the path was, he stumbled and fell. He was in agony and started to limp he knew he was going to hold up the unit and had let them down again. It was becoming a habit.

The unit were nearly at the checkpoint when they did a headcount to ensure they arrived as a whole unit. William was missing from the unit this made everyone feel hostile, once again they were being delayed by the lad with no stamina and no guts. He was the one that always seemed to let them down. William was fearful as he knew the rest of the lads were not happy. They were sick of him bringing the unit down.

Edward decided to go to the checkpoint, when he turned around, he saw William limping, the others turned on him, they were shouting in his face. He held his hands to his ears and began shouting back,

"no I can do this, I'm a good soldier, and I am part of this unit". As the others backed off, he and the rest of the unit ran and met up with Edward. The unit fell silent as Sergeant Peters arrived,

"you took your time! All the unit here? I expected you would have left one of them behind........but no. Good to see the unit working as a unit, no individual is bigger than the unit.

William was really angry and hurting inside, he was going to show the lads he wasn't a pathetic lad, that he had his uses, and he was every much a soldier as they were......... they would see!

The lads thought the exercise was done, but there was one more task. Sergeant Peters handed them an envelope. Inside was another mission, this time the unit had to retrieve a package from a farmhouse in the valley. What they didn't know was that it would be guarded. The unit went to the truck that was waiting for them and retrieved their equipment. William was determined he would get this right. The farmhouse was a short walk; they ran and hid. One of the lads Jack ran ahead he didn't see the dogs coming from the back door. It was too late they got him, growling and barking... the great black dog bit down on his leg, the screams were blood-curdling. William ran to get him; he kicked the dog so it let go. It retreated into the shadows as the unit ran past him, he carried Jack to safety and set about cleaning the wound, bandaging him. He was at last showing what he could do. The unit retrieved the package and returned to the truck, with William still looking after Jack. For the first time .... the unit saw him as part of the team, he had risked himself to rescue Jack. The lads thanked him, and he felt now as he was part of it...... this new family.

THE EXERCISE WAS over and Sergeant Peters said they were to go back to the barracks and pack their belongings. The lads were given a day's leave to go home and put their effects into order and say goodbye, as after they had done that and returned, they would be dispatched for their first assignment. They were not to know until the moment they were shipped out........ it was top secret by all accounts. The concerns on everyone's face were a picture of what was about to come. The boys had all been trained, but in an environment where they were protected. Now they were about to step into the unknown. Edward was happy that he would get to say farewell to Dorothy. He could not wait to surprise her.

The ride back in the truck was sombre the lads didn't know what to say or think. Their brains were going over the idea of putting their effects into order and saying goodbye. No idea of where they were going or what was coming next, all of a sudden this was real ...... the war was coming as clear as day to meet them. Although just for tomorrow they could forget for a short time when they all went home or to who home was.

As the bus arrived at Edward and William's stop, they both let out a heavy breath. They gathered their bags and got off the bus.

"Brother, I am going to the factory for a while," said William. Edward knew William just wanted some time alone. He could sense the fear in William, something that William would always deny.

"I will go and see Dorothy," said Edward. The boys parted ways and Edward headed home to see Dorothy. As he got to the house, he opened the door and went inside. Anna was sat on the chair alone.

"Hello ma'am," he said softly.

"Edward it's you," cried Anna.

"It's so lovely to see you." Anna stood up off the chair and embraced Edward with a cuddle.

"Dorothy is at the doctors helping out," she said. Edward smiled, he thanked Anna and left the house to head to the doctors.

Edward was smiling and whistling away as he walked to the doctors, when he arrived he walked confidently inside. He approached the receptionist.

"Excuse me ma'am I am here to see Dorothy," said Edward. The receptionist smiled,

"please take a seat sir, I'll let her know you're here". Edward sat down on the chair in the waiting room. After a few minutes, Dorothy came into the room. Her eyes lit up when she saw him. Edward stood up and Dorothy ran over to him and wrapped her arms round him.

"Edward you came back, and wow you look so handsome in uniform". Edward blushed, his cheeks going bright red.

"I am only back for today my lady, tomorrow I must return, I'm being sent on a mission". Dorothy's smile started to fade, she did not like the news she was hearing. Edward on a mission she needed to know more.

"What is this mission"? she asked him.

"My lady, I do not know. They have told us all it is top secret and that they will tell us when we are in transit". Dorothy was worried, but as she only had the day she did not want to ruin it. She told Edward she would take the rest of the day off and that they could spend some much-needed time together. Dorothy grabbed her coat and told the receptionist to let the doctor know that she would not be back helping out today. Dorothy then skipped back to Edward and linked his arm and walked outside with him.

"How is William"? she asked.

"He is struggling, he struggled with the training, he was ridiculed but I think now he has found his purpose," replied Edward.

"Where is he"? asked Dorothy.

"He is at the factory; I think he wanted to be alone for a while,. he replied.

"Well let's go and see him, I would like to see him before you both go," asked Dorothy. Edward smiled and agreed and the two walked arm in arm to the factory.

WHEN THEY ARRIVED at the factory William was sat on the step, holding a cigarette in one hand and looking at his sketchbook with his other hand.

"William, I do wish you would stop that awful habit," asked Dorothy. William smiled and looked at her

"it's good to see you Dorothy," he said. Dorothy sat down on the step next to William, Edward sat the other side of William.

"It is going to be ok," said Dorothy to William.

"You are brothers and you will both look out for another," she said. William started to relax; he liked the fact that Dorothy started to show compassion for him. He did not want to be useless, and he did not want to let anyone down, especially Edward.

"Thank you, Dorothy," he said. He then proceeded to hand Dorothy his sketchbook

"please take care of this for me when I am away," he asked. Dorothy gasped she did not expect this, she took the notebook and gave William a hug.

"I will take care of this and as soon as you return, I shall give this back to you". Edward loved that Dorothy and William had seemingly managed to put the past behind them. William then stood up and said he was going inside for a short while.

"Want us to join you"? asked Edward.

"No, it's fine, I need some peace," replied William. William then walked into the factory and left Dorothy and Edward sat on the stairs together.

Dorothy gazed deeply into Edward's eyes,

"shall we"? she said. Edward knew what she meant

"certainly my lady," he replied. They both stood up and Edward took Dorothy's hand. They then walked together to their sacred spot the sycamore tree. When they arrived, they sat down in their usual spots. At first, they just listened to the sounds of the birds, then Edward spoke out

"my lady, if anything happens to me when I am at war, I want you to continue living your life and being happy". Dorothy did not like this talk, her bottom lip began to quiver.

"No Edward, you are going to be ok. Please do not say things like this, I cannot lose you. I love you". Edward sighed, he did not know what he was going to face, but he could remember George's stories about the bloody battles of the Somme.

"My lady, I just want you to know, if anything were to happen that I would want you to love again. I would want you to achieve your dreams. I want you to be a nurse, I want you to get married." Dorothy's eyes were now swelling up. The emotional conversation was so hard for her to take in.

"But I will be getting married, to you Edward. I will become a nurse. We will be together forever". Edward knew that Dorothy did not want to think the worst. He placed his arms around her shoulders and pulled her into his chest. Her tears dripping down his uniform. He knew that he had to return for Dorothy, but he wondered if that would be impossible not knowing what mission was lying ahead.

As they both sat there holding each other close, the sun began to set. This would be the last night that Dorothy and Edward would spend together. Edward did not know if this would be the last time that he would ever see Dorothy. Dorothy, on the other hand, did not want to think that, she was enjoying being so close to her beloved Edward. As the sun finally set and the stars came out Edward softly said

"No matter what happens, I will love you now and in the afterlife" A single tear poured out of Dorothy's eye, she simply replied,

"I love you to the far end of the stars". As they sat there gazing at the stars, they knew it was time to head home. The walk home was slow, Edward would squeeze Dorothy's hand three times. She would always smile; her eyes were very red from all the tears. When they arrived at home, Dorothy took off her coat and held onto Edward's hand. She led him upstairs to her bedroom. Where she wanted to declare her love to Edward one final time before his inevitable mission.

SOON IT WAS MORNING, Edward was up early and in his uniform. His pick up at 08:00. Dorothy was still fast asleep in bed. Edward did not want to wake her or make her feel even more emotional than she already had. Edward simply kissed Dorothy on the forehead and told her that he loved her. He quietly walked downstairs, the house was silent and the stairs begun to creak. He wanted to leave without waking anyone. His heart was already hurting, he could not handle anymore heartache by having to say his goodbyes again. He got to the bottom of the stairs he picked up his bag and left the house. He quietly closed the door and looked up at the house.

"My lady, stay strong," he whispered to himself. He then set off to catch his bus. As he arrived at the pickup location he was greeted by William.

"Where is Dorothy"? he asked.

"She is asleep, I couldn't bear to break mine and her heart again," he replied. William could see that Edward was hurting. He could see the pain in his eyes. The truck shortly pulled up and the boys stepped onto the truck. As the truck drove off all Edward could vision was Dorothy and her beautiful loving smile.

STEPPING INTO THE UNKNOWN

Not knowing what path lies ahead can lead to one becoming
fearful. Many embrace the unknown and will happily walk
that path. Not knowing can lead to many variations in life,
mainly fear or excitement. A person must walk that path once
in their life, this path may even lead to one's destiny.

EDWARD AND WILLIAM were greeted by Sergeant Peters
as they got off the truck. They were told to line up with
everyone else and fall in. Sergeant Peters stood tall over
everyone, walking up and down the line eyeballing
everyone as he walked past.

"Lads, we are going into France, we will be trying to
push the German army back, not all of you will survive.
But this is our mission. We are one unit and no one
person is greater than the unit, you fall behind we will
leave you". William was shaking at the knees; this was real
now, and he had no idea what he was about to face in
France. Edward stood tall, remaining confident.

"At ease soldiers," shouted Sergeant Peters. Everyone

picked up their bags and headed across the airfield where the military transport plane was waiting. They loaded up and sat down in their seats.

"Brother have you ever been on one of these flying machines before"? asked Edward.

"No, I have not," said William in a very croaky voice. Edward could sense the fear flowing through William's veins he knew that this was not going to be a simple stroll across France.

As the plane started to move down the runway, Edward could feel the vibration tearing through his spine. Before long, they were up in the air. William was holding onto his harness as tight as he could. Edward was thinking about Dorothy, wondering what she was doing and if she would be thinking of him. Jack shouted across to Edward

"you ok friend, you look lost". Edward looked over to Jack,

"I.I.I.I am fine," he stuttered, Edward then started to worry, he had not stuttered in a very long time. Was this because he was missing Dorothy or was he afraid of what would happen once he stepped foot off the plane. He then regained his focus and said to Jack

"I am just thinking about my lady". Jack smiled,

"aren't we all my friend," he replied. Jack then turned his attention to a terrified looking William

"It's going to be ok. We have got your back; you have helped me and I will stand by you". The tensions in William's arms started to relax, he did not feel so worried anymore. He had Edward and Jack for support. He simply replied,

"Thank you, Jack".

As the plane landed in northern France, Sergeant Peters made his appearance.

"Gear up soldiers, it is time to get off this bird". Everyone started grabbing their items and bags and made their way off the back of the plane. And they stepped outside the air was cold and damp, the weather was much like they were used to in Birmingham. As they fell into line they looked around, they appeared to be in the middle of nowhere stood on an old abandoned airfield which was overgrown with moss and surrounded by trees. There was a strong smell of stagnant water, it was very unpleasant and hard to bear. As they all fell into line, Sergeant Peters started today's talk.

"We have a very long walk ahead of us, the enemy is about 30 clicks to the east of us. We stay quiet and we follow the orders at all times, now let's go two and two formation and follow me". William quickly made sure he was in the formation with Edward. He did not want to be away from his brother for too long.

It did not take long before they were off the airfield and into the woodlands. The trees were towering over them almost blocking out any light. It was damp and the ground was sodden. The overgrown shrubs were particularly difficult to navigate around. As they continued to walk, they noticed that there was a huge lack of wildlife.

"William, I honestly thought being in a different country would be so vibrant," Edward whispered.

"So did I brother, it's too quiet and I don't like it,"

replied William. Before long they had managed to navigate to an old dirt road.

"Halt," shouted Sergeant Peters,

"We follow this road and we meet up with some other squads that will be waiting for us. When we arrive, further instructions will be given."

Everyone geared up and started the walk down the long dirt road. The road was very loose and very slippery, it appeared to go on forever. Edward and William had never walked this far before. They didn't think anyone had done. They could hear Jack behind them, complaining that this was very extreme and surely, they could have landed closer or had vehicles waiting for them. Edward rolled his eyes; he did not want to hear complaining all the time. He heard enough of that from William. As they continued the temperature started to drop and it was getting cold. Then there was a huge thunderclap from the sky, the rain started to pour down. It was heavy and very thick. In a matter of minutes, everyone was soaked through. They could not stop though. They had to reach their rendezvous point.

It was now pitch black; the rain was intense as it had been when it started to rain. Sergeant Peters then raised his arm with his torch, indicating for everyone to stop. Everyone stopped and paused. In the distance, they could see some light. Sergeant Peters signalled to the lights in the distance. Edward felt tense, he could see William shaking, cold and soaked through. Was this the enemy, were they about to engage? No one in the squad had seen military action before.

"Come on soldiers, this is where we will be staying for

the night." William let out a loud sigh which everyone heard. Edward smiled, this was their rendezvous point, what they had been waiting for all day. As they arrived at the location, they set up their shelters and all started to relax.

"It's you," William froze and Edward's jaw dropped, a familiar voice, one that could not be forgotten came from behind them.

***

WILLIAM COULD FEEL the hairs on the back of his neck standing up, he turned around slowly stood before him was Clara's father. He was alive and William had no idea if he knew that Clara was deceased.

"Boy, how is my Clara"? William gulped, how could he explain that Clara was killed in the bombing. What could he say to this man? Edward could see how frightened William was,

"Sir, she was tragically lost in the blitz last November". His face turned red with rage, he reached forward and grabbed William by his collar and raised his fist

"boy, you promised me you would look after her". William started to panic, his breaths getting faster and faster.

"Sir, I tried to save her and I failed you, I have to live with this every single day myself. I love her," cried William. Her father's face started to change, he let go of William and turned to Edward

"Is this true"? he asked.

"Yes sir, I lost someone too that day, George. He was

my hero, he died trying to save Clara". Clara's father then said

"my name is Richard". He then turned his attention back to William

"you stay out of my way". He then pushed his way past William and walked off to his own tent. William was still trembling and sat down on a small chair.

"I cannot believe that he is still alive," said William.

"I never thought he wouldn't be, but I honestly did not think we would see him here," replied Edward. Edward knew that William and Richard would have to find some peace, to be able to fight together.

The following morning Edward knew he had to do something to help Richard and William work together. He went for a short walk and bumped into Jack, then he had a brainwave.

"Jack, I need your help to calm tensions down". Jack nodded; he was willing to help. Together they walked around trying to find Richard, they found him playing dominoes with some other soldiers.

"Richard, can we please talk"? Richard turned his attention to Edward and Jack

"if it's about that traitor I do not wish to know". Edward sighed,

"he is no traitor sir, he loved Clara and he looked after her so well". Richard stood up and charged over towards Edward and Jack

"he is a coward, he let my daughter die, what has he ever done for anyone other than himself?"

"Excuse me sir, I'm Jack and that coward you are calling helped save me, I don't know him like Edward does, but what I have seen shows me a man with a heart, who would do anything for the people that he cares about". Richard lowered his head to the floor. He then turned and walked back to the table to finish his game of dominoes.

"No harm will come to him from me," he said softly. Edward smiled, he was relieved,

"thank you, Jack," he said. He then headed back to William to tell him the good news that Richard no longer wanted to beat him. William felt that a massive weight had been lifted off his shoulders, suddenly the bellowing voice of Sergeant Peters could be heard,

"line up, fall in".

EVERYONE FELL INTO LINE; Sergeant Peters took his place at the front of the squads with the other sergeants. They then stood very still and tall and saluted. An older man wearing a much smarter uniform started to walk up and down the line.

"I am Colonel Watson; I am the commanding officer here and you will all know that what we are going to face is the reality of your worst nightmares. Many of you will die, many of you get wounded. But together we will win this war, and we will push the German army back. Get your gear and get ready, we have a long road ahead and a mission to complete." William was so scared; he had now heard twice that many of them would not survive. He did not want to die, he wanted to go home now. He had changed his mind about the war. Edward wanted to get this mission complete, so that he could head home and see Dorothy and feel the warmth of her body pressed next to his.

They were soon on their way, walking along another dirt road carrying their heavy bags. Clothes still damp from the day before. Today was a new day and there wasn't a cloud in the sky. It remained eerily quiet, something that petrified William to the soul of his body. As they pressed forward William could see Richard in front of him, he wanted to apologise over the loss of Clara, but he knew that Richard would not accept this. Edward could see that William was worried again and that he wanted to make peace.

"Now is not the right time or place, make peace when the time is right," said Edward to William. William knew Edward was right, they were in the middle of nowhere and there seemed to be no benefit of trying to make amends with Richard. Before long, they arrived at an old small village, it appeared to be completely abandoned. The buildings were heavily damaged and there were clear signs that war had come to this small village. The Sergeants stopped everyone, Colonel Watson informed the Sergeants to break formation and stay and to keep their squads together.

The four squads were all given an area of the village to cover, William and Edward's squad approached the west side of the village. It appeared to be heavily abandoned, there was clothing and boots on the floor and the windows in the houses had been taken out. There was a sudden bang from one of the houses. Sergeant Peters raised his arm to indicate everyone to stop, He crept on slowly and waved the soldiers to follow on one at a time. As everyone made their way to the entrance of the house Jack was ordered to go in and scout first. Jack went into the house. You could hear the floorboards cracking under his feet from outside. Sergeant Peters then indicated for Edward to go into the house. As Edward made his way inside the smell of burnt wood hit him hard. He looked around to see nothing but burnt furniture. Everything was broken. He could not see Jack. Perhaps he is upstairs Edward thought to himself. As Edward climbed the stairs, he couldn't hear a thing, only his own footsteps on the creaking wood. As he arrived at the top of the stairs, he saw Jack. Jack was leant down next to a body.

"Sir, it's clear," shouted Edward. Sergeant Peters entered the house and the rest of the squad followed in shortly after. Edward looked down at this body, it was a young man maybe only 19 years old, he was holding a pistol in his hand and a fresh bullet hole in its skull. The blood was everywhere. This was the loud bang that everyone had heard. He couldn't look at it anymore, the memory of his father taking his own life when he was young caused a flashback in his mind. He ran downstairs outside; he began to hyperventilate. He had not seen anything like this not since his father. William came outside to see Edward.

"Brother, it's horrible". Edward started to catch his breath back. He would start to think about Dorothy and their sacred place. His happy thoughts always made him feel more relaxed. The squad then all made their way outside.

"Suicide," said Sergeant Peters, probably thought we

were the enemy. Edward remained quiet he did not know what to say, he fell in line and followed the orders to meet up with the other squads to the north of the village. There was nothing else to see, other than more abandoned homes that had suffered heavy damage from the war. As they continued their walk along the path they all knew that they were stepping into the unknown.

MEANWHILE, back in Birmingham Dorothy was starting to feel nauseous and being sick in the mornings, it never stopped her from helping at the doctors. She would always freshen herself up and get ready to face the day. She was eager and keen to become a nurse. It had been several weeks since Edward had been sent to France. Dorothy would always worry when there was a knock at the door. She always feared the worst that something had happened to Edward. She kept herself busy working long hours to help out where possible to take her mind off the tragic circumstances that may fall before her.

Dorothy was headed to work one morning; she could feel cramps and pains in her stomach. She was used to feeling sick, but she did not know what was causing this. As she arrived at the doctor's, she began her duties by assisting the doctor with patients. The cramps and pains would come and go throughout the morning until Dorothy could bear no more.

"Excuse me Dr Bennett I need to go and freshen up". Doctor Bennett smiled at Dorothy and indicated that this was fine. Dorothy slowly started to make her way to the restroom. As she arrived in the restroom she collapsed to her knees.

"What is wrong with me"? she said out loud. She then vomited on the floor, the sound of her retching alerted the receptionist who came into the rest room to check on Dorothy.

"Oh, my goodness my dear. I will go and get Dr Bennett," she said in a panicked voice. The receptionist ran out of the rest room and after a few minutes arrived back in the restroom with Dr Bennett.

Dr Bennett immediately began to tend to Dorothy after a few minutes of examining her on the floor he did not appear to show signs of concern. Dorothy still felt very sick, but the relaxed look on Dr Bennett's face made her feel somewhat relaxed.

"Dorothy, I need to get you to my treatment room so I can run a test," asked Dr Bennett. The receptionist and Dr Bennett helped Dorothy stand up on her feet, they then walked her arm in arm to his treatment room where she was laid down on the table.

"I am just going to examine your stomach." Dorothy nodded she was more relaxed and knew she was in safe hands. Dr Bennett seemed very confident in what he was doing. He felt her stomach and then listened.

"Dorothy, I think you might be pregnant." Dorothy felt her heart stop. Her eyes widened like saucers, and she started to breathe heavily.

"Slow down your breathing Dorothy," asked Dr Bennett. All Dorothy could think about was Edward, that if she was pregnant and Edward never came home then what would happen.

"Dorothy, to be sure I just need to run a test," said Dr Bennett.

Dr Bennett left the room and came back with a tube.

"I need you to urinate into this tube Dorothy". Dorothy took the tube and slowly walked back to the restroom with the receptionist. Dorothy managed to pass some urine and returned it back to Dr Bennett. Dr Bennett then pulled out a needle and drew up a syringe of urine. He then took it into a back room. After a few minutes, he returned back.

"I can confirm that you are pregnant Dorothy". Dorothy was stunned,

"how can you be sure"? she asked.

"I injected the urine into a rabbit, the rabbit displayed heat. It shows the correct hormone for pregnancy," he replied. Dorothy was terrified, she was only 18, and she was now going to be a mother to a child who does not have a father around. She was worried about what her mother would say and how her father would feel if he were still alive. Dorothy could not feel anything other than fear, her whole body was limp, and she was staring deeply into space.

"May I go home Dr Bennett"? asked Dorothy.

"Of course, you must go home and rest". Dorothy still stunned, shocked and terrified by the news walked very slowly out of Dr Bennett's office. Now she had to go home and tell her mother.

AS DOROTHY SLOWLY STEPPED OUTSIDE, the light

blinded her. The sun was intense, and she was in a state of shock. She raised her hand above her eyes to block the sun out. She then began a very slow walk back home. Terrified and afraid of what her mother would think of her she deviated towards the canal. As Dorothy stood over the canal she looked down. She saw the water and thought to herself

"I don't have to do this. I can stop this now. I can throw myself in there and it will all be over. Mother will not need to know I can't be a mother, not without Edward". As Dorothy pondered what to do, she continued to stare at her reflection. The water then started to ripple and Dorothy's reflection changed, it was no longer her reflection, but a reflection of her father.

"Father, can that be you?" she said in a very soft voice. Dorothy could not believe what she was seeing this could not be real, she rubbed her eyes and looked again only to see her father's reflection still smiling at her". Dorothy then closed her eyes

"father what should I do." After a few minutes she re opened her eyes. The reflection was Dorothy again. She smiled at her reflection, turned around and started to head back home.

As Dorothy came into the house she shouted for her mother. Anna came in from the garden

"what is it Dorothy"? she asked.

"We need to talk mother". Anna stared deeply at Dorothy

"I will make us a pot of tea," she said. As Anna made the pot of tea, Dorothy sat down on the sofa feeling very anxious. She was rubbing her hands together and muttering to herself on how to tell Anna. As Anna brought the teapot in, she poured two cups.

"Mother I have something to tell you, I just do not know how". Anna smiled at Dorothy and softly said

"you are pregnant aren't you". Dorothy's jaw dropped she was gobsmacked

"how did you know"? she asked.

"I'm your mother Dorothy, I could tell, the sickness in the mornings, the tiredness. Don't forget I was pregnant too". Dorothy could not believe what she was hearing. Why was her mother not angry? Why was she not screaming at Dorothy for being stupid?

"You are not angry with me mother"? asked Dorothy.

"No, how could I be"? she replied.

"I got pregnant with you at the same age as you are now." Anna then put her cup down on the table and reached round and pulled Dorothy in for a hug. Dorothy felt so relieved and relaxed. This could not have gone better for her. She now knew that she had her mother for support. She wouldn't be alone, and she would have all the help she needed until Edward would return.

EDWARD AND WILLIAM had now been away for 6 months. They were exhausted, tired and dirty they had walked for hundreds of miles. They had seen very little conflict, and they did not know when things would really heat up. It was cold, winter had arrived and the nights were freezing. The frosts would form on the top of the canopies of their shelters. Icicles would hand down from the sides. It was bitter and everyone was freezing. As Edward and William woke that morning, they knew they were in for a long winter ahead. It did not take long, for Sergeant Peters to start shouting at them all to get up and get ready to move on.

As they packed their gear and started their march, they could see a town up ahead. It looked so familiar to all the other towns abandoned and destroyed by the war around it. The air was so calm, yet so cold. As they continued their walk towards the town Edward could sense something was not quite right. He broke formation and walked up to Sergeant Peters.

"Sir, something is wrong. I can feel it".

"Get back in formation, do not break formation that's an order soldier". Edward was deeply concerned his gut instincts were not usually wrong.

"Sir, we need to stop now". Sergeant Peters raised his arm the squads all stopped. Colonel Watson made his way to the front

"why are we stopping Sergeant?" he asked.

"The soldier is right, that is not an abandoned town". The colonel then looked ahead; they could see behind the houses what looked like military vehicles.

"Sergeant, they could be abandoned," shouted the Colonel.

"No sir, they are clean and look well maintained. We need to plan and strategise this". Colonel Watson took another look with his binoculars

"holy shit," he said in a deeply concerned vehicle. He passed the binoculars to Sergeant Peters who could see many soldiers in the vicinity of the town.

"Looks like they are holed up in there," said Sergeant Peters. "Or they are protecting the area," said Edward. Sergeant Peters glared at Edward "get back in formation". Edward walked back to William.

"Brother, what is going on? Why have we stopped?" asked William.

"The town up ahead is occupied by the enemy. If we continue on this path we will be ambushed," replied Edward. William started to get worked up

"so what do we do, I don't want to die here. Not now not anytime". Edward grabbed William by the shoulders

"we are not going to die today; we are aware of what lies ahead. We wait for our orders and if we want to stay alive I suggest that we follow them". William closed his eyes

"yes, follow orders," he repeated.

"Is he ok"? asked Jack who was in the formation line behind Edward and William.

"He will be fine," replied Edward. William was very fidgety. He was struggling to stand still and maintain his composure. This started to unsettle a few others around him.

"William, please calm down I am here," said Edward in a very strong deep voice. William kept closing his eyes and kept repeating the phrase lets follow orders.

"Will you shut up"? said one of the other soldiers. William opened his eyes and started to take deep breaths. He did not want to be responsible for any failures in the mission.

SHORTLY AFTER SERGEANT PETERS indicated to his squad to go to the east. The squad was joined up with Richard's squad. The other two squads were leading away with Colonel Watson to the west. As they got into cover Sergeant Peters asked everyone to come close in a very quiet voice he said

"this is it soldiers, we have to take this town. Our plan is to flank them. We attack from the east, the others from the west. First squad will enter the village to the north east, the other to the south east. We cover all angles. Make sure you protect each other's backs. May god have mercy on your souls". The reality was now surreal, William was sweating, even in the ice-cold air the sweat was pouring off him. Edward was holding it together. Many of the other soldiers were scared, you could sense the fear among all the soldiers.

"William, we have to do this. I will have your back; I will protect you," Edward said very calmly.

"I will also protect you, you helped me. I will have your back," said Jack. As they began to get ready to head to the north east they noticed Richard approaching. Edward and William stood still. What now Edward thought. As Richard got close to William he put out his hand

"we stand together," he said. William accepted the handshake

"together," he replied. Richard then turned away and caught up with his squad. Peace had been made between William and Richard. William started to feel more energised now. He felt protected that he would be saved if the time came. The boys then headed to the north east to regroup with Jack and their squad.

Edward and William approached the squad, they were quiet and kept low. Edward was called up front to stand with the sergeant.

"The area is swarmed; we have to do this carefully and quietly," said Sergeant Peters. Edward nodded he looked and could see armed patrols walking around others stood conversing. The time was now to start to make the approach. The squad slowly started to move behind one of the buildings in the town. They remained in single file formation and waited for their following orders.

"Brother, I don't like this," said William in a very nervous voice.

"Neither do I," muttered Edward. As they slowly made their way around the back of the next building there was a loud burst of noise.

"Open fire," shouted Sergeant Peters the squad from the south east had been spotted and were engaged. Now everyone was engaged and the sound of the rifles firing was deafening. William ran inside a building and put his hands over his ears, he sat on the floor in a dark corner hoping no one would see him. Edward ran into the building to get William, but when he saw him cowering in the corner, he knew this was not his fight.

"Stay here William and wait for me". Edward left the building and went outside. Bullets were flying all over the place. Edward could see the Germans advancing he opened fire with Jack taking several soldiers down. As the battle went on the smoke from all the weapons started to fill the air. The ground was soddened with blood from the deceased and wounded. There were cries of pain and screaming in the distance. Edward started to make his way back to the house where William was taking refuge along the way a bullet flew by his head hitting the wall behind him. He jumped into the doorway and took cover. He peered outside and another bullet flew past his face. He felt trapped, he started to think about Dorothy his beautiful woman who he missed dearly. He closed his eyes and waited for what he thought was the end.

Suddenly the squad ran past the doorway, shooting at the enemy. Edward walked out the doorway and looked up to the sky

"thank you," he simply said. As he followed the squad he detoured to where William was

"it is time to go," he grabbed William's hand and dragged him up. They left the house and caught up with the rest of the squad. Sergeant Peters was at the front, he was looking at everyone and doing a head count.

"We are missing two men; we need to go back and look for them". William started to panic again, he was hidden before and now he was exposed. He did not want to go back into battle once more. As they made their way back into the town the sound of gunfire had vanished. Once they reached the middle, they regrouped with the other three squads. Richard was staring at William, he could see that he was unscathed, clean with not a spec of dirt on him. He knew that he had held back and stayed hidden.

Before long all the bodies from the fallen soldiers had been collected. They were placed in the centre of the town where some of the soldiers from the other squads started to dig graves for them. It did not take long before the bodies were placed into their shallow graves, and they were covered. William could not stop staring at the graves. He knew that this should have been him. He felt so guilty that he did not help and that now someone has had to pay the ultimate price. Jack turned to William,

"I know you was hiding, so do many of the others, do not let us down again." Jack then walked off; William looked to see Richard staring deeply at him before he turned to walk away. Edward grabbed William by the arm

"we stick together," he said. William nodded he knew that he could not let the squad down again. As the squads regrouped and headed out to the town Edward could only think of one thing Dorothy.

BRUTALITY OF WAR

The savagery of war can bring great cruelty to many. The loss of a loved one due to a fight which was no fault of their own can be brutal. Having to tell someone that they will never see their loved one again is one of the hardest conversations one could ever have.

THE WAR CONTINUED IN EUROPE, the German military had only got stronger and were pushing back the allied forces in many places. It has been two weeks since Edward and William were involved in the skirmish in the town. They had new orders now to head to Poland to help assist the polish people.

"Brother, I am so sorry about before, I was afraid. I just could not go and face that," said William. Edward looked at William

"You are going to have to face it sooner or later if something happens to me who is going to take care of you"? replied Edward. William shrugged his shoulders and he sighed. The squads continued to make their way forward walking through every terrain possible. It was rocky, wet and slippery. Then it would be boggy and their feet would sink as they took a step forward.

As the day drew on darkness started to fall. Sergeant Peters wanted to ensure that they were in a safe location to set up camp for the night. They found this old disused road either side of the road was very tall trees. You could smell the soaked wood off the trees and a slight haze had begun to descend onto the road. It was eerily quiet, no noise except the footsteps of the squads walking in front and behind.

"Something is not right," muttered William. Edward felt the same he could feel the shivers down his spine.

"I know," he replied to William. Jack looked back towards them, both

"we should not be here," he said. The feeling was mutual with many around them. They all felt exposed. It was dark, misty and wet, and they all knew that this was a bad omen and could sense the fear in all the others around them.

You could hear the heavy breathing around. People were scared, everyone was scared except Sergeant Peters who continued up front walking with his strong presence. As the rain started to fall and the mist became more intense Sergeant Peters raises his arm to indicate for everyone to stop. Colonel Watson made his way to the front

"why are we stopping"? he shouted.

"Sir, because I can no longer see clearly". Colonel Watson was not amused by this, he called forward another Sergeant and asked them to lead the way. The squads started to move forward again. They were now all cold and soaking wet. William just wanted to go to sleep. Edward was starving and was also beginning to feel tired. They had walked all day long and everyone needed a much-deserved rest.

As they continued to press on, they could feel their legs turning to jelly. Up at the front, the noise was quiet then all of a sudden there was a huge flash and a massive bang.

"Fall back, fall back." The intense shouts of the Sergeant at the front, someone had stood on a land mine causing it to explode. Panic started to erupt; everyone was looking around them. Carefully placing their feet on the floor, so they would not trigger off any more land mines. As they started to step back lights appeared in front and behind. The sound of humming could be heard in the distance. Edward ran forward. As he ran he saw the body of one of the sergeants, the sight made him feel sick to his stomach. As he squinted to see the lights, he realised It was headlamps from vehicles. Edward now knew this was an ambush. He ran back to William,

"It's an ambush," screamed Edward. William's heart started to race, there was nowhere he could hide, not this time. As the lights got closer gunfire started to erupt. Bullets reigned down from the vehicles. German soldiers started to approach from the sides out of the woods shooting at the troops. The squads were exposed and many soldiers were mortally wounded after the first few rounds of gunfire.

"Into the woods," shouted Sergeant Peters. Edward grabbed William and dragged him into the woods, there was a small mound where they could gain cover from the fire. Edward pushed William down and told him to stay there. As the gunshots intensified William placed his hands over his ears. He began to cry. He began to call for Clara. Edward knew William was not in the right frame of mind. But he had to help the others. He hesitated for a few minutes, but then he knew what he had to do.

Edward ran to help others; the presence of the enemy was so intense that Edward clearly knew they were outnumbered. He could see some of his fellow squad members holed up behind a tree, he managed to take out two German soldiers from behind as they were attempting to shoot at the tree.

"Guys come on we need to keep moving". As they ran through the woods there was an intense barrage of bullets. Two of the squad were downed. Edward looked at his fallen squad-mates. He knew there was nothing he could do at this point.

"Jack, we need to get William, we have to get out of here". As they ran through the woods they leaped over broken trees until they saw they had nowhere to go. In front of them were two German soldiers with their rifles pointed at the faces of Edward and Jack. As they both closed their eyes waiting for the inevitable, they could hear the sound of bodies falling to the floor. They opened their eyes to see Richard, armed with a knife stood over the German soldiers.

"This way boys," he said. Edward and Jack followed Richard back to the mound where William was still cowering.

"Come on, let's go," Richard said to William as he

dragged him up to his feet.

The four of them carefully made their way around the woods, checking to see if anything was coming.

"Where is everyone else?" asked William. Richard snapped at William and told him that they were all dead, killed in an ambush whilst he was hiding. William could not respond, for once in his life he was speechless as they made their way through the woods, they stumbled across one of their own. It was Sergeant Peters; he was laid on the floor bleeding from his mouth. His legs were no longer attached to his body. He had stepped on a land mine in the woods. Edward looked at the injuries that Sergeant Peters had sustained. He knew that there was nothing that could be done.

"Sir, it's going to be ok," said Edward. As he knelt down, he noticed the severity of Sergeant Peters injuries. Even though his legs had been blown off in the explosion he also had massive blood loss from multiple bullet wounds to his abdomen. Edward sighed; he could hear that Sergeant Peters breaths were slowing down. He knew it was his time to go

"Sir it has been an honour serving with you". Sergeant Peters started to cough in his last words he said

"the honour has been all mine." With that he let out his last breath and passed away. Edward closed his eyes and stood back up.

"You are free now," he said softly. Richard then called to everyone

"We need to keep moving."

As they turned to move, they could hear the sound of the enemy making their way towards them. They ran as fast as they could and jumped down into a small trench-like hole in the ground. As they took cover, they thought that they were safe, then suddenly something fell into the hole.

"Grenade," shouted Jack. Edward lent over and placed his hands securing his helmet on his head. As he closed his eyes, he could see Dorothy sat next to him under the sycamore tree

"I love you Edward." He did not know if this was him passing into the afterlife. Jack then jumped down onto the floor curling up into a ball. The grenade had landed right next to Richard and William. Without any hesitation, William threw his body on top of the grenade. Richard desperately tried to grab William to stop him from sacrificing himself, but it was too late. The grenade detonated sending William a few feet into the air. The blast went off creating an almighty noise. Edward then slowly opened his eyes and turned around he stopped and stared at the carnage before him. He was frozen, Jack got to his feet

"Edward, Edward," he shouted. Edward shook his head he could not comprehend what had just happened. He slowly stepped towards William. William was face down in the mud, his body still as if he were in a deep sleep. Edward sat down on the floor next to William he did not want to believe what he was seeing. He then rolled William onto his front. William had significant injuries to his chest cavity and abdomen. Edward's heart started to sink to the bottom of his chest. He was meant to protect William, to keep him safe. They were brothers. He desperately started to shake William.

"Wake up, please William. I love you." There was clearly no response from William. Richard knelt down next to Edward. He looked him in his eyes and shook his head. Edward now knew then that William was no longer with him. He held William's head in his hands and placed it on his lap.

"Brother, no." Tears started to pour from his eyes, they dripped onto William's motionless body. Richard quietly said,

"he saved me, I tried to stop him, and he saved me". Jack stood back,

"he is a hero after all," he said softly. As Edward held onto William, he knew he could not bring him back. His heart heavy and emotions pouring through his veins. What could he do now?

"We need to go," snapped Richard.

"I am not leaving him," replied Edward. Richard knew that they would be stronger together, but he also knew that the enemy knew where they were. That they were no longer safe and that they were all in great danger. Jack started to tremble; the fear was ever-present in his body language. Richard knelt back down,

"listen boy, if we do not get out of here, we are all dead." Edward did not respond, he continued to hold onto William. The grief of losing his blood brother was more than he could have ever truly understood. With the sound of heavy footsteps drawing nearer Richard knew it was too late to retreat. He stood tall with Jack as they waited to see their fate.

It was not long before they were surrounded by German troops. Richard and Jack threw down their weapons as Edward sat on the floor holding William's body. Some German soldiers jumped down into the trench and grabbed Jack and Richard, they then grabbed Edward who couldn't talk. He had lost his brother, all that was going through his head was what could they possibly do to him now. He had just lost his blood brother; he did not care if they wanted to execute him. As they were dragged away, they were bound together at the hands and feet. They were then forced to walk through the woods as they reached the road they were loaded into vehicles. The vehicles then drove off, with Jack, Edward and Richard unsure of where they were going and what is going to happen to them. The fear had hit Jack hard. Richard remained calm, fearless as ever. Edward could not lift his head. The image of William's body flowing through his mind wishing instead that it was him who sacrificed himself.

BACK IN BIRMINGHAM a now heavily pregnant Dorothy was helping her mother tend to the housework.

"Tell me Dorothy, when will you become a nurse"? said Anna.

"Not before I have the baby," replied Dorothy. Anna smiled and Dorothy smiled too, they were both happy and content and were hopeful of the arrival of the baby.

"I shall make us a pot of tea," said Anna. Dorothy smiled at her mother and thanked her. Then there was a knock at the door.

"I wonder who that could be?" asked Anna.

"I do not know, but I shall get the door," replied Dorothy. The knocking continued,

"hold on I am coming," shouted Dorothy. As she opened the door her heart sunk to the bottom of her stomach. There were two military men. They both immediately took off their hats.

"Miss, may we come in"? Dorothy did not speak, she held the door open and allowed them to come inside. As Anna came out of the kitchen carrying the teapot she froze. She turned back into the kitchen, after saying she needed two more cups.

The teapot was placed on the table and Anna poured four cups of tea. "I have some terrible news ma'am, I must tell you that Edward Fisher is currently missing in action. Dorothy was frozen she was in a state of shock, she did not know what to say. Anna knew that Dorothy was stunned she had to ask.

"what does that mean missing in action?" The man looked at Dorothy knowing she was in a very fragile condition, he then looked at Anna.

"It means that we do not know of his whereabouts. His squad was hit in an ambush about a week ago. We recovered many bodies, but his could not be located." Dorothy then looked up,

"does this mean he is still alive?" she asked.

"Yes, ma'am he may still be alive, but it is very unlikely, they were deep in enemy territory. I can confirm that his friend William was killed in action." Dorothy's tears started to intensify; she knew if William had been killed then that would weaken Edward. She looked to the ceiling and simply said, "father, please watch over Edward." As the men left the house Dorothy collapsed into her mother's arms. She was as heartbroken as Edward had promised that he would safely return. She held onto her mother and cried into her arms before taking out Edward's pocket watch from a drawer and kissing the picture that William had drawn of him for her.

DOROTHY GRABBED the watch and William's sketchbook. She left the house and headed over to the factory first. She went inside and up the stairs to where William's old room was. She wanted to find something. She was looking at finding a location that William loved. After she searched and searched, she found some drawings. She picked them up and had a look. It showed that William had a liking to the canal, there were so many pictures of the canal, the birds on the canal. She knew what she had to do. She left the factory and headed back to the canal. Her back was starting to become sore, but she had to do this. She found a large rock and tied it to William's sketchbooks. She then dropped them into the canal and watched as they sunk.

"Goodbye William, may you rest in peace my friend." She then blew a kiss at the sinking sketchbook and heading to her and Edward's favourite place the sycamore tree.

As she arrived at the tree, she was grateful to see her old mound was still there. She sat down and looked at the tree. She looked at the pocket watch, she wanted to bury this at the base of the tree. As she looked at the watch, she looked at the tree. In the distance, she could see a beautiful rainbow. She then started to hum the song that she and Edward both loved. Her heart started to flutter. She had a feeling; she could feel that Edward was still alive. She could not take her eyes off the watch. The sound of it ticking would remind her of when she used to rest her head on his chest to listen to his heartbeat. She put the watch back in her coat pocket. She looked up at the tree then up at the sky.

"Edward, I love you. Please come home," she said. She remained sat down, thinking and remembering all the amazing times they had in their favourite place. She remembered the first time they had a picnic. Their first kiss, the first time they made love. Dorothy began to smile for the first time since she was told the tragic news. Missing in action was not killed in action, she kept repeating in her mind. As the day dragged on, she forced herself to stand up and started to walk slowly back to the house.

As she walked down the canal she would stop and pause. She could feel the movement in her abdomen. She would rub her abdomen and talk to her baby. She would listen to the sounds of the birds she would continue to hum 'over the rainbow' the song gave her hope that things were going to be ok. As she got to the market she looked around and remembered back to when her, Edward, William and Clara were all friends. It made Dorothy feel sad, as now it was just her all alone on her own without her friends. She started to think, what do I do now? Where do I go from here? She walked through the market and headed back home. She was exhausted and needed much rest, she held onto the pocket watch tight refusing to let it go. As she got home and walked through the door she burst into tears. All of a sudden, she felt hit by a wall of sadness, she did not know where this sadness had come from, but it was a pain that was beginning to absorb her mind. Anna came running to the entrance and out her arms around Dorothy. She walked her slowly towards the sofa where they both sat down and embraced in a cuddle.

"Mother what do I do?" she asked.

"We stick together," replied Anna.

BACK IN EUROPE, a dirty bloody Edward was being escorted by vehicle with Richard and Jack they were blindfolded and had no idea where they were being taken. The journey was long and very bumpy. After a few days of travelling the door to the vehicle opened, and they were dragged out of the truck. Their blindfolds were removed and a very clean looking German officer started to talk,

"welcome to Stalag". Edward was pushed forward by someone's rifle digging into his back. Edward, Richard, and Jack were forced to walk forwards through the gate and into this very large prison.

"This is a prison of war camp," whispered Richard. Edward knew this already. They had been captured, and he was now very worried about Dorothy. He could not stop worrying he needed to know if she was ok. As they were marched into the camp, they were told to report for work duty.

The camp was a mess, the living accommodations

smelt of urine and faeces, there was the smell of death, it filled the air. There were large buildings with no windows. Edward would look at these unsure of what they were. Everyone in the camp was filthy, underweight and looking extremely malnourished. Edward knew that this could be the last place he would ever call home. The frightened look of the captured men would sink into his heart. Richard was more reserved, Edward felt like he knew what this would be like, perhaps he was in one before. Jack was terrified the look of fear was all over his face. You could even smell the fear dripping from the pores of his skin. The other prisoners would stop and stare at the three men as they made their way through the camp. Jack was that frightened that he urinated himself. This was noticed by a German officer who pointed and started to laugh. The other officers would join in and Jack became a laughing stock between the officers.

"I don't want to be here," cried Jack. Richard tutted

"we have no choice boy, do as you're told, keep your head down and you will stay alive". Edward agreed with Richard

"he is right, we do not want to draw attention to ourselves. We can get out of here alive." As they got to their spots for duty, they were greeted by an officer who took one look at Jack and burst into laughter. He had noticed that Jack had urinated through his clothes. Edward and Richard did not respond they knew better, however, Jack couldn't contain his anger

"stop laughing at me you kraut," he shouted. The officers face dropped and his smile faded into an angry frown. He walked over to Jack and stared him deep in the eyes, as the officer went to turn away, he swung his rifle butt straight into Jack's face knocking him to the floor. The officer then proceeded to repeatedly hit Jack with the butt of the rifle until his face was nothing more than a crimson mask. Edward was shocked. He wanted to intervene, but he knew this would only result in the same for him. The beating continued until Jack was motionless in a pool of his own blood on the floor. The officer blew a whistle and two other soldiers came over. They dragged Jack up to his feet and put his arms over their shoulders before dragging him away.

The officer then looked at Edward and Richard.

"Right, get to work." He sent them both over to a wooden hut and ordered then to grab a shovel each. Their job was to dig holes. Edward thought what am I digging holes for? He couldn't see the benefit of digging so many holes in the ground in a prison such as this. But he did as he was ordered. Richard on the other hand knew exactly what the holes were for, they were for prisoners who would not survive. Dig the holes and already be prepared for the inevitable. He did not want to tell Edward this as he did not want to cause him a panic. They dug and dug, digging as many holes as they could. As the day started to draw to an end there was a loud explosion. Edward fell to his knees trembling the noise caused him to have a flashback of William his brother lying motionless on the floor. He could see the blood all over William's face the flashback felt so real. He kept his hands over his ears, he did not know what was going on. The bang had triggered a memory, one that brought him great sadness. As he sat there on the floor holding his ears in fear something happened, a familiar voice. It cannot be can it he thought to himself. The familiar voice was that of George.

"Get up Edward, you are no longer a little boy. You are a man who's strong and determined. The hero that I never was and you have a job to do. I need you to fight your enemy and return home. I expect you to look after my daughter. Remember Edward, I will always be with you, to guide you. To help you regain your focus. You have so much to live for. You may get knocked down, but you will always get back up. No matter how hard life hits you, you must continue. It is not about how many times you get knocked down. It's about how many hits you can take and keep pushing forward. I am so proud of you, you've come so far in your life. Now get up and be the man that I know you are."

Edward rose to his feet, had George really just spoken to him from beyond the grave. He wasn't sure, but the wise words of wisdom gave him the motivation to continue and to never give up. He turned to Richard

"what was that explosion?". Richard looked at Edward,

"animal stepped on a land mine just outside the fences." Richard could sense that Edward had an epiphany. He could feel the strength flowing through his veins. Edward wanted to get out. He knew he couldn't just leave. But he could survive until the day came. He wondered about Jack, was he injured or dead? He did not know. What he did know was that one day he was getting out of there and going home to his beloved Dorothy. As he continued to dig, he would sing "over the rainbow" in his head. The song that Dorothy had fallen in love with. It would keep him smiling and it would keep him working hard knowing that his love for Dorothy would never die.

Edward stood tall, knowing that he could never give up. That now he had hope, something to cling on to. As a few weeks had passed Richard and Edward would continue to be forced into working. What seemed like every other day they were burying someone. They mostly appeared to be soviets starved or dying of disease. It was a hard moment for both Edward and Richard as they did not know who would be next. Would it be them? Edward would think about Jack, was he ok? It had been many weeks since they had last seen Jack, and he was growing deeply concerned.

"Do you think Jack is ok?" Edward asked Richard.

"We haven't buried him yet if that's what you're asking, so I would say he is still alive." Edward stopped and thought about what Richard had said. It all started to make sense, perhaps he was in the infirmary. He wanted to find out, but what could he do? He thought to himself about asking someone but knew that he wouldn't get the answers he was looking for.

DURING THE ALLOCATED RECREATIONAL TIME, they would often sit and play cards or dominoes. One particular day they were sat with a small table, Richard and Edward were playing dominoes.

"Do you think we will ever leave here alive"? Edward asked Richard. Richard placed his domino down on the table, looked up at Edward and replied

"no".

"Really, no," said a figure from behind them. They

knew the voice. As Edward and Richard turned around there was Jack, still bruised on his face.

"So, did you miss you me then"? Jack asked. Edward stood up and gave Jack an enormous cuddle.

"Easy there, I am still very sore," Jack said.

"Sorry, I am just glad to see that you are still alive," replied Edward. Richard stood up, he extended his hand and shook Jack's hand

"it's good to see you," he said. Everyone then sat down and shuffled up the dominoes.

"Let's play," said Jack. The three of them then engaged in a game of dominoes and it was like none of them had ever been apart.

IT WAS a foggy gloomy day in back in Birmingham. Dorothy was struggling now; she could barely take herself up and down the stairs and started to have pains in her abdomen.

"Mother, I really think something is happening," called Dorothy from the living room. Anna appeared from the kitchen carrying her traditional teapot. She looked at Dorothy

"I am sure everything is fine. The baby is due anytime soon," she said. Dorothy frowned, she was in pain and her mother was not exactly being helpful towards her. As Dorothy stood up, she felt warm liquid run down her leg.

"Mother," she shouted. Anna came over and saw the fluid on the floor.

"Oh, good gracious Dorothy your waters have

broken. We need to get you to the hospital to see the midwife," replied Anna. As Anna attempted to walk Dorothy she started to cry out. Anna knew that this was going to be impossible. She helped Dorothy lie down on the sofa and ran to the front door. Opening it very quickly.

"Can someone, please help"? she shouted out.

"Mother, please help me," wailed Dorothy from the sofa. Anna started to panic, she did not know what to do, she could not leave Dorothy to get help but had anyone heard her calls for help. She left the front door open and ran back to Dorothy. She took her hand and told her to breathe in and out slowly. Dorothy started to breathe, her face turning red. The painful expression on her face terrified Anna.

"Hello," there was a voice from the doorway.

"Please get us a midwife," shouted Anna to the passer-by.

"Certainly," called the passer-by. As the door closed Dorothy continued to become more and more agitated.

"This really hurts mother, please help me". Anna moved to the front of Dorothy. When she looked she could see that Dorothy was dilating. Anna thought to herself that she may have to deliver this baby. She had to help Dorothy, she could not bear to continue her screams, seeing her daughter in so much pain was heartbreaking for her.

"Ok, Dorothy, I am going to ask you to push." Dorothy screamed out

"push but it hurts so much mother."

"Just push Dorothy you are doing fantastic," Anna

shouted back over Dorothy's screams. As Dorothy began to push Anna started to smile, she could see the head.

"Keep pushing Dorothy." Dorothy continued to push and push. After a few exhausting minutes there were cries. Cries of a newborn baby. Anna smiled at the baby and wrapped it in a blanket. The front door then flew open. The passer-by managed to get a midwife from the doctor's surgery. The midwife made her way to Anna and looked at the baby, she smiled. Congratulations it's a baby boy. Dorothy however was still in immense pain. "It hurts so much," she cried. The midwife then took a look.

"There is another baby," she quietly said to Anna. Anna's face looked startled. The midwife then called to Dorothy

"you need to push and push," she said. Dorothy began to push and push, screaming out in agony. Shortly after there was another baby. The midwife then said,

"congratulations, you have two baby boy twins". Dorothy smiled, the pain had subsided, and she wanted to hold her boys. The midwife placed the boys on each of Dorothy's arms. Before telling her that they would have to go to the hospital to make sure that everything was ok.

An hour later an ambulance arrived at the house. The two baby boys and Dorothy were taken into the back of the ambulance with Anna. They were then taken to the hospital to be checked over to ensure that everyone was healthy. The ride to the hospital was short, Dorothy was in love with her boys, the look on her face. She was now a proud mother. She thought about Edward and how happy she would have been if he had been around for the birth of his children. She wondered what had happened to him if she would ever see him again. In her mind, she now had to be strong for the children. She had a reason to carry on the two amazing lives that she had brought into the world. As they arrived at the hospital, they were all taken in. They were checked over by the doctors and midwifes.

"Everything is good and healthy," said the doctor.

"Oh, thank goodness," replied Anna. Dorothy just wanted to go home with her babies and take care of them herself. But she was told that they would all remain in hospital for a couple of days just to make sure that everything is going to fine.

As Dorothy lay down that night to go to sleep, she would look at her boys, she could see her beloved Edward in both of them. They had his eyes; she placed her hand on their tiny hands.

"I love you so much," she said to them both. She then leaned down and kissed each of the boys on their forehead.

"We will be home soon, and one day I will tell you all about your grandfather and of course your father. Goodnight my angels." Dorothy then climbed back into her hospital bed and looked up at the ceiling. Her mind started to wander back to Edward and how much she deeply missed him. A single tear slid out of her eyes.

"Edward, I miss you. I love you," she whispered. She was hoping that somewhere, anywhere that Edward would hear this.

1 2

OUT IN THE OPEN

The open wilderness is perhaps the most amazing natural wonder the eyes can behold. However, nature is more powerful than any army or anything and it can bite back whenever it wishes to do so.

IN THE DARK of the night, Edward was lying down on his hard bed. His eyes wide open, he briefly closed them where he could hear Dorothy saying

"I love you." He smiled and thought back to the good old times where he and Dorothy would spend all day sat under the sycamore tree, cuddling, holding hands and having so much fun together. He missed her so much wondering what she was doing at that very moment in time. His mind would then wander to William, his blood brother. Wondering where his body was taken. He was proud of William, for making the sacrifice to save everyone else. Edward knew that William had finally shown his potential, that he was not weak and that he would do what he could to save the people that he cared about. Edward closed his eyes and tried to clear his mind; he soon fell asleep. Before he could even start to dream the sun was up and a new day was ahead.

As Edward pulled himself together for the day he met up with Richard and Jack.

"Have you heard the news"? asked Jack.

"What news, what is going on?" replied Edward. Richard looked dumbfounded he had no idea what Jack meant.

"Well then, explain," snapped Richard. Jack knew that Richard did not really have the patience for cryptic discussions. Jack knew that he may as well just spit out what he had heard.

"So, apparently our allies have been dropping crates, things for us to do when we are having the recreational time. I have heard from some of the others that there are board games and maybe even Monopoly." Richard rolled his eyes; he could not care less for board games.

"Is that all you have to share boy"? shouted Richard at Jack. Edward agreed with Richard

"it is hardly useful for us. I was hoping you was going to say the war is over." Jack could sense that both Richard and Edward were disappointed, and they were more hopeful for happier news. Jack dropped his head down in shame,

"best get to it then," he said very quietly. A disappointed looking Edward and Richard followed Jack out of the accommodation block and into their work assignment for the day.

It was pouring with freezing cold rain. The air was very misty and it was bitterly cold. As they walked towards their assignment, they had already become drenched by the enormous raindrops that were falling around them.

"This is horrible," moaned Jack.

"Well boy we ain't got any choice so suck it up," replied Richard. Edward continued to walk; he knew there was no point in moaning. They couldn't change the weather, or the situation that they were in. They had to do what they were told, because he knew that he did not want to face the consequences of what could happen if he did not do as he was told. They reported for duty to be told that they were now going to be completing landscaping duties. They were marched over to a large metal cabin. Inside it was full of old tools. The smell was not pleasant it was very musky, it was dark and damp inside. An officer stepped inside the cabin he was shouting something in German. After the officer rummaged around in the cabin, they were given some rakes and forks to tend to the grounds with.

"What am I supposed to do with this"? asked Edward. Richard looked at Edward's rusty splintered rake and shook his head

"mine is not much better," he replied. Jack looked at his rake,

"well this is just as useful." They were then shouted and instructed to follow an officer. They followed the officer across some small fields to an area near the fence. As they got close to the fence Edward paused. He looked at the fence and could see the freedom beyond the metal mesh. He looked the fence up and down, the razor wire at the top was a sign that he could not just climb over it. He sniffed deeply and could smell the sense of freedom just a few feet away on the other side of the fence. As he closed his eyes and continued to sniff, he felt a hard nudge in his back.

"Get to work," shouted the officer, Edward looked to see that both Richard and Jack were raking away the leaves and grass around them overturning the soil as they had been instructed. Edward grabbed his rake and began to help complete his duties. They raked for what seemed like an eternity before it was time for their recreational activities.

As THEY MADE their way to the recreational area there was some commotion. A crate had been picked up by and was being brought in on the back of a truck. The prisoners started to gather round, the commotion was high and everyone was excited to see what was inside the crate. Edward pushed his way toward the front of the crowd. As the lid was taken off the crate items were handed out to the prisoners. As Edward waited his turn, he could see playing cards, dominoes, magazines and books being handed out. Soon it was his turn, he was handed a game of Monopoly. Edward smiled and laughed as he looked down at the board game. Only this morning Jack had mentioned about crates with this game in them. He took the game over to Richard and Jack.

"What have you got there"? asked Richard. Edward held up the box and showed it to Richard and Jack.

"Brilliant," cried Jack as he started to clap his hands.

"Let's set it up and have a game shall we." Richard again rolled his eyes, "sure, why not," he replied.

Jack could not wait to get his hands on the game. He had been itching to play it for such a long time. As he opened the box, he started to set the game up. He handed out the money to Edward and Richard. Then begun to finish setting the board up.

"We all roll whoever scores the highest goes first," said Jack. Jack rolled and scored a 6 with both die, it was then Richard's turn, and he rolled 7.

"Ha," said Richard. Edward then picked up the die,

"it is not over yet," he said. He rolled double 6.

"Yes," he shouted it was a 12. Edward knew he was now first. He picked up the die and rolled. He got an 8. He moved forward and the game started to continue. They all took their turns and managed to get around the board a few times. Edward was ready to take another turn. He rolled and he landed on the chance space. He picked up his card to see what his chance was. As he looked at the card his face changed. He looked confused and startled.

"Boy what's your card say"? grunted Richard who was too impatient.

"It says inside the board," replied Edward.

"What? Let me see that?" grumbled Richard. He snatched the card out of Edward's hand and read it.

"Bloody hell," he said.

"I think this is a message." Edward started to run his hands around the board. It only took a few seconds and he found a crease. Edward lifted the crease to see that there was something stashed inside the board. He slowly pulled it out.

"What is it"? muttered Jack. Edward looked at this silk cloth, he opened it up and gasped.

"It's a map," said Richard. Edward turned the cloth over to see that it was double-sided. They now had a map of the area they were in. Was this their opportunity to escape and be free?

As the sirens went to signal the end of recreational time Edward quickly shoved the cloth up his sleeve. Jack quickly packed away the game and the three of them made their way back over to the landscaping area. As they started to rake Edward would continue to make his way to the fence, he was looking for a weak spot. Somewhere that they may be able to get out from. The fence looked strong, it appeared that they would not be able to just go through the fence. Not there anyway. Richard would swap over with Edward, and check the fence out. Then he had an idea. He started to rake at the bottom of the fence purposefully catching the fence with his rake attempting to bend the metal. After several long hours of going back and to from the fence Richard had managed to bend it enough to get your hands under it. He then cleverly raked back some soil so the damage to the fence was not noticeable. He made his way over to Edward and Jack

"It's done, we can lift that when no one is around." Edward smiled. Richard replied with

"it is best we do this at night. When it is dark. No one will see us". Jack and Richard agreed, and they continued their duties until it was time to head back to their bunks for the night.

Deeper into the night, Edward approached Richard.

"What is the plan"? he asked. Richard rolled over to face Edward,

"we need to understand where the guards are and their patrols before we try anything," replied Richard. Edward nodded to indicated that he agreed with Richard. He headed over to Jack.

"Hey Jack," whispered Edward. "What is it"? asked Jack.

"We need to study the patrols of the guards, to see where they are, learn and understand them before we can get out of here." Jack nodded, they now had to fully understand where each guard was and problem solve the best point in the night where they could make their escape and head back to the safety of their fellow soldiers. Edward got back into his bunk, they had to plan this carefully. He thought to himself that they may be executed if they get caught. He did not want this, he wanted to get home to Dorothy. He closed his eyes and thought about what Dorothy was doing.

DOROTHY HAD BEEN SPENDING all her time with her boys. She had not returned back to work yet. Anna was helping out; Dorothy had no idea that two baby boys would be such hard work. She was exhausted from the sleepless nights, having to wake every hour to feed one of the boys and sometimes both boys. Her hair was a mess and her eyes had very large bags underneath them.

"Sweetheart, why don't you get some rest. I can look

after the boys," said Anna. Dorothy looked up; her eyes so bloodshot.

"Oh mother, I would love to get some sleep. But I would also like to go out for a walk and for some fresh air," she replied.

"Yes, of course. But please be careful," replied Anna. Dorothy grabbed her coat and headed out the front door. She walked into the market and paused. She looked around and felt somewhat lost. It has been a few weeks since she had been out of the house on her own.

The market was noisy and busy, much like it was prior to the war starting. As she left the market, she chose to go down the street where she first met Edward. She stopped at the bakery and looked in the window. She smiled as it brought back the memories of her first encounter with Edward. She continued to walk down the street, she stopped as soon as she got to the spot where Edward bumped into her and knocked her down onto the floor. Her bloodshot eyes started to fill with tears. She sat herself down on the floor and begun to sob into her hands, as she sat there crying a hand appeared on her shoulder.

"Are you ok miss"? said a deep voice. Dorothy removed one hand from her face and looked up. Stood in front of her was a tall handsome man, wearing an expensive suit. He had dark brown eyes and jet-black hair.

"I am fine sir," said Dorothy. She could feel her heart racing, who was this handsome stranger stood before her?

Dorothy rose to her feet. The man held out his hand, Dorothy was unsure at first but took his hand and steadied herself.

"The name is Charles," he said.

"I'm Dorothy," she replied.

"Well I am pleased to meet you; may I walk you home"? Dorothy was still unsure about this man, but he was so handsome and his charm was winning her over.

"Yes, please I would like that," she replied. Charles then extended his arm for Dorothy to link it. Dorothy paused and then decided to just link Charles' arm, she didn't see any harm in this. As they walked down the road Charles would ask Dorothy about her life. At first, she was very reserved and did not say too much. She did not know this man and was keeping her heart closed.

"Are you married?" asked Charles. Dorothy smirked,

"no I am not married, I was going to be married. But he is missing in action in the war. I do not know if he is alive. There has been no news in a long time now," she replied.

"I am terribly sorry, how long has it been"? he asked.

"Months," Dorothy replied.

"Well I hate to say this but it has been that long I doubt there is any hope left."

Dorothy started to weep again. She believed Charles. If Edward was ok surely she would know about this. Surely someone out there would be able to shed some light on his whereabouts. She did not reply, she continued to walk with Charles through the market.

"Do you have any children?" asked Charles. Dorothy looked up at Charles,

"yes I have two boys they are twins," she replied. Charles stopped and stared at Dorothy.

"That is rare, is the father your missing fiancé?" he replied.

"Yes," said Dorothy solemnly. Dorothy then closed up and did not speak until she reached her house.

"Thank you, Charles," she said. "My pleasure," he replied. Dorothy then opened her front door and walked inside her house. She slumped on to the sofa and burst into tears. Anna came running down the stairs.

"Dorothy what is wrong"? she cried as she grabbed Dorothy and wrapped her arms around her firmly.

"He's not coming back is he, he's gone. My Edward is gone," she wailed. Anna held Dorothy close and tight to her body

"I am sorry," is all she said. She took Dorothy upstairs to her room where both the boys were fast asleep.

"It is now your time to rest my child," said Anna. Dorothy laid down on her bed, her eyes were stinging from all the tears and being overtired. She rolled onto her side, she closed her eyes and fell into a very deep sleep.

THREE DAYS later back in the camp Jack had been closely watching the guards. He knew exactly when they would change over shifts and who would be guarding where. His tactical plan was to feedback to Richard and Edward and make sure the three of them would find their way out through the gap in the bottom of the fence that Richard had created. During recreational time when they were playing dominos Jack finally spoke,

"the guards change shifts every four hours. When they change, they temporarily leave their posts this is our opportunity." Richard started to giggle "they leave their posts, why on earth did we not know this sooner?" Edward also laughed;

"well I guess it's a straight forward get out then," Jack scowled,

"it is not that easy the posts are only not covered for about 15 seconds. This gives us little to no time." Richard stared deeply into Jack's eyes

"15 seconds eh, that's all we will need to get around the buildings." Jack thought deeply, he knew Richard was right. There were no overnight guards on the fence that they would be using. The three men smiled, tonight was going to be the night that they would escape the hell that they were living in and seek the freedom that they had sought for so long.

As the day came to an end, the sun set. They made their way back to their bunks. They lay in wait, for the darkness to completely fall over the camp. It was eerily quiet that night. The sounds of the guard's footsteps could be heard as they were walking and doing their routine checks. When the sound of the footprints died down Edward grabbed the silk cloth. He climbed out of his bunk and crept over to Jack.

"It's time," he said. Jack slipped out of his bunk and followed Edward over to where Richard was laying. Richard was laying in his bunk wide awake. He knew they were coming. As they arrived, he looked at them both,

"let's do this," he said. The three men then quietly tiptoed out of the sleeping quarters and out into the dark of the night.

Outside the mist had descended into the darkness making it very difficult to see, the air was thick with moisture and the feel of a storm was in the air. This was good news for the men, as they now not only had the cover of darkness, they had the mist to their advantage too. They slowly made their way around the back of the guard station. The sounds of the guard's footsteps drew closer. Edward indicated for everyone to pause, the sound of footsteps drew nearer and nearer. Then they stopped, nobody moved. They ducked down and hid. The sound of the footsteps then started to draw away from them. They quickly moved around the next few buildings. Listening out for the sounds of the heavy boots from the guards. They knew they would never have a long window of opportunity to move between all the buildings. They would watch, listen and wait for the right opportunity to step out into the open remaining unseen.

The fence was in sight, they ran to the fence. As they arrived Richard pulled at the bottom of the fence making a gap large enough for Edward to crawl under. Next it was Jack he crawled out.

"You boys need to pull that fence; I will not fit through this gap," said Richard. Edward and Jack dropped to their knees, they pulled at the fence, it was very strong, and after several attempts at pulling they made the gap slightly larger for Richard to crawl under. As Richard stood up on the other side of the fence, he proceeded to kick the fence back into position. Edward pulled the silk cloth from his pocket.

"We need to head west," he said.

"We need to watch out for landmines," replied Richard. The three men paused and looked around. In the deep mist they had to be careful, they could not risk setting off any of the landmines.

They carefully made very small steps looking at the ground below them for signs of disturbed ground. Edward's heart was racing, the intensity and fear of where they were had started to kick in. He could hear the deep breaths from Jack, he could feel the tension from Richard. They all took their time in navigating their way through the field. They eventually arrived at a wooded area and made their way into the cover of the trees. There were no sounds of any sirens or people around. Edward knew that no one had noticed that they were missing. He knew they had to make ground. He told Jack and Richard that they must continue west, that they had to do this quick to get a head start before the German's would start looking for them. Jack was anxious, he was rubbing his hands together. Edward could see the anxiety flowing throughout his body. There was no return now. They all knew that if they were caught that the punishment would ultimately be death.

The woods were silent, you could not even hear the sounds of the wind. Everything was silent, it was dark and the mist had started to disappear. It was so cold; they were underdressed for this.

"Maybe we should go back," cried Jack. Richard scowled at Jack

"go back, don't be a fucking idiot. They will execute us if we do that."

"He is right," said Edward.

"We have to keep moving, according to this map we are not that far from where we need to be, perhaps only a few hours walk." Edward started to lead the way deeper into the woods, Richard quickly followed. Jack lowered his head and sighed. He knew he had no choice now but to follow Edward and Richard further into the woods. As they slowly climbed through the undergrowth and over the large roots of some of the trees, they could hear a faint noise. The sound of tapping in the distance.

"What is that noise"? whispered Jack.

"Sounds like some kind of bird," replied Edward.

"Well it is nothing to worry about, now let's keep moving," said an irritated Richard.

They continued their journey; it had been a few hours since they managed to escape. As the woods started to come to an end, they noticed a clearing.

"We need to keep low, and we need to keep quiet," said Richard. Edward knew that in the clearing they would be exposed and visible to anyone who would be potentially looking for them. They carefully stepped into the clearing, walking slowly, checking for possible landmines along the way. As they got into the middle of the clearing, they could hear faint shouts in the distance coming from behind them.

"They know we are missing," wailed Jack as he started to panic. Edward and Richard looked at one another.

"Run," called Edward. They all ran as fast as they could through the clearing. The ground was soggy in places, they didn't care about landmines at the moment. They needed to get back into the safety of the woods. To be protected from sight.

They managed to pass through the clearing. They stopped to look behind them and there was nothing they could see. The sound of the shouting sounded far away. But they could not be so sure that they would be safe.

"We must carry on," said Edward.

"Agreed," replied Richard. Jack was clearly scared; he did not respond but followed behind Richard and Edward as they made their way over some fallen trees. They continued to walk for what seemed like miles.

"Do you know where we are"? asked Jack. Edward pulled out the silk map, he took a look at where they were.

"Well we have walked this way for a few hours, so we are somewhere around," Jack cut Edward off

"you have no idea where we are do you?" Edward sighed,

"no I don't." Richard started to pace up and down. He was clearly agitated

"what do you mean you don't know where we are. What the bloody hell are you playing at? We've been walking for hours and could have been in the wrong direction," shouted an angry Richard.

Edward was getting tense; he was not William, and he was not going to back down from Richard shouting at him in his face. He could feel his blood starting to boil and his heart starting to race. He was not about to be bullied by Richard, not here and not anywhere, he took a step towards Richard and shouted

"I got us out of there, I got us where we are now. We are safe and we are free." A shocked Richard took a step back

"well boy, you surprised me there. I didn't think you would be the type that doesn't take shit." Richard then smiled and patted Edward on his shoulder.

"Come on, let's get the fuck out of here," said Richard. Edward smirked and followed Richard on. Jack begrudgingly followed on.

Everyone was starting to become tired. The night seemed endless, no one knew what time of day it even was. As they progressed on, they heard more noises around them. The sound of the cracking of fallen branches.

"We are not alone," said Edward. They all paused and looked around. It was too dark to see.

"This way," called Richard. They walked back towards a small mound. The sound of the footsteps on the ground now appeared to be all around them. As they turned to go in a different direction they stopped, completely frozen. There were five German troops in front of them. They could hear the rustling behind them, they knew they were surrounded.

"Runter auf die Knie," shouted a German soldier.

"What did he say"? shouted Jack.

"He said down on your knees," whispered Richard as he slowly placed his hands on his head and lowered to his knees. Edward followed suit he did not say a word. Jack looked at both Edward and Richard. He started to panic and dropped to his knees and put his hands on the top of his head.

Edward could hear Jack's heart beating fast, Richard remained extremely calm. Edward just did not know what to expect. Suddenly stood before them was a German officer dressed very smartly.

"Did you really think you could escape and get away"? he said.

"No sir, I didn't," cried Jack. Richard's face grimaced,

Edward saw this, and he knew that this was a very bad mistake for Jack to talk back.

"You tried to escape, but now you will be going back," said the officer. The officer then nodded to the soldier who stood behind Jack. There was an almighty bang, there was a huge spray of blood which covered Edward's face. Jack's body slumped down on the floor in front of Edward and Richard.

"Let this be a warning to you both. If you try this again this is the consequence." Edward was trembling throughout his body. He was covered in Jack's blood. He could see the damage the shot had inflicted on the back of Jack's head. Richard did not show any emotion he continued to stare forward.

Edward and Richard were then dragged up onto their feet with soldiers aiming their guns in their directions. They were pushed forward to walk. Edward was terrified he had a very bad feeling about what was going to happen next. They were marched very quickly to nearby vehicles where they were bundled in the back. Jack's body was slung in the back of a vehicle with them. Edward could not believe he lost another friend. Everyone who he cared about around him had died. Was it his turn next he kept thinking to himself? Richard remained extremely quite. He looked so calm, Edward could not understand how Richard managed to stare death in the face so easily and yet not show any emotions around it. The journey back to the camp was very quiet. Edward just stared deeply at Jack's motionless body. He kept saying to himself this could have been me. Richard did not say a word his body language was very relaxed. He did not look at Jack once. He just sat on his seat with his hands on his lap.

The vehicle door flew open, two soldiers dragged Jack's body out of the back and carried it off. Shortly after Edward and Richard were dragged out of the vehicle. The soldiers were speaking German and Edward did not understand what they were saying. However, Richard knew exactly what they were saying. Edward was worried he started to feel like the scared little boy again when he was younger and living on the streets

"w.w.w.where are we going"? he asked. He was pushed forward and into the camp. He and Richard were marched to a tiny wooden building. Where they were taken inside. There they were stood before the smartly dressed officer. He looked at both Edward and Richard,

"you will now remain in solitary confinement until I say otherwise." Edward gulped he was a bloody mess covered still in the remains of Jack. Richard continued to remain silent. He stepped forward into a small cell and turned around as the door was locked before him. Edward did not want to go into that small cell. He was now very fearful and all his confidence had left him.

"P.p.please sir, please," Edward cried. The officer looked at him and showed no expression or emotions. Edward was then pushed to the floor from behind by a soldier. He was grabbed and dragged into his cell. The floor was soaking wet, there were no windows only a small gap that let in a tiny streak of light. The smell of urine, feces, and death was so overpowering that it made him feel sick to his stomach. As he lay there on the floor, he burst into tears. The doors was closed and locked. He lay there screaming out for Dorothy.

"Please my lady." He wailed and wailed but no one was coming to his aid.

He lay there sobbing uncontrollably. Not knowing how long he would be in the cell. Richard could hear his cries from the cell next to his. Richard sat down on the floor, showing no signs of emotion. As he sat there all he could hear was the heavy breathing and cries of Edward next door. It was dark, cold, damp and inhumane. What could Edward do, there was no escape this time. He was trapped in this tiny room, unable to leave and having to wait for someone to open the door for his freedom. He hoped that day would come. He did not want to stay in there for the rest of his life. His claustrophobia getting the better of him. He did not want to open his eyes, he just wanted to lie there and let the world swallow him whole.

LIFE GOES ON

There is a time when we have to find a way to move on with our lives. We never give up hope. But leading a life of unhappiness will only cause one to fall into despair.

MANY MONTHS HAD PASSED since Edward was placed into isolation. There had been no information given to Dorothy about his whereabouts or if he was still alive. Dorothy was always hopeful, and she wished Edward would come home. But deep down in her heart, she could sense that she may never get to see him again.

"Mother, it has been a year since Edward went to war, we have heard nothing." Anna walked towards Dorothy; she placed her hands on her shoulders

"I know," she replied. Dorothy then leaned into her mother and embraced her; two teardrops dropped down her cheeks. She wanted Edward to come home, but she was beginning to understand that this may never happen.

"Mother would you please watch the boys for me

whilst I go out and get some fresh air"? asked Dorothy. Anna squeezed Dorothy tight.

"Of course, you go and gather your thoughts." Dorothy kissed her mother on the cheek and then headed to the front door.

Dorothy stepped outside; she took a deep breath to smell the fresh air around her. She headed down the lane and into the market. She did not stop, she walked through the market to the canal. When she arrived at the canal she stopped and stared at it.

"Hello William," she said. She then skipped along the canal and headed for her safe spot. As she got to the clearing, she looked at the large sycamore tree before her.

"Hello old friend, it has been far too long," she said to the tree. Dorothy grabbed her place at her mound. She sat down and pulled out Edward's pocket watch from her jacket pocket. She opened up the watch to look at the picture of Edward that William had drawn for her all that time ago.

"Oh Edward, what do I do? I love you so much. Please tell me what to do? Are you ever coming home"? she asked. Suddenly there was a huge burst of wind, it was so strong that it nearly knocked her off her mound.

"Edward is that you"? the wind had died down.

"Edward come back," she cried. The wind fell silent and Dorothy sat back down on her mound. She closed the pocket watch and placed it back in her pocket. She then stood up and kissed the large trunk of the sycamore tree and headed back to the canal.

She began to hum some music as she skipped her way

through the field back towards the canal. There was another burst of wind again. She paused,

"Edward, please talk to me," she shouted. There was nothing, she was confused and had no idea what was going on. She continued her walk back down the canal. She was going to head home, but she could feel a chill down her spine. She detoured and headed to where her father was laid to rest. As she headed to the graveyard she continued to hum away. When she arrived, she stopped at Clara's grave.

"Hello Clara, I hope you and William are together again and behaving," she said as she giggled. She then headed over to where her father was buried. As she arrived at his grave the huge burst of wind hit her again.

"Father is it you?" she asked. The wind came back and almost knocked her off her feet.

"Father it is you," she cried. Dorothy dropped to her knees and stared at her father's headstone.

"Father what are you trying to say?" The whistling of the wind around Dorothy sounded like something was trying to talk to her.

"Please father, tell me what to do?" She started to weep in her hands then a whisper of

"be happy, live your life and follow your dreams," was heard. She removed her hands from her face.

"Father was that you?" she cried. The wind then died down. The whistle had gone.

Dorothy stood up. Could George have really sent her a message? She repeated the message in her head

"be happy, live your life and follow your dreams." She kept on repeating this to herself. Was this George telling her that it was ok to let Edward go? To move on with her life to allow herself to be free from the hurt and the pain that she was going through every single day? She started to make her way back to the market. She was confused still and unsure of what had actually just happened. As she stopped off to buy some vegetables, she heard a familiar voice.

———

"HELLO." She turned around. It was Charles. Dorothy blushed her cheeks going bright red. Charles was as handsome as ever and dressed very smartly.

"Hello Charles," she said in a croaky voice. She had clearly been caught by surprise and did not expect to see Charles again.

Charles extended his arm.

"Would you care to accompany me"? he said. Dorothy grinned and let out an embarrassed giggle.

"Where would we be going"? she asked.

"Well I would like to take you for dinner," said Charles. Dorothy froze, was this a sign? Was this the right thing to do? Was she truly ready to spend time with another man? What if Edward came back, he was her true love.

"I am not sure Charles. May I have a think about it"? asked Dorothy.

"Yes of course, would you like me to walk you home?" Dorothy smiled,

"yes please that would be lovely," she replied. Dorothy then linked on to Charles arm, and they walked arm in arm back to her house. As they arrived at the house Anna opened the door.

"Dorothy, who is this handsome man"? she asked. Charles took off his top hat and bowed before Anna.

"My name is Charles ma'am I am just walking your daughter home to make sure she is safe." Anna had a very pleased look on her face

"thank you, kind sir," she said. Dorothy hurried into the house and thanked Charles for the walk. Anna then closed the door and wished Charles a good day.

"He is very handsome, and very well-dressed," said Anna.

"Mother please, he wants to take me out for dinner," moaned Dorothy.

"I do not see what you are moaning about, he is handsome and clearly upper-class. You should go for dinner with him. This could be a new fresh start for you," replied Anna. Dorothy just stared at her mother before telling her that it was too soon and that she still loved Edward and no one could ever replace him. Anna walked into the kitchen, she shortly returned with a fresh pot of tea.

"Dorothy, I know how much you love Edward. But he has been missing for such a long time. You should move on with your life, you are still young. You have two beautiful sons. Think of them, the life you could live, instead of living with me here. It's your time." Dorothy burst into tears, overcome with emotions. She liked Charles and enjoyed talking to him, but this made her feel unfaithful to Edward. What to do she thought then it clicked. The whisper in the graveyard. She looked at her mother with her eyes red and tears pouring down her face.

"I will go for dinner with Charles, you are right mother. The children deserve happiness from a loving family. Dorothy then headed upstairs she gave her boys each a kiss. One day I will tell you both about your very brave father.

DOROTHY STAYED WITH HER BOYS, she sat down on the old wooden chair in the corner of their room. She looked at them both, she smiled, and she started to tell them a story about a little boy who did not want to grow old. That this little boy was rescued by a fairy and taken to a land far far away. It was a land where he couldn't grow old. But was filled with pirates. This boy would then leave the land and visit his home where he met a young girl who he used to take back with him for their adventures. Dorothy was getting deeper into the story, then she stopped. They were both fast asleep.

"Goodnight my beautiful babies," she said. Dorothy then gave both boys a kiss on the head and left the room to go and spend the evening with her mother.

Dorothy and Anna had a long talk, they spoke about the boys and how beautiful they both were. They spoke about George and how much they both missed him.

"Sometimes I still wait and hope for him to walk through that door," said Anna. Dorothy placed her hand on her mother's hand.

"I wish for that too mother, I remember when father

and Edward used to walk through that door together. Oh, I do wish for that to happen one day." Anna squeezed Dorothy's hand, Dorothy's heart then skipped a beat. This was what Edward used to do to show his love for her. Dorothy closed her eyes; she could see Edward stood before her. She stared deeply into his eyes.

"I want to be happy, I need to live my life," she said. Edward looked back at Dorothy

"be happy," he said. She opened her eyes to see her mother looking somewhat concerned.

"What is wrong?" Anna asked.

"Nothing mother," smiled Dorothy.

TIME HAD STOOD STILL for Edward; he was still locked away in isolation. His hair had grown and he now had a beard. He was dirty, filthy and the stench was so powerful that it would make him feel physically sick. He had no idea how long he had been in isolation. There was no concept of time, what day? Month? Or even year? The only thing he did know was whether it was day or night and that was due to the small crack in the wall that would show some light. He was starving and had lost weight, his only meals fed to him off a flat metal tray. Food that was always cold, hard to chew and no doubt not that safe to eat. He was given water three times per day, but the water was never clean. It would be murky, grey or brown. Many days he would sob and cry himself to sleep. He could never hear Richard in the room next to his. It was always so silent. However, Richard could clearly hear Edward's cries and whimpers.

Richard would sit in his cell all day. He would not cry; he would not whimper. He showed absolutely no emotion. He was fearless, not afraid of death. He had already lost his daughter, to him there was nothing else to lose. Occasionally Edward would bang on the wall to try and get Richard's attention. However, Richard would not respond, he would just continue to stare in space as if his time on this earth was coming to an end.

There was a bang on Edward's cell door. It startled him, and he stood up to look at the door. His eyes bloodshot, his beard messy, his hair so long and matted. He smelt terrible but who was banging at the door. Suddenly the door opened ever so slowly. In stepped a well-dressed German officer

"We can hear you cry; we can hear you scream. But no one is coming. Do you really think your brave Winston Churchill will come to your aid? You are to remain here and to keep quiet, under Hitler's orders." A startled Edward stepped back. He didn't know what to say or how to react. Had Hitler really given the order directly himself for Edward to keep quiet or were they just trying to scare him into remaining silent? Edward tried to regain his focus, but this was the first time he had seen another person face to face in a very long time. He shook his head and then nodded at the officer. The officer then stepped back outside and a guard closed the door on Edward locking it after.

Edward slumped down onto his bed. He placed his head in his hands. He was scared, and he did not believe that he would now ever get out of there alive. The fear of death was looming. All he could think about was Dorothy and how she was coping without him being there for her. He lay down on his bed and turned to the wall. He tapped it three times

"Richard, I am sorry," he said ever so softly.

"It is ok, our time will come. Soon we will both be at peace," replied Richard. A shocked Edward sat up. This was the first time that Richard had spoken in a very long time. He was speechless he had no idea what he could say. He gathered his thoughts

"Is there any hope"? he asked. A deep sigh could be heard through the wall followed by a very stern

"no" from Richard. Edward started to believe now that all hope was lost. He lay back down on his bed and closed his eyes. He started to vision the day he first made love to Dorothy under the sycamore tree.

DOROTHY WAS GETTING ready for dinner with Charles.

"Mother I really do not know what to wear."

"Oh, my dear you have so many outfits to choose from, what about this lovely mustard dress you have here?" Dorothy turned to look at what Anna was holding. Her jaw dropped when she realized it was the dress that Edward had bought her many years ago.

"No mother, I cannot wear that. Edward bought me that dress. It would not feel right." Anna placed the dress back on a hanger and placed it into the wardrobe.

"How about this one?" Dorothy looked again and saw her mother holding a lovely red velvet dress.

"That is not mine," said Dorothy.

"I know it is not, it is one of my old dresses. You could borrow this if you like." Dorothy smiled, she walked over to Anna and gave her a kiss on the cheek.

"Thank you, mother." Anna smiled. Her and Dorothy were as close as they had ever been.

"You do not mind looking after the boys tonight?" said Dorothy.

"Not at all, you go and enjoy yourself," said Anna.

Anna left the room and Dorothy started to get ready. She could feel her heart racing. She was very excited about going out for dinner with Charles, but she was also worried that this would mean she was no longer faithful to Edward. She would take heavy breaths from time to time. She carefully started to put on her dress. It was a perfect fit. She had a look in the mirror she absolutely loved the dress. Dorothy then sat down at her dressing table and started to brush her long golden hair. Shortly after she was ready. She went to see her boys who were playing downstairs.

"Be good my angels," she said as she kissed them both gently.

"Thank you, mother," Dorothy then turned as there was a knock at the front door.

"I shall answer that," said Anna. Dorothy smiled; she knew it was Charles she could tell by how he knocked on the door. As Anna opened the door she could hear the well-spoken voice of Charles.

"Hello ma'am I am here to take Dorothy for dinner."

Anna smiled and held the door open. Dorothy hurried to the door. She paused when she saw Charles, he was dressed with such elegance. His smile beaming from ear to ear. Dorothy could see how handsome Charles was and it made her feel very funny inside. She then headed outside with Charles. She linked his arm. Charles then led Dorothy to his car. Dorothy was shocked, Charles had his own car and even had his own driver.

"Charles, this is wonderful." Charles smiled.

"Yes, it is truly wonderful." Charles then opened the door to his car and allowed Dorothy to step in. she lifted her dress, so she could step up into the car. She sat down on the back seat and Charles soon followed in after. He closed the door and informed the driver to take them to the restaurant.

"You look so beautiful," said Charles. Dorothy started to blush, her cheeks going bright red.

"You're very handsome," she replied to Charles. Dorothy was struggling to hide her blushes. She could feel the nerves pouring through her veins. This was all new to her, she had not even been out to a restaurant with Edward. Edward was the only man she had ever been out with for anything. Now there was this very tall handsome man showing her a lot of attention and being extremely generous towards her.

"What is this restaurant like?" asked Dorothy. Charles laughed,

"This is one of the best restaurants in the whole city. You will love it." Dorothy started to feel a little more relaxed and content. Charles had been so lovely and friendly towards her; it made her feel wanted again something she had not felt since Edward was around.

The car pulled up to the restaurant. The driver then got out of the vehicle and opened the door. Charles stepped out of the car and lent back in extending his hand. Dorothy took his hand and lifted her dress, so she could step out of the car. As she got out of the car her eyes lit up. This was not just any restaurant but a really fancy restaurant. A place that Dorothy could only have dreamed of in the past. She linked onto Charles' arm and walk with her head held up very high and her back straight with him into the restaurant. She wanted to look good for Charles and not the lost girl that she sometimes felt.

"Reservation for Charles." The waiter looked at Charles and smiled.

"Yes sir, follow me your table is ready." Charles and Dorothy were led by the waiter to their table. The waiter pulled out the chair for Dorothy, and she sat down. She was amazed by the table before her. The beautiful wine glasses, the champagne flutes. The cutlery a fine silver. The table cloth pure silk. It was luxury like she had never seen before.

"Would you like some wine ma'am"? asked the waiter. Dorothy was stunned. She had never drank wine before. But before she could reply

"We will have a bottle of your finest champagne," called Charles from across the table.

"Yes sir," said the waiter. He then scurried off leaving Charles and Dorothy alone sat at the table. The candles were lit and everything was beautiful. Charles picked up a menu "are you going to have a look at your menu Dorothy"? he asked.

"Oh, yes Charles," said a startled Dorothy who was still in amazement of her surroundings. Dorothy picked up the menu, she had a look at it then started to panic. She had not heard of anything on this menu, but she did not want Charles to know that.

"What can I choose"? she said to herself. Charles then said he was ready. Without thinking or hesitating she ordered a Rabbit stew. She placed her menu down on the table and placed her hands on her lap.

"Charles how does a restaurant operate like this when rationing is in place"? she asked curiously.

"Food's that are rationed are not on the menu, all the food you can get in the restaurant is foods that are not on the list of rationing," he replied. Dorothy then smiled but she was still curious,

"what about all the people who have lost their homes due to bombings or have run out of ration cards?" Charles looked at Dorothy,

"well this restaurant helps those people, every day it opens its kitchens in the morning and late at night to help feed those less fortunate," he replied. "That is a lovely thing to do," said Dorothy. She loved the idea of charity and that people were getting the support they needed. "What would you like to be?" asked Charles.

"I have always wanted to be a nurse; I have helped Dr Bennett many times and I have done some training," she said softly. Charles had an admirable look on his face, he thought it was fantastic that Dorothy wanted to be a nurse to help others.

The waiter returned shortly with the food. Dorothy looked at her rabbit stew. She picked up a spoon and was not expecting anything special. However, she was taken by surprise. She found it absolutely delicious.

"Charles, this food is amazing," she cried in excitement.

"Yes, it truly is special here," he replied. They continued their meals, with Dorothy telling Charles all about her dreams to help others in need. They both had a wonderful evening together, and they really enjoyed the champagne.

"Thank you for such a wonderful meal Charles." Charles then stood up

"no thank you, it is all my pleasure." He then walked around the table and extended his hand. Dorothy stood up with him, and they walked back to the car.

"Let's get you home." Charles opened the door for Dorothy and helped her back into the car. He then got in the car and closed the door.

The car drove off and Dorothy was feeling so happy. She had an incredible evening and it had been so long that she had been in the company of others. It was a night that she did not want to forget. Charles would talk about his business and how he enjoys owning a hat factory. Dorothy was amazed that Charles was so successful when he was only a few years older than she was. Shortly after the car pulled up and it was time for Dorothy to go. Charles stepped out the car and helped Dorothy out.

"I will walk you to your door," he said. They linked arms and slowly walked to the house. Dorothy got to the door and as she was about to open it turned to face

Charles. She gave him a kiss on the cheek and thanked him again.

"Goodnight," said Dorothy.

"Goodnight, I look forward to seeing you again soon." Dorothy then headed inside and closed the door. Anna was sat on the sofa reading a book.

"Hello, how was your night"? she asked.

"Oh mother, it was just amazing," Dorothy replied. She then sat down next to Anna and leaned into her for a cuddle.

"How were my angel's mother"? Anna held onto Dorothy.

"Wonderful those two boys are truly wonderful. I am so proud of you" Dorothy felt so content and relaxed, a feeling she had not felt since her father and Edward were around. Things were finally starting to look up for Dorothy.

She went to bed that night feeling excitable, all she wanted was to feel loved again. To be happy and to be able to move on with her life. She would think about Edward, she would often wonder if he was alive and where he may be. But as so much had time had passed, she started to believe her mother that perhaps he may never come home. Her heart would feel so heavy at such thoughts, the feelings of worry that he may not have been laid to rest. The feeling that he may never be found and that he could be laying somewhere rotting away would often make her feel so stick to her stomach. Her thoughts would often lead to her boys, how she wanted a father figure in their lives. She closed her eyes and drifted off into a deep sleep.

She began to dream; she was walking through the field towards the sycamore tree when Edward arrived.

"Why didn't you wait for me my lady"? he yelled. Dorothy froze, she could not think of what to say. She was so shocked and startled. She never expected to see Edward again. She walked up to him and placed her arms around him

"where have you been?" she asked.

"I have been with you all this time," he replied. Her dream started to become dark, darkness surrounded the sky above her and a storm started to come in. The winds picked up and thunder could be heard in the distance coming closer and closer. Edward started to change, his skin turning a blood-red.

"I love you Edward," screamed Dorothy. A huge bolt of lightning then hit the sycamore tree, causing it to burst into flames.

Dorothy screamed as she sat up in bed, she was soaking wet with sweat. A terrible nightmare had taken over her subconscious thoughts. Her breathing was heavy, what had just happened and why was she having these dreams she thought to herself. Was Edward trying to send her a message that he would return and that she shouldn't move on? She got out of bed and took herself to her washroom. She cleaned herself up as much as she could. The makeup she had used on her face had all run down her cheeks. The dream felt so real. It was so intense and left her still in a state of shock. She went to check on her boys who were both fast asleep. She felt relieved that her screams did not cause them to wake. She got back into bed and stared deep at the ceiling. She was afraid to go back to sleep, she did not want to experience those dreams again, but she knew she had no choice. She wanted to be happy, she wanted to be strong for her boys and to give them a life that they truly deserved.

MORNING CAME and Dorothy had struggled to sleep through the night. It was a restless night full of tossing and turning, and she felt so exhausted. She pulled herself up and forced herself to climb out of bed. She walked to the boy's room to check on them. They were not there. Hmmm mother must have already got the boys up she thought to herself. Still in her nightwear and her hair being a mess she headed downstairs. When she got to the bottom of the stairs she shrieked. There was Charles sat with Anna drinking a cup of tea whilst the boys were playing. Dorothy felt so embarrassed she was a complete mess. She had not sorted her hair; makeup was all over her face, and she was in her bed wear.

"Good morning," said Charles. A very embarrassed Dorothy started to blush, she couldn't get her words out properly she started to mumble. She did not expect this, she turned around and ran back upstairs feeling very embarrassed. She ran into her room and jumped into her bed.

There was a knock on her bedroom door,

"it is only me," said Anna. She slowly and carefully opened the bedroom door and walked into Dorothy's room where Dorothy was slumped on her bed.

"Why did you not warn me that Charles was here?" she cried.

"I'm sorry," replied Anna.

"Why don't you get yourself ready and come back downstairs and have a cup of tea with us"? she asked. Dorothy buried her face in her pillow in embarrassment

"yes mother, I will be down soon," she said in a very muffled voice through her pillow. Anna smiled and headed out of the room and back down the stairs. Dorothy continued to lay on her bed for a few minutes before deciding to get herself freshened up and dressed to come downstairs for tea with mother and Charles.

In a hurry Dorothy threw on a blue and white dress, she quickly brushed her hair to get it as neat and tidy as she possibly could. She wiped off all her makeup and quickly headed downstairs to meet Charles and her mother.

"I apologize about before," she said still embarrassed from Charles seeing her in the mess that she was in. Charles let out a cheeky laugh

"It is not a problem," he replied still grinning. Dorothy was nervous and Anna could sense this. Dorothy clearly liked Charles and how much of a gentleman he was. They all enjoyed a nice hot cup of tea together.

"Your boys are truly wonderful," said Charles.

"Thank you, they mean the whole world to me," replied Dorothy. She was so proud of her boys and the fact that Charles was fond of them only made her feelings grow for him. Finally, Dorothy was happy again.

"Would you like to come for a walk with us?" she asked Charles.

"With the children?" he asked.

"Yes, of course," she replied. Dorothy started to trust Charles now and wanted him not only to be a part of her life but to also be a part of the boys lives also.

The walk was lovely, the wind was settled and the air was clear. The sun was shining and it was a lovely day to be out walking with Charles and the children. As they walked past the canal, she could see the sycamore tree in the distance. The dream she had come back to her, she paused and stared intensely at the tree in the distance.

"What is wrong"? asked Charles.

"Nothing, everything is fine," said Dorothy. They continued their walk. She did not want to take Charles to the sycamore tree. This was always hers and Edward's spot. It was sacred and she could not share that with anyone else.

"I would like to help you with your dreams, I want to help you become the nurse you wish to be," said Charles. Dorothy grinned

"how can you do that"? she asked.

"I have spoken to some friends and you can start your formal training next week if you wish." An absolutely shocked Dorothy stopped where she was stood. She wrapped her arms around Charles and kissed him firmly on the lips

"thank you that is so kind of you," she wailed in excitement. Charles taken aback by the kiss was amazed. He had very strong feelings for Dorothy and now it seemed as if their relationship was in full swing.

The rest of the walk was perfect. Dorothy was loving having her boys with her, and she loved the company of

Charles. Charles had invited Dorothy over to his home for dinner and of course, she could bring the children. Dorothy was so happy she gladly accepted. It was now new beginnings for her. Her dreams of a nurse were now going to become true, and she now had met a man who was willing to step up and support her and her children. She still felt bad for Edward, but she could no longer live in hope that he would return. She would keep telling herself that Edward would wish for her to be happy and with for her to move on with her life. This was her coping mechanism to help hide the guilt. When she returned home with her boys, she kissed Charles goodbye. She went inside and told her mother that she was so happy, that she had been invited over for dinner and that she had feelings for Charles. Anna was so happy with this that she embraced Dorothy with a very long cuddle, before telling her that she loved her so much and that she is so proud of her.

An excitable Dorothy skipped her way upstairs to her room. She took off her dress and got into some more comfortable clothes, she was humming away and finally felt like she was back on top of the world. Once she had gotten changed, she headed back downstairs. She sat on the floor with the boys and begun to play with them. She was smiling and laughing. Anna was so pleased to see this; she had not seen Dorothy this happy in such a long time.

"It is so good to see you happy again," said Anna. Dorothy looked up at her mother, she gave her a beautiful smile that could warm anyone's heart. Happiness had come back to the household and now Dorothy finally had hope again, hope that things were finally starting to go well for her and her family. Dorothy could feel in her heart that it was finally the time for her to move on.

EDWARD WAS STILL LIVING in his awful squalor. He had lost so much weight and felt weak. He did not know how much more he could possibly take. He started to eat the meals that were given to him by the guards. He wanted to survive, his whimpers and cries had stopped. Conversations with Richard through the wall were becoming more regular. They were both helping each other to survive. Edward would often tell Richard that he was wrong. That there was hope, and that one day they would both be free from the hell that they were subjected to. Richard would smile, he loved Edward's enthusiasm, and his never give up spirit. Time would pass, but hope would not leave their souls not anymore.

ALL THINGS COME TO AN END

There is always one guarantee in life, that life will come to an end. It is the only guarantee that we can make from the day we are born. This not only just happens with life, but happens with everything. Many believe love lasts forever. Is love strong enough to last for all time?

IT WAS NOW LATE 1944, it had been two whole years since Edward had been sent to war. Dorothy had a very strong relationship with Charles now. They had been courting for almost a year. The boys were now toddlers and were walking around and grabbing anything that they could.

"Will you boys stop that," called Dorothy. They had been playing with all of her hairbrushes and hiding them from her.

"My dear they are only having fun," said Anna.

"I know mother, but I wish they would stop hiding my belongings all the time." Anna smirked and left the room. Dorothy picked up all her belongings and put them away. She then picked up the boys one on each hip and headed downstairs to continue conversing with her mother.

"Mother, I have been thinking. I have been seeing Charles now for almost a year, I think that it is time that the boys and I move in with him." There was a smash as Anna dropped her cup on the floor in shock. She did not see this coming; she did not want to be alone. Dorothy was all she had left in the world. But she knew she could not stop her from following her dreams.

"I understand, you need to do what is right for you. But what about your nursing?" replied Anna.

"That is fantastic, I am doing so much now at the hospital," said Dorothy. Dorothy had been working incredibly hard at the hospital to become a trained nurse, she was now able to do so much more than she could have ever done helping Dr Bennett. Anna still worried about being alone but knew that she had to let Dorothy go and live her life. They had breakfast together until there was a knock at the door.

It was Charles, he was here to take Dorothy to the hospital. She had a full day ahead of her, and she would be looking after the elderly patients today. Dorothy was always so excited about working in the hospital. It made her feel so warm inside, that she had a purpose and that she was giving back to people who needed it the most. Dorothy gave her boys a kiss goodbye and headed to the car with Charles.

"Have you thought about my offer"? Charles asked.

"I have, and we would love to move in with you," replied Dorothy.

"Wonderful, I shall get everything organised," replied Charles. Dorothy's eyes lit up; her life was going so well now. She had a family for her and her boys, stability and a father figure who could provide for them all. The warmth she could feel flowing through her veins would reignite the fire deep within her, to be successful and to live a long happy life.

THE HOSPITAL WAS BUSY, it was a cold winters day and a lot of elderly people had been admitted due to having bad chests and breathing difficulties. Dorothy could not believe the scale of what she had to do. There must have been 50 patients crammed into her ward. The doctor nowhere in sight. People coughing and crying, it was very upsetting to Dorothy, but she could not just give up. she wanted to help each and every one of them. She started making her way around the ward. Stopping off at each bed and introducing herself to every individual patient. Dorothy thought it was very important to know everyone by name and that they should also know her name.

As she made her way from bed to bed speaking to the patients and asking them about how they were feeling she noticed something. There was a man, he was not old. He looked so much like her father. She had to look away and look back. She walked over to the bed

"Hello, I am Dorothy and I will be taking care of you." The man started to cough; he was clearly not in a healthy condition.

"Hello, I am Peter," he replied between his coughs.

Dorothy handed him some tissues and sat down on the bed next to him.

"You look so much like my father," she said. She just stared in amazement the resemblance was surreal.

"Thank you," Peter replied.

"My father was killed many years ago, in the bombings that took place over the city. It's just so strange," she said softly.

"I am sorry for your loss," replied Peter. Dorothy grabbed Peter's hand and held it softly.

"I will be here and I will ensure that I check on you," she said. Peter gave Dorothy a gentle smile as she stood up from the bed and started to walk across to the next patient.

"Nurse," shouted this voice from across the ward. Dorothy stopped, turned around and could see the doctor not looking impressed at her walking around and talking to the patients. She made her way over to the doctor

"I am sorry sir; I think it's very important that the patients get to know us all." The doctor frowned

"this is not a social gathering; you have work to do and I expect you to do it," he said very angrily. The doctor stormed off to complete his rounds. Dorothy was very upset, she just wanted to make people feel less afraid, to feel secure and feel that they are in safe hands and are being looked after. She solemnly headed back to her station where she started to look through the paperwork. She could not get over the fact that Peter was so much like her father. It brought back many fond memories that she had of him and all the wonderful adventures he took her on when she was only a child.

Dorothy continued to sort through the mountain of paperwork that was set before her, however, there was this urge to go over and speak to Peter. She did not want to get herself in any more trouble. She waited patiently for the doctor to leave the ward. Once he had left, she took her opportunity she went over to Peter's bed.

"Hello, Peter is there anything I can do for you"? she asked.

"No thank you," he replied. Peter then started to cough, he coughed so hard that there was blood on the handkerchief that he was holding in his hand. Dorothy now very concerned did not know what to do.

"Peter, I will go and get help," she said as she was struggling to get her words out. She ran out of the ward to the doctor.

"Sir, Peter is coughing up blood," she cried. The doctor did not look overly concerned. He remained very calm and relaxed and walked with Dorothy over to Peter.

"I think it is just a case of coughing too hard and tearing the throat muscles," said the doctor. Dorothy started to feel relieved. She headed back to her station and finished off with her paperwork.

HER SHIFT WAS NOW OVER, and she was going to make the big move, her and the boys would be moving in with Charles. She left the hospital to be greeted with Charles, who had arrived to take her home to help move her belongings. Dorothy was so excited and ran back in her house. She grabbed each of the boys and gave them a big kiss.

"Today we are moving in with Charles," she yelled in happiness. She knew the boys did not really understand what she was talking about, but she didn't care. This was new beginnings for her. Anna was sat down, looking sad.

"What is wrong mother"? asked Dorothy.

"Nothing my dear, I guess I just don't want to be alone." Dorothy sat down next to Anna; she placed her arm around her shoulder.

"Mother, we will always visit you and father is always with also," she said. This made Anna smile but at the same time her eyes filled with tears. Dorothy gave Anna a cuddle and reassured her that they would always remain close.

"You better get a hurry on," said Anna. Dorothy jumped up and ran up the stairs. She started to take her clothes out of the wardrobe. She loaded them into suitcases. Then she saw it, the mustard dress that Edward had got her. She carefully took it off its hanger, folded it very neatly and placed it on the top of her suitcase. She walked over to the dresser, there was only one thing left for her to collect. Edward's pocket watch, she opened up the watch and was surprised that it was still keeping time. She looked at the picture that William had drawn of Edward for her, it made her smile and feel warm.

"Edward, I will always love you," she said softly before closing the watch and giving it a kiss. She then slipped the watch into her coat pocket.

She headed downstairs with her suitcases, Charles was

stood at the bottom of the stairs, seeing Dorothy struggle he ran up the stairs to take the cases off of her.

"Thank you, Charles, they are very heavy," she said. Charles took the cases out to the car. Dorothy then sat down with Anna, who was looking very emotional.

"I will come and visit you all the time mother, please do not worry. The boys and I will always pop by and spend time with you. Of course, you can always come and see us if you like." Anna smiled, she loved how much Dorothy cared for her and how close they had become over the years. Anna gave Dorothy a cuddle,

"I love you," she said softly,

"take care of those beautiful boys."

"Of course, I will mother, we will see you soon." Dorothy then grabbed the boys and took them out to Charles' car. Anna got up off the sofa and walked over to the front door. As everyone was loaded into the car with all Dorothy's and the boy's possessions the car started to pull away. Anna stood at the door and waved to Dorothy who waved back blowing kisses.

The boys were amazed with the journey. They would just stare out of the window at the scenery. They had never been in a car before and were so excited that they were climbing all over Dorothy.

"Boys will you please settle down?" Charles started to laugh.

"They are just being children; I do not mind," he said. Dorothy started to relax and allowed her boys to just be boys. She was smiling all the way to Charles' house. Charles lived only a few minutes' drive towards the outskirts of the city. He had a large house with beautiful gardens. She knew the boys would be very happy here. There was so much space for them to run around and just be children.

The car pulled up the house and Charles' driver opened the door for them. They managed to grab all the suitcases and items between them. Charles then opened the door to his house. It was so luxurious and smelt incredibly clean. Everything was pristine and immaculately clean. Dorothy was amazed, she never expected to live such a life of luxury.

"This way," Charles said. He led Dorothy upstairs to the master bedroom.

"Let's help you unpack."

"It is ok Charles, if you don't mind, I would like to do this," said Dorothy. Charles nodded and left the room. Dorothy began to unpack her belongings and started hanging them in the wardrobe. She lay out her dresses on the bed. All her hair products were placed on the dressing table in the corner of the room. She then looked at the pocket watch briefly before putting this back in her pocket. She did not want to leave that lying around, she just didn't want Charles to feel jealous or worried that she was still madly in love with Edward.

She turned her attention to the dresses on the bed, some were very worn and needed to be discarded, but she did not want to rely on Charles to purchase all of her clothes for her. She wanted to become a nurse, to earn the wage and to be able to provide for herself and her boys without relying on Charles' wealth. She sorted her dresses and begun to hand them up on the hangers in the wardrobe. She organized them neatly. She did not own much and this did not take her too long. Shortly after she was finished, she headed downstairs to see the twins and Charles.

Everyone was sat in the luxurious lounge. The boys were playing together on the beautiful rug in front of the fireplace. Charles was sat talking to his maid. Dorothy was in awe at the amazing oil paintings that were hanging on the wall. The feel of the rug on her bare feet was so mesmerizing. This was such a beautiful house and now somewhere that she could always call home. She sat down and sunk deep into the softest armchair that she had ever had the privilege to sit in. the comfort was so relaxing that she was worried that she may fall asleep if she sat there for too long. The feel of comfort in a large beautifully taken care of home was starting to sink in very quickly.

DOROTHY WOULD RETURN to work the following day; she was upbeat about her upcoming day. She walked into work with her usual smile and positive attitude. She signed in and made her way down the long winding corridors to her ward. As she settled into work at her station, she could see that Peter was still there, he was looking brighter today and not as unwell as he had the previous day. She raced through the paperwork that was set before her and headed over to Peter.

"How are you feeling today?" she asked.

"Better," he replied. Dorothy smiled. She headed back to her station and waited for the nurse in charge to arrive,

JAMES KEITH

so they could complete their rounds. She did not want to aggravate the doctor today by talking to all the patients.

Dorothy followed the nurse around taking down all the notes that she was given. She enjoyed the rounds as she loved being close to the patients, spending time with them and getting to know them. It made her feel so warm inside knowing that she was bringing joy and happiness to people who were feeling unwell. Dorothy only had a few months left of her nurse's training, and she could not wait to be the one giving out the treatment to the patients. She always paid attention and focused on what the nurses were doing, she wanted to be the best nurse that she could be and one that would always put the patients first before anything else.

The next few days Dorothy was in her element. Peter had recovered well and was being discharged to go home. She had spent so much time with Peter that she had built a good strong bond with him. Now though it was time that they both parted ways. Peter was fit for going home and Dorothy knew that she possibly may never see him again. The resemblance from the look of her father and the sound of the voice would not leave her mind. Dorothy ensured that she gave Peter an enormous cuddle before he left.

"Thank you, Dorothy, I have enjoyed spending time with you," said Peter.

"The pleasure has been all mine," she replied. Peter soon walked down the corridor and left the hospital. Dorothy felt sad, however, she also felt happy at the same time. She had helped to make someone feel welcomed and cared for. Her dreams were now becoming a reality, and she could not wait for the day to come where she would be the nurse in charge of the ward.

———————

FIVE MONTHS HAD PASSED since Dorothy had moved in with Charles, the boys were happy as was Dorothy. She had now completed her nurse's training and was a nurse at the hospital. She was working as many shifts as she could, even though she did not need the money due to Charles' business she wanted to do her part. She wanted to make sure that when her boys grew up, they knew that they needed to provide for themselves than to rely on others to do this for them. She loved her job so very much; she couldn't stop thinking about the boys and if they were behaving for her mother that day. Anna would occasionally look after the boys when Dorothy would be at work and if Charles was unavailable. She did not want a stranger to take care of her children when she was busy at the hospital. Dorothy always remained very particular about this.

———————

BACK IN THE heart of Europe in what was now early hours of April 29th 1945. Edward barely alive was starving, he was nothing but skin and bones. Struggling to keep the food down him that was being fed into his cell. All hope had been lost; he was waiting to die for the first time in his life he wished death would come to him soon, so he could not suffer any longer. Richard was still in good health, managing to eat the meals and drinking the dirty water. The stagnant smelly conditions seemed to have little to no effect on him. It was like he was used to living in such squalor, he remained calm even though they had both been in isolation for the best part of 3 years now. As the morning went on Edward thought it would just be another day of hell and misery, he was truly suffering. He could barely stand on his own two legs as his body had become that weak. It was not long until Dawn started to break.

There was this rush, a huge noise outside. Richard stood up and walked to the door, the commotion was intense. There were sounds of gunshots, sounds of cheering. Edward laying on his floor opened his eyes; he could hear the sounds of people sounding really happy. The sounds of doors being opened and heavy footsteps all around. He pulled himself to his knees, but he was far too weak to stand up now. The sound of the footsteps drew closer and closer. The door then suddenly flew open.

"We have live one's here," shouted a soldier in a thick American accent. Edward coughed; he could not believe what he was seeing. Was this him dying or dreaming that the allied forces had come to liberate the camp?

"We need a medic here now," shouted the soldier. Edward just lay on the floor, not truly knowing if he was about to enter the afterlife.

The medic came running into the room and sat down next to Edward

"This one is extremely malnourished and dehydrated we need to get him out of here now." The medic ran back to get a stretcher and Edward was lifted onto this. He was carried out of the room he looked across to see Richard stood there, bearded and long hair like himself.

"Stop, just for a minute," Richard asked the soldiers. The soldiers paused and Richard took Edward's hand, he lent down to him and softly said

"we are free." Edward closed his eyes and thought of Dorothy. He was finally free to eventually be reunited with his long-lost love. The soldiers continued to walk carrying Edward, as they stepped outside Edward had to close his eyes. The sunlight was burning his eyes, he couldn't look. The feel of the wind against his face was surreal, he had forgotten what the feeling was like.

The camp was finally liberated. The rest of the prisoners were all being checked by the soldiers. The German's had surrendered the camp. The war was changing and the allied forces were beginning to advance further and further. Richard walked behind the stretcher with the American soldiers. He stopped and sniffed the air; freedom was finally theirs. They were no longer locked away in isolation, something that Edward had feared would consume him and take his life. This was the end of the war for both Edward and Richard and Richard knew this. A disorientated Edward was loaded into the back of a vehicle and was taken away to the nearest allied forces medical camp where he was going to be treated for his ill health before he would be allowed to travel back to England.

Edward was not out of the woods yet, he needed to recover his health, build his muscle strength back up before he could even reconsider heading back home. When they arrived at the medical center, Edward was immediately cleaned, he was then given some treatment by the doctors. Edward was never sure of what they actually did when he first was treated. His memories were a blur just like his eyesight was that day. He just remembers not having to stay in the darkness, no longer waiting for death to come. He had finally stepped out of the darkness and back into the light. He would often sleep through the days as his body would recover from the starvation.

Richard did not need much treatment he remained in fairly good health. The first thing he did was cleaned himself up, before cutting off his long-matted hair and beard. Richard would often stay with Edward and was refusing to head back home until Edward was well enough to do so as well. Most days Richard would just sit by Edward's side watching over him. As Edward's health started to improve, they would often play dominoes.

"They have told me that soon I will be able to go home," said Edward.

"Good, I have had enough of this shit hole," replied Richard. Edward laughed, which caused him to startle himself. He realized that he had not laughed now for many years, an emotion that he had thought was only a part of his past. A simple laugh started to make him feel so hopeful about life once again.

AFTER FIVE LONG months of support and treatment in medical, it was time for Edward to head home. The war was over, Hitler's army had surrendered and the news that Hitler was killed was spreading like wildlife. There were huge celebrations all over Europe and the allied forces were so happy that now the fighting had stopped and that they could all go back home to their loved ones. Edward and Richard boarded a train to France where they would then catch the ferry across the British mainland. The train journey seemed like an eternity however as the day was dawning, they arrived for their ferry. Richard paused

"when we get back, I would like to see my daughter." Edward nodded,

"yes I will take you," he said. They both boarded the ferry and set back off to England. Hoping that the final train ride after back to Birmingham would not be so long.

A day later Edward and Richard got off their train in Birmingham. There were so many people waiting at the train stations looking for their loved ones when they got off the train. Richard knew that no one would be there waiting for him, all he had in the world was Clara, and she was taken from him. Edward frantically looked around hoping to see Dorothy. He looked for her long golden hair but could not see anything.

"Please wait with me Richard," asked Edward. Richard sighed and sat down on a bench

"very well," he said. Edward ran up and down the platform looking in hope. He could not find Dorothy anywhere, so he decided to sit with Richard and try to wait and see when the crowd dispersed.

People started to leave; the crowd was becoming less by the minute. Yet there was still no sign of Dorothy.

"Let's go," moaned Richard.

"No, we can't. She must be here, please, a little longer," begged Edward. Richard rolled his eyes. He knew that

Dorothy was not there, but yet Edward was not letting his hope go. More people left the platform, women happy to see their husbands returning from the war, embracing with cuddles and kisses. Edward was still sat there, now there were only a few people left on the platform and the realization that Dorothy was not there started to hit Edward hard. He slowly stood up from the bench

"come on I'll take you to Clara," said Edward. Richard stood up and placed his hand on Edward's shoulder.

"I'm sorry," he said. They both then left the train station and headed back home.

The walk back was very short only 20 minutes. When they arrived in the market Edward stopped and looked around, the houses had all been rebuilt, the market itself looked exactly the same as it did all those years ago.

"You coming"? said Richard. Edward then hurried along to catch up with Richard. Together they walked through the market and towards the graveyard where both George and Clara were laid to rest. The entrance to the graveyard was starting to look overgrown. Richard moved some of the branches from the tree overhanging the entrance and walked through the gate. Edward then walked in front of Richard to the spot where Clara was resting. Shortly after they arrived at her gravesite.

"Can I have some time alone"? asked Richard.

"Of course," replied Edward who then headed over to George's resting place. Richard knelt down onto one knee and removed his hat.

"Hello sweetheart, I am so sorry that I was not there for you. I have let you down and it has taken me so long to come back to you. I want you to know that I met William again

and that we finally made peace. I am sorry I cannot bring him back to you here, but I am sure you are both together again with your mother in the afterlife. I want you to forgive me for letting you down. For not being able to save you, for not being able to save William. You are my little girl, and you'll always be in my heart. Always and forever." Richard then laid down a single red rose on Clara's grave. He then kissed the ground where she lay

"I love you." He stood back up and headed over to Edward. He placed his arm around Edward's shoulders

"You are a brave man, I will always be around, look me up some time." Edward smiled and nodded at Richard. Richard then turned and walked away from Edward heading out of the graveyard and finally out of sight.

Edward then turned his attention back to George's grave.

"Hello sir, well things did not go so well out there really. I spent the last three years in a hole in the wall," Edward joked as he told George all about what had happened in the war and how he did so well until he was captured. *"I am going to go and find Dorothy now. I thought she may have been waiting for me at the train station, but then maybe she did not know that I would be coming home today."* Edward then put his hands in his pockets and started to walk away. He was going to head home now, to see his beloved Dorothy. It had been far too long, and he could not wait to have her back in his arms once again. He skipped down the street, thinking about what he could say. He worried that she may not even recognize him, but nothing was going to deter him from seeing her.

THE HOUSE LOOKED QUIET; it still looked the same as the last time he saw it. He walked up the door and knocked three times. He waited, there was no answer. He knocked again after a few seconds he could hear the lock in the door turning and the door slowly opened.

"Edward? Is that? Can it? No, it can't be you." Edward smiled

"Yes ma'am it is me Edward. I am finally home." A shocked Anna dropped her cup of tea onto the floor smashing it. She then flung her arms around Edward and squeezed him ever so tightly

"you came back? It has been far too long," said Anna softly into his ear.

"It has ma'am, is Dorothy home?" Edward asked.

"Oh Edward, I really do not know how to tell you this, but Dorothy does not live here anymore, she's moved to the cobbles." Edward started to cough

"The cobbles, that's a wealthy area, which house?" he asked.

"Number 9," said Anna. Edward quickly turned around and started to run down the street"Edward wait, I need to tell you something," shouted Anna. Edward did not hear Anna's shouts he wanted to find Dorothy.

He ran and he ran until he could not run anymore. Soon as he stopped running there was a clap of thunder followed by intense heavy rain. It did not take long before he was soaked to the bone. When he got his breath back, he started to run and this time he did not stop until he reached the cobbles. As he walked down the road, he was counting the numbers of the houses. Eventually, he reached house number 9. He was soaked and cold, not an ideal entrance to see Dorothy after all this time, but he needed to tell her he was back. He started to approach the house, he walked through the lovely iron gate and headed for the front door. He slowly walked down the path thinking about what he was going to say, but then something caught his eye. He looked into the window and could see Dorothy; she was not alone. She was slow dancing with another man, a tall man. Edward was confused. Was she learning to dance? He proceeded to walk closer, then he stopped. Dorothy and this man started to embrace with a kiss. Standing in the pouring rain Edward stared straight at Dorothy.

Inside the house, Dorothy started to dance with Charles again, as she turned around to face the window she froze and stopped dancing. She could see the silhouette of a man in the pouring rain. She walked towards the window the figure sent chills down her spine.

"Edward," she said softly. Charles walked up behind Dorothy

"is everything okay?" Dorothy turned to look at Charles then looked back at the window. The figure was now gone.

"Yes Charles, it is nothing," she said. They continued to dance for a short while, but Dorothy could not get the image of Edward out of her mind.

"I need to go out, I'll be back soon." Dorothy pushed Charles back and ran to the front door. She grabbed her jacket and headed outside. The rain was continuing to pour. She looked around the garden and there were no signs that anyone was there. She had to be sure, she could feel something inside her. She had to follow her instincts. She started to run, and headed straight for the canal. She was going to go to the sycamore tree. If this was really Edward, he would be there waiting for her.

The rain did not stop, Dorothy was now soaked to the bone. The clearing to the sycamore tree looked as if someone had recently been through. Dorothy could see some footprints, as she stepped through and looked into the distance, she could see the silhouette once again. She slowly started to walk towards the tree. As she got closer all she could see was the back of a person. She could feel a lump in her throat. She was terrified, yet at the same time she was wishing that this was Edward. She was now within touching distance she went to touch his shoulder then

"Hello, my lady." Dorothy gasped and her heart skipped a beat. It was Edward, he turned around and gave her an empathic smile.

"Edward, I thought you were killed. They told me and mother so long ago that your squad was killed, you were missing." Dorothy could not contain her emotions. She burst into tears of joy and flung herself at Edward. The two embraced with pure emotion with not a care in the world of anything else around them.

"I was taken to a prison of war camp," said Edward. Dorothy did not want to let Edward go, but then she thought about Charles. It was an awful dilemma.

"It is ok my lady, I always wanted you to be happy." Dorothy was so happy to see him again.

"I have fallen in love with another man Edward, I am so sorry." Edward could feel the pain of heartache flowing through him. But he would not stand in the way of Dorothy.

"Tell me what has happened in all this time," asked Edward.

"I am a nurse now; I am also a mother of two beautiful boys. They are twins," she said.

"You have children with this man that is amazing," replied Edward. Dorothy let out a huge breath.

"No Edward, they are not his. They are your boys." Edward's eyes flung wide open, he did not know whether to scream with happiness or burst into tears of sorrow. Why did he go to war, why did he have to leave when he had children on the way?

"I would love for you to meet them," she asked.

"I would love to meet my children," replied Edward. Edward and Dorothy then embraced in another long cuddle, as they pulled away, they looked deep into each other's eyes. The love, the attraction was still there, they both leaned into one another and shared a long passionate kiss. As Edward pulled away, he slowly opened his eyes. Dorothy was there giving him that beautiful look that he always loved from the past.

"Time to go," he said. Edward stood tall and slowly started to walk.

"Edward wait," Dorothy shouted. She ran over to him and reached into her pocket where she pulled out his pocket watch.

"You kept it all this time?" he asked.

"Yes, I did, but there is one thing missing," she replied.

"Well, what is that?" said a confused Edward. "The picture that William drew of you, I am keeping that," she said with a huge grin on her face. She then wrapped her arms around Edward again. Before grabbing his hand and squeezing it three times. Something that Edward used to love doing to tell her that he loved her.

Edward stayed still, after a few seconds he squeezed Dorothy's hand three times. The magic was still there. They both still loved each other so much. Edward leaned in for one last kiss. It was passionate and they could feel the rumbles in their stomachs one again. After the kiss Dorothy kept her eyes closed and could feel Edward's hand slipping away. She slowly opened them to see Edward walking away into the mist.

"Edward will I ever see you again?" shouted Dorothy. Edward stopped and turned around

"You most certainly will my lady." Edward then continued walking; Dorothy watched as he vanished into the mist.

SHE WAS SAD, yet she was happy. He was back, he was alive and the spark between them was still very strong. She headed back home; the rain had now stopped but the mist was thick. She hummed the song 'over the rainbow' all the way home, this was the first song that her and Edward had listened to. When she got home, she opened the front door. She headed straight upstairs to where the boys were. She walked into the room and kissed them both on the head before saying,

"goodnight George, goodnight Edward………"

THANK YOU FOR READING

I HOPE you enjoyed ***Under the Sycamore Tree***. Please consider leaving a review where you purchased it.

Several readers have requested more about George and his backstory. If you would like to know more about George's life from when he was born until Dorothy came into the world, please keep an eye out for the release of ***Tears of the Poppies***, book two in the Forever Love Trilogy, by signing up for my newsletter or visiting my website.

www.jameskeith.co.uk

ACKNOWLEDGMENTS

For my amazing and wonderful wife Claire and my beautiful daughter Leah-Jane.

A huge thank you to Leanne for helping me.

An extra special thanks to Amanda and Rene for helping me get this far.

ABOUT THE AUTHOR

James Keith is a knowledgeable professional with almost 20 years of proficiency in the healthcare industry. James has always been an activist for mental health due to his own experiences in the field.

James wants people to be aware of how to deal with emotional, psychological, and social well-being issues and how to stop them from affecting their lives.

Follow James at
www.JamesKeith.co.uk

facebook.com/jameskeith86

twitter.com/JamesKeith86

instagram.com/jamesikeith

Printed in Great Britain
by Amazon